PERFECT STORM

COLLAPSE: BOOK ONE

RILEY FLYNN

SYNDICATE PRESS

NOTE FROM THE AUTHOR

Hi!

Thank you so much for picking up a copy of my debut novel, *Perfect Storm*. It's the first instalment in the *Collapse* series, which I have been working on for months, and planning for years. In fact, it's my second go around, after an extensive re-edit. It has been a tough few months, hacking away at this draft, but I think definitely worthwhile!

I've been dreaming about the end of the world for as long as I can remember. I'm not sure that that's an entirely healthy pastime – or that I should be admitting it to you – but it's the truth. Zombies, EMPs, computer viruses, deadly plagues, you name it, I have wondered how I would survive it. I've spent my time on the forums. Prepared. Believe me, my bug out bag is packed and waiting by the door. I just don't know how it's going to happen.

But time after time, I keep returning to one terrible conclusion: that our networked world, where information flows along undersea cables and through satellites in milliseconds, where I can hop on a plane today and be in Beijing before the sun sets at home, is just a hair's breadth away from disaster. A man coughing in Tokyo today can be a full-blown flu outbreak in Berlin by the middle of next week. It's the butterfly effect on steroids.

And most of us are simply not prepared to survive the apocalypse. Central heating, electricity, the networked smart phones that most people stare into hour after hour, day after day: they have made us weak.

What if it all went away? Maybe it happens on purpose – Iran or North Korea decide that America's weakness is the Internet that we all rely on so much. Or maybe it's an accident – a solar storm that takes out the power networks, and our way of life as we know it.

It doesn't matter how it happens – only what happens *after*. To us. The children of the electric generation. People who have forgotten how to kill for the food on their table, how to survive in the wilderness – and how to protect themselves – and their families…

I've been writing for years. Dry academic reports locked away in the dusty basements of half a dozen universities and companies, thrillers, you name it I've tried my hand at it. But *Collapse* is the story that had to be told.

Perfect Storm is just the beginning. Hunted, the second book in the Collapse series, and the third instalment, Storm Front, are both available now. Not only that, also out now is the Collapse: New Republic spinoff series, written in the same world with my co-author and good friend Mike Wolfe. That's a total of six novels - almost half a million words, to get stuck into! So buckle in. It's time to kick the tires and light some fires!

Riley Flynn.

PERFECT STORM

Everybody has a plan until they get punched in the face. What's yours..?

When the end came, it came fast. The Eko virus emerged from behind the North Korean DMZ. It spread like wildfire, burning through the world in a matter of weeks. Rumors spread that it was a weapon: a dying regime lashing out with deadly fury.

Millions died. Then billions. And then the blackouts began.

The cyber weapon hit hard, bringing a staggering world to a shuddering stop. Our cars, planes, power grid, communications networks, the internet … everything failed. It might have been humanity's last shot at stopping the spread of the virus. But by then it was already too late. Society wobbled on the edge of disaster, and then plunged right off.

For Alexander Early, surviving the apocalypse was the easy bit. He played pool and drank warm beer while a perfect storm destroyed the world. But when the lights went out, Alex knew it was time to get the hell out of Dodge. Five years before, tragedy had forced him away from the family farm in Virginia to a life in the city. Now the end of the world called him back.

Getting out of the city is only the start. Alex will face a virus he can't even see, and an enemy he's ill equipped to fight. But he'll have to learn fast.

Because he'll soon discover that the end of the world was no accident...

CHAPTER 1

*P*eople have plans. Then people get punched in the face.

The words echoed around Alex's skull, each regretful syllable a ricochet that rattled around behind his eyes. Alex did not have a plan. So he ran through the darkness, alone.

A siren screamed. Shots fired on the other side of a wall. Sometimes, he thought, the only sure part of a plan was that it was doomed to fail. Plans were for other people.

And then someone punched Alex in the face.

The concrete floor caught him on the chin. He could feel the flesh around his eye unfurling into a bruise, the blood already bitter beneath the skin. Even with the mask, the force of the blow caught him off guard. The assailant had stepped out from a dark corridor and laid Alex flat. Then vanished.

The flicker of the old-style fluorescent lights was no help. All Alex could see were ghosts and shadows, shapes painted on the walls. The inside of the mask began to steam up again.

On the other side of the room, more shots rang out. Another shout. Someone was hit. His gloved fingers scratching on the ground, Alex rose to his feet. There was no time to wait, no time to stand still.

Weighing his pistol in his hand, he knew he was short. Always bring more bullets, Timmy had told him. But Timmy said a lot. Alex found an unlit niche and stepped inside.

From here, he could see the room. It was a worn-out warehouse. Spray cans and paint had done their work on the walls. There were surfaces made to seem like corrugated iron, thick plastic mats placed on certain parts of the floor. The lights hung from heavy chains, swaying and unsteady, their yellow light littering and chattering.

Above the lights, the ceiling was far, far above. It was all cloaked in darkness. But there were people up there, waiting and watching. Deep down here in the belly of the machine, Alex was almost alone.

But he was only wasting his own time standing in the shadows. The gun was light, he knew, but he still had his fists. His elbows. Perhaps his legs, if these thick, heavy pants didn't weigh him down. They were padded, protective. Restrictive, Alex now realized. But there was no denying that his heart was bellowing up out of his chest and into his mouth. The most excitement he'd felt in years.

The siren screamed again, beckoning Alex toward the end. This place had been a car factory once upon a time. The owners seemed aware of that: they'd left relics and burned-out shells lying around to hinder people's progress. When it was everyone against everyone, he knew, the only way to progress lay through your opponents. Hidden away for the moment, he began to think.

There were a few essential truths: He needed to get across the room. He didn't have many bullets. He didn't know his way around, or how to shoot straight. His head was still reverberating and his mask only made things harder.

Timmy was nowhere to be seen. This wasn't Virginia. Hell, this wasn't even Detroit. One day, he might go home. Something deep in his bones told him he'd see the farm again. One day. But not today. His parents' house had never seemed so far away. The pain in his chest was either nostalgia or internal bleeding. But it felt good.

With the blood was rushing through his ears and his veins, Alex noticed, and he was actually enjoying himself. So, he thought, time to act.

Alex dipped his head out of the shadows. The layout of the room was clear. He had fixed it in his mind. A wide-open space, about twenty feet across, punctuated by waist-high barriers, the skeletal car wrecks, and darkened corridors leading God knew where. Last time he checked, Timmy had been on the other side. Find Timmy. That seemed like a decent plan. Decent enough, at least.

Bursting out of the darkness, Alex ran to the nearest wall. Ducking down, he heard the siren once again. Time was running out. The light was glowing electric above, finally holding steady for more than a second. He looked up. Opposite him was a steel wall, polished and shiny. A mirror.

Lifting the mask, he stole a breath. The plastic had covered his whole face with a cheap, thin material. Protective gear made by the cheapest bidder. It felt good to rip it away, if only for a moment. The air wasn't fresh. The fetid, dank warehouse interior hung heavily overhead. Peering deep into the mirrored surface, Alex saw nothing. He was lost.

Alex the unfamiliar clothes felt uncomfortable. Combat fatigues, basically. Rugged, rip-proof clothes a far cry from the worn jeans and T-shirts that had served him well for so many years. He'd have to get used to this.

But, Alex realized, if he could see himself in the mirror, then so could his enemies. This was a bad place to be. A more experienced man would have known that instinctively, he thought. Timmy wouldn't be able to hold the laughter in. Life and its lessons.

Like a rat from a pipe, Alex ran from behind the wall. He ducked down, back flat, and ran across to the car.

A thud, thud, thud clanged near his head.

Someone was shooting. They must have been watching the mirror. Alex felt his breath heat up beneath the mask.

But they'd missed.

For now.

Lifting his gun above the hood of the gutted Chevy, he fired a shot, and then another. Alex had no idea where he was aiming. The modified pistol kicked against his wrist. The siren screamed again. What had been minutes was turning into seconds. He fired one more shot, felt the recoil twist his wrist, and heard someone lumbering on the other side of the vehicle.

They were close.

There was no choice. Alex had to run the last fifteen feet to safety. Reach the other side of the room, hope Timmy was near, and get his help. Or give help. Whatever it took to win: to survive.

An idea struck, arriving quietly and making itself heard over the clamor. He needed a distraction. Still crouched behind the car, he felt around in his pockets. Nothing. They'd emptied them. Something to make some noise, to put off the attacker. Anything.

Alex undid the buckle on his mask. It was all steamed up, at least he'd get some use out of it. The flat transparent face stared back up at him. He weighed it in his hand. It was light. Plastic and mesh, mostly. Hardly designed to block much. Couldn't stop a fist. They just gave them out for the sake of it. He held the mask in his hand, scraped it against the side of the Chevy, and then rolled it along the floor, away from the wall.

A flurry of shots followed. They lit up the wall above the mask. But Alex was already running. He was gone, out and away from the car, his legs opening up. It was ten feet. Then seven. Then five. He was almost there, his eyes scanning the wall for any sign of his friend or any place to hide before the siren let out another, final scream.

The man's shoulder caught him full in the gut. The impact knocked the breath out of him. Alex dropped his gun. Together, the two of them rolled across the plastic floor. Not as hard here. Hard enough to hurt.

They tussled, tangled up, arms and legs locked together. Alex hit out with a fist. It found the man's mask. Only hit the buckle. Didn't do much. The man caught a wrist, wrapped one leg around Alex's neck and leaned back. It was a tight grip.

Choking.

The assailant pulled back hard on the arm, his thighs locked around Alex's collar and shoulder, squeezing. Every drop of blood began to crawl to a cold stop and he feel the edges of his eyes darken.

He flung his free arm against the man's shins, against his ankles and legs. Nothing. The man tugged tighter. Alex flailed, twisting and struggling. The man had him in a lock.

It was impossible to escape. There was nothing he could do. He felt around, finding only the floor. Then: there it was. The pistol. Alex's own. Light on ammo. But enough, maybe.

Alex turned the gun into his grip. He was losing sight. Losing breath.

He lifted the gun up, over his face. He fired. Once. Twice. A third and a fourth time. A red splurge burst across the man's chest, dripping down onto Alex's face.

But the man would not let go. Alex felt himself falling deeper and deeper into unconsciousness. His body was light. He fired the gun again. He couldn't feel anything. Squeezed the trigger again. It was empty. Nothing left.

THE LIGHTS WENT UP. The siren screamed for the last time. The man's legs loosened, and Alex's eyes widened as he lay on the floor, relishing each breath. Applause was sputtering into life above, the hasty patter of busy feet moving around the warehouse toward them. He drew a deep breath, feeling his mind creep back to the real world. Then, piercing it all, came Timmy's voice.

"I told you: never take off the mask, man," he laughed. "They don't like it."

Timothy 'Timmy' Ratz was standing above, his own mask perched atop his head, his crooked teeth barely containing the cackling rattle of a laugh as he stretched out a hand. Alex allowed himself to be dragged upright. Timmy was slightly taller and thinner. His skin was a pasty white, immune to any sort of sunlight, and near-translucent compared to Alex's own. They were wearing the same clothes, still holding the same weapons. Around them, others entered the room and began to clean up.

"It's like this every time?" Alex asked. "I don't think I could handle it."

"You did good, man," Timmy said, gesturing with his gun and handing Alex his discarded mask. "Well, mostly. I did tell you to get more ammo. We all saw you running out."

Alex waved away his friend's comments and turned around. The man who had tackled him was talking to a judge, pointing to a fierce bloom of red paint dashed across his chest. The man was still wearing his mask, but Alex could see the anger in his arms and body. There was an argument brewing.

"What's his problem?" Alex asked his friend.

"Oh, Freddy? He thinks he had you, says you shot him after the final siren. What did I tell you, man, people take this stuff seriously."

Timmy took both paintball guns, one in each hand. Using his thumbs, he flicked the safety switch, holstering one weapon and carrying the other. With deft fingers, he began dismantling his own pistol, raising it to the light and staring down the barrel. As Timmy turned, Alex could see a wash of smudged blue paint spread over his friend's back.

"They got you," he said. "I thought you were the pro."

"I'm no judge," Timmy replied, his tongue poking between his lips in concentration. "But I'm certain the aim on this is off. Should really invest a bit more in my own gear. The rental stuff they give you is crap."

The pistol clicked mechanically as Timmy lowered it from the light and reassembled it without looking.

"Come on," he said. "Let's go get changed and head out, before Freddy accuses you of anything."

Leading the way, Timmy motioned over his shoulder. Alex turned. The man was shouting, now, the mask barely containing his fury. Even now, he remembered the way the darkness had been setting in, the way the corners of his vision had edged toward the center. It had been exhilarating.

He felt like he should shake the man's hand. But he knew better. That same hand was now pointing in his direction.

Alex stepped lightly and caught up with his friend.

Timmy had a knack for escaping danger. Alex still had a lot to learn. The world was full of threats and there was no place quite like home.

CHAPTER 2

*T*he warehouse corridors were spartan: long, thin concrete tunnels which twisted around the arena like an ant's nest. The innards of the warehouse had been painted up like the end of the world. The walk to the changing rooms from the arena was short but strewn with all the artefacts of some post-apocalyptic, burning Hollywood vision.

It wasn't hard to find burned-out cars in Detroit, but hoisting them up on the walls must have taken some effort. This new sport was where the money was, Alex figured. He hadn't paid tonight, just tagged along as Timmy's guest. His skin still tingled, remembering the rush to beat the final siren. They gave you the first hit for free.

"You liked it?" Timmy asked, holding the changing room door open.

"I've never done anything like it," Alex replied, following him in.

Even the changing rooms were riddled with the same aesthetic. Someone had taken to the metal lockers with red paint, giving them a rust flavor.

"I remember my first time," Timmy replied. "Feels like only yesterday."

Timmy turned on his best thousand-yard stare. "You kids today," he said, "you don't know how good you got it. Back in my day, we had fights and paintball separate. Two whole different things. Why, I went to an MMA match with one of my pals and we didn't see a firearm all night. Could you imagine? What kind of hellish past was that?"

Alex jerked open his locker, throwing in his mask and finding the holster ready for the pistol. It was well-organized, this place, and well-funded. Start with an internet video spreading round the world like a virus, he knew, and soon you'd have everyone infected. They had franchises all across America now.

Timmy had been bugging him for months to try this out. Every day, his head poking around the cubicle, that mess of red hair arriving first, passing through some leaflet or printout, the word 'GUNPLAY' splattered everywhere.

There was a mirror in the back of the locker, coated in the filth of a thousand rounds of underground paintball fights. Peering through the grime, Alex he could see himself. Six feet on the dot, beard barely trimmed, though no more than two days old. Black hair short and cropped, anything long on top pushed to the right side but now muddled with sweat. The green of his eyes was being joined by the purple-blue of a bruise swell right above his cheek-bone. It'd be shining bright by morning. Tough one to explain to the boss.

Alex began to remove the heavily padded clothing. As he eased off the vest—Kevlar-lined, the advertisement assured—he felt a twinge in his neck and his shoulder. That man had turned something, had twisted a muscle in a way it was never meant to be twisted. Even to raise his arm up brought a world of pain crashing down on Alex's shoulder.

"Maybe I should have tapped out," he suggested. "Do they still call it that?"

"You got him in the chest though, man. Final shot. Boom. Then the siren. It was poetic. Honestly. Never seen anything so cool. Wish I'd done that well on my first time."

Trying his shoulder again, still expecting the pain, Alex didn't have the heart to tell his friend that the so-called poetic shot had been a last, desperate move, the product of not knowing what to do. Terror was not a good look, not these days.

In the locker were his familiar clothes, blue jeans and a shirt fixed with the faded logo of a company he couldn't remember. Someone else's store-bought nostalgia. Normality was rushing back to him, the pain in his shoulder and the rolled-up pair of socks tucked neatly into his sneaker a pointed reminder to Alex of why he was destined to sit in an office all his life.

"You coming for a beer later?" Timmy asked. "We can stop by my place. Got something I want to show you…"

Alex shrugged. A mistake. Wincing, he shook his head.

"Smarts, does it? One evening here and you think you're in Korea. You should see it when a blackout hits. Twice the fun. Kids these days, I tell ya."

Timmy was a year older than Alex, he knew. They both knew. But in certain worlds, in certain ways, Timmy seemed two hundred years old. Ask him about the news, the wars, the state of the world today–as Alex knew all too well—and Timmy would take on a morbid tone.

No one else at work made that mistake any more. No one but Alex. To him, Timmy's well-ripened pessimism was a soothing break from the grinning idiots who anchored the news, splashed across every screen.

It was nice to have a little doom and gloom in the world once in a while, even if most of Timmy's answers fell apart under any scrutiny.

Adjusting his socks, sliding into his canvas sneakers, Alex felt a rush of air as his locker slammed shut. He looked up. A weathered hand was holding the door closed, pressing so tight that the knuckles and joints were white. He followed the hand, up the wrist and the hirsute arm, past a faded green tattoo and over a gnarled shoulder, all the way up the turkey neck to see a man, seething, staring down.

"What the hell was that?" snarled the man. "What the hell?"

Words stumbled on his tongue.

Alex, his hands still trying to tie a shoelace, found his thoughts had deserted him. He felt a twinge in his shoulder. He understood. This must be the man from the arena. Wordless, he dropped the laces and tried to stand, but the man pushed him back down, finger pointing right into the aching shoulder.

"I had you down, maskless, and wrapped up. You should have tapped out. Given up. I shoulda won."

"I don't know what you're talking about," said Alex.

The red paint was dried, speckled across the man's chest. His mask hung from his hip, his pistol holstered. It wasn't the regulation, company-owned kind that Alex had tried. The metal gleamed, he could see, even when it was tucked away. It was twice the size of the regulation-issue guns, fitted with an extra-long clip and all sorts of bells and whistles.

"You know damn well. Now, what are you gonna do about it?" the man said, leaning down hard and close in front of Alex's face.

A hand split the air between them. It was Timmy, insinuating himself into the conversation with the care and guile of a drunken lover.

"Freddy, buddy, listen. This was Alex's first time. We know you got this." Timmy dusted off the man's shoulder, "That was a hell of a hold you put on him there, nearly wiped him out. Just telling me how close to tapping out he was. You been practicing? I know you weren't that good last time we played."

The anger fell off the man, like fall leaves from the trees. The rushing red skin gave way to a gentler auburn. Freddy blew a long snort through his nose. He cocked a head.

"Well, you know, Ratz," he said, "I been thinking about the service again. Got to get myself in shape."

Timmy patted the muscle on the man's arm. "Looks it, my friend. They'd be lucky to have a man like you. I've never seen you in such good form."

Smirking, Freddy turned away from Alex. Timmy slipped an arm over the man's shoulders, guiding him away and out of Alex's orbit. Even from here, Alex could overhear them talking. They'd switched into gun chatter, regaling each other with weapons and specs. Soon enough, Freddy had his pistol out of his holster and Timmy was turning it over in greedy fingers.

Now that the man was out of his face, Alex could see him as a whole. The arms might have been strong, the fury potent and fresh, but there was a sag about Freddy which had set in for good. A paunch hung over his tactical belt, and there was a slight limp when his attention slipped. The tattoo on his arm was real, probably from the service. But if the forces were welcoming back vets like Freddy, then things in the world must have taken a turn.

They'd nearly recruited Alex once. See the world, they said, get out of Virginia. For a farm boy with a broken heart, it had been more than tempting. Alex got all the way to the parking lot in front of the recruitment office when he'd overheard something on the radio. All the news came out of China and Korea, even back then.

But it had been enough. The sharp slap of awareness hit him hard across the face. People were dying out there; it wasn't a game anymore. Alex had driven home right away and packed up his possessions. It had been a long drive to Detroit, but the flight to the far east would have been much longer. They tried to recruit everyone, eventually.

Men like Freddy went back for a second bite.

Alex fiddled with his socks as he watched Timmy talk. He smelled an armpit; his shirt wasn't the freshest. Neither was he, for that matter. Once upon a time, these kinds of places had showers. Soap. Shampoo. Everything.

Nowadays, they had safety codes to cover all that. Couldn't have running water at a business like this. Pipes carry all sorts of things. Who knows what's in the water? That was what they said, anyway. Alex wondered whether it was just the company trying to save money. It sure made trips on the bus less tempting.

The pistol had been returned to Freddy's holster. Alex watched Timmy–Ratz, as they called him here –stroll back across the changing rooms. Timmy had been quick to change, though had hardly changed at all. He'd switched out one set of tactical-looking pants for another, his skinny legs bolstered by the extra padding. The man had more pockets than he had possessions. Black trousers, a gray T-shirt, and a khaki waistcoat worn over the top, it must have taken Timmy ten minutes to find his keys. Probably not. The man probably had a specific place to store them; a plan for every pocket.

"He was not pleased with you," Timmy announced.

"I did something wrong?" Alex knotted his shoelaces. "You told him this was my first time, right?"

"Sure. Everyone's a bit on edge now, especially round here. You see the news? Crazy stuff. Anyway, I smoothed it all out. This wouldn't have happened if you'd just bought more bullets. That thing with the mask though? Still love it."

"You saw that?" said Alex, gathering his possessions together, ready to leave.

"You kidding me? We were all watching, couldn't believe it. Taking your mask off in a paintball fight? Takes balls, man. Those things can have your eye out."

Alex hadn't considered this. The praise felt undeserved, almost enough to redden his cheeks.

"It kept misting up on me."

"You gotta spit in it, man." Timmy mimicked spitting into an imaginary mask. "Deals with that no problem."

The pair closed their lockers. Following the labyrinth corridors out of the warehouse, Alex felt like an ant all over again. Losing an eye? That was never the plan. Getting punched in the face was never the plan, either. He'd just reacted. All that effort to appear as normal as possible. Fitting in.

"You won, Alex. First time and you won," Timmy said, slapping Alex across the back. "Or you didn't lose, at least. We're drinking tonight."

"Work tomorrow, you know that."

Timmy pushed open the last door, bringing the two men out into the cool air of a Detroit autumn.

"Tomorrow can wait, my friend. Let's live a little."

CHAPTER 3

The wind was brittle. It cut up and under the shirt sleeves, around the ears, and across the parking lot. There was an ice on the air, a sign that Michigan was already thinking of winter. This part of Detroit was hardly paradise; there were plenty of warehouses, factories, and other empty spaces out here, waiting to be snapped up by companies looking to make a quick buck. It was a long way to the city center. Together, Timmy and Alex walked across the asphalt. They were quiet but in a comfortable sort of way.

"Back to my place?" Timmy asked. "Want to follow me?"

Timmy's place was in Grosse Pointe, almost on the shore. Alex lived in Forest Park. From their position in Riverside, that meant driving out twice as far and back again to get home. But what damage could a few miles do?

"Sure." Alex shrugged. "Let me just get my car."

He pressed the button on his keys, expecting a flash of amber lights from the darkened row of cars in the lot. Nothing happened. Timmy had already found his spot, an all-black SUV with worn-down tires. Walking along the row, Alex arrived at his Lincoln. It was beaten up. It was busted. But it was his. It was the same car he'd driven up from Virginia.

Inside were the same seats where he'd sat with Sammy and they'd driven around together for years. Stuffed up in the wheel arches, Alex assumed, there were still chunks of farmyard life: mud and corn husks and everything else that never seemed to shift. Once a car got driven onto the farm, it'd never be clean again.

With a longer, harder press at the key fob, the car finally woke up. The turn signals blinked, the interior light spluttered into life. Too many things were breaking these days. Opening the passenger door, Alex threw his bag into the spare seat. Riding solo tonight. Timmy pulled his car around, waving from the window. He was pointing at something uncomfortably close to Alex's car.

Down on the wheel.

The clamp was painted yellow, striped with black. Like a wasp, a warning. It was the last thing Alex needed. He searched around the lot. There were no signs, no warnings against parking in this particular place. Could be a fine from somewhere else. He already had a stack of parking tickets as high as an elephant's eye.

Forgetfulness and disinterest were a worrying combination, turning him into a rebel without a cause. No point in paying a city council which always seemed on the verge of collapse. Easier to just wait them out. But they must have finally caught up with him. He walked across to Timmy's window.

"Rain check for me."

"They get everyone, man," Timmy agreed. "Got me just last week. You need a ride?"

"Nah, I'll walk. It's not far. I can eat on the way. I'll see you tomorrow."

"Walk? In this city? You're braver than I thought, man."

"Compared to your driving? I'll take my chances."

When Timmy finally took no for an answer, driving out into the night, Alex returned to the clamp. There was a number fixed down the side. Call for help, it said. Fishing out his phone, he dialed. An error message appeared on the screen. The phone went dark. The long, familiar reboot. These Chinese models were glitchy as hell. Alex knew he should have sprung for something local.

Without the phone, there was no way the car was moving tonight. Alex didn't want to wander back into the warehouse. That was Timmy's world. He might as well leave the car. No one was going to steal that hunk of junk. Even thieves had standards. What was the worst that could happen, he thought, they'll clamp me again? Double negative. Two wrongs don't make a right. Either way, he'd need to start walking soon. His stomach rumbled.

Retrieving his bag from the car, he locked the doors. The lights shut off. Dead for the night. He'd have to come back the next day. Timmy would already be using it as an excuse to play again. Checking his wallet, Alex considered cab fare. But there was no cash. Rookie mistake.

Out here, in Riverside, at this time of night? Cash was the only thing that would get him home quickly. With an empty wallet, he started walking.

THE CITY HAD CHANGED in the last five years, even Alex knew. When he'd arrived, fresh from the farm, the very thought of the city was enough to excite him. Then he'd grown used to the sights and the smell, grown used to how the people moved and how the sidewalks felt beneath his feet, and he'd settled in.

Once he'd become acquainted, he could see how the world changed.

Even here, China was the name on everyone's lips. They'd knocked down half of Detroit and put up new factories on the same old spots. Spending American dollars and Chinese renminbi in equal measure, all on empty space. Alex was walking through them now. There'd been a boom, a time when people were flocking to the city to get a job alongside an army of foreign robots, building pretty much anything that could be sold to Americans.

Alex had done just that.

Now he worked in an office.

Times change.

The warehouses, the factories, and pretty much everything else in

Riverside had been thrown up in a boom, had weathered almost instantly, and now lay–mostly–abandoned. As Alex walked farther and farther from his car, the style of the street started to change.

Because that was how cities grew, he'd come to learn; they moved about like the oceans. People throw around money, somewhere upstairs, and then there's different signs above the doors, different names above the buzzers. Ships in the night. The previous people left, or were pushed, and a new wave of people washed ashore.

Then they'd go, chasing the tide in some other direction. What was left behind was the high-water mark, a pile of sticks and stones and wet detritus which told the world how high the sea had been and how far it had crawled back. Detroit – the whole world, really - felt caught in a rip tide, the money streaming out to sea.

Sink or swim.

THE SOUNDS WERE the same everywhere. As the city darkened, the shouts and sirens made themselves heard. All Alex needed was to get home safely. Sometimes, that meant moving toward the shouting.

Passing block after block, he could already hear trouble ahead. Yelling, running, and the sound of glass breaking. Another night in the city.

As he turned a corner, Alex saw the trail end of a crowd. They were walking ahead of him, marching through the streets. No direction in particular. Making their presence felt.

The protests and demonstrations had become common place. Walking across the city without seeing angry people was impossible. Alex marched on into the night, taking a backstreet through the block. If he could cut them off, he'd avoid the crowd altogether.

Halfway through, he knew he'd failed.

Shouts and screams. No one chanted anymore. Alex glimpsed the chaos through the alley ahead and walked on anyway.

As he stepped into the street, he was caught up in a current of bedlam.

Shoulders barging, jostling from place to place, people knocked him around.

Up above, flags and placards mixed with flaming torches. Old school anarchy.

There was no time to read the signs. A young man bounced Alex back, sending him stumbling.

"Hey, watch it!"

The man disappeared into the crowd before Alex could respond. He'd only stepped out from the alley a second ago and already he was lost. The people marched forward, pushing him along.

Deep inside, there was something about the protesters which appealed to Alex. The ability to care that much about anything, to feel that zeal and energy pumping through the veins. To know, entirely, that everything should change and to believe that stamping down the street would have an effect.

But Alex hadn't felt that way since leaving the farm. Since leaving Sammy on that porch and abandoning the recruitment office plan while still in the car park. He'd mortgaged his ambitions and his optimism in exchange for a comfortable, easy existence.

Existence and nothing more. Maybe one day he'd go back. But he was almost tired of telling himself that. Cruise control for the mind, making those long journeys easier. Running down the days, one at a time.

Snapping back from his thoughts, Alex felt himself propelled along by the protesters, fighting. He pushed and shoved, dragging his bag into any empty space on the road. All the time, people were shouting.

"Hey!" A strong arm pushed back against Alex, throwing him to the ground. "Out of the way!"

The bag broke his fall, scratching and skidding along the asphalt. Even before he could stand up, people were walking around him, on top of him, over him.

A knee caught Alex in the neck, knocking him back to the ground. The bag disappeared into a tangle of legs. He cursed. Nothing but dirty laundry inside, but it was his dirty laundry.

Alex dived toward the place it had just been, knocking up against the denim knees, tripping up the protestors.

The noise was immense and incalculable. A hundred people, everyone making their presence felt, everyone chanting to their own tune. From the ground, Alex looked up at the signs.

Anti-government. Anti-China. Anti-trade. Anti-gangs. Anti-everything.

Everyone knew what they hated.

Alex looked around and saw his bag between two feet. He grabbed at it, snatching hold of a handle. As he dragged it toward himself, the feet came too.

"Stop that!" A voice called from above. Alex looked up. A man with a nose ring and no hair, shouting. "Get out of here!"

"I was just getting-"

The skinhead didn't listen. He kicked Alex in the arm.

"I don't care what you say, you were stealing that bag!"

"I wasn't," Alex tried scrambling to his feet, clutching at his possessions. "It's my bag."

"Like hell it is!"

As the crowd moved around them, all chanting and marching, the man with the nose ring stared at Alex. There was hardly any space between them. He swung an arm.

Ducking to the side, Alex pushed into a petite woman with a placard. She swung the wooden stick, nearly clattering him in the head. It missed.

Alex straightened up, holding his back.

"Sorry," he said to the woman. "That man was-"

"Bag thief!" the skinhead was shouting. "Get the thief!"

Heads turned toward Alex. The light flickered from the flaming torches.

A wave of silence fell over the crowd. Starting from the front, it washed back, chasing away the noise.

"Get him!" the skinhead shouted again, pushing his way through to Alex. "Thief!"

"Cops!" someone yelled.

"Cops!" Other people took up the shout, spreading it around, hearing it echoed back.

As one, the crowd broke in every direction. Holding his bag tight to his chest, Alex ran.

Choosing a direction was easy. Anywhere the skinhead wasn't. Spotting an alley, Alex ducked down.

Behind, the sound of breaking glass and cracking skulls reverberated against the bricks of the buildings. But it was quite in the alley. Alex walked, dusting off his shoulders. That wasn't his fight. He'd seen too many protests and demonstrations to know they did nothing. Just people, lashing out in any direction they could.

Checking over his shoulder to make sure he wasn't followed, Alex picked up the pace and left it all behind. The cruise control switched on, guiding him back to his apartment.

CHAPTER 4

*H*alfway home, Alex noticed how hungry he was. Shoulder hurting, adrenaline dried up, he needed to eat. He was out of Riverside now, the streets changing their shape, the sounds of the protest dying behind him, others emerging ahead. By now, the demonstration would have become a riot. Something to catch later on the evening news.

Closer to the center of Detroit, he was passing shops, more and more, restaurants and all the other signs of civilization as he'd come to know it. But first, he knew, he'd need cash. This was a problem. Most places got picky when you tried to pay with anything else. Nobody trusted the banks anymore.

There was a police presence patrolling. They seemed to be headed back toward the riot. Alex couldn't see through the black masks they wore. Riot helmets, more rugged than the GUNPLAY equipment. If he got close enough to see himself reflected in the visor, he was too close. People kept their distance. They walked slower. Quieter. The police walked on past.

The first ATM was nothing but a smashed screen, but the one after that seemed to be working. Alex joined the line, waited his turn, and took his dollar bills. He had heard people in the line talking, chatting to one another. The same stories seemed to be bouncing back and forth between everyone he overheard. It was like trying to piece together current events by standing on newspaper scraps blown down the street by the wind. Half a headline here, a few sentences of comment there.

Along one street, Alex found himself outside of an electronics shop. It wasn't one of the upmarket American ones. People here still resented the Riverside factories after they'd shut down. But most people, at least on this side of the city, imported. Chinese phones, TVs, computers, and all the rest. The pieces were cheap, tacky, and almost disposable. But they were all most people could get their hands on.

Alex watched through the store window. They'd turned the TV screens to different channels. There was no sound and trying to watch through the barred windows was inconvenient at best. North Korea, one screen read. Boats at sea, said another. Floods, swarms, strikes, sickness, gangs, riots. They only talked about one Korea these days. They only talked about the boats when they sank. The gangs seemed to slip by unnoticed. Probably how they liked it.

One screen was leading with the story of a plane. Sick pilot lands plane, the headline read, scrolling across the bottom of the screen. A news anchor smiled from ear to ear as she read the story. Alex couldn't hear the words but he could see the photographs of the sick pilot. The man seemed close to death, his skin a pallid sweaty gray, but he'd managed a grin. Why fly at all if you're sick? There was no mention of what illness he had.

Flying too close to the sun.

Feel-good fare and no one asking the real questions. Alex turned away from the report before it finished. They wouldn't say anything of value.

Crowds were gathered at the foot of the staircase beneath the plane, hands waving as the man stepped down. Those same hands reached out, touching his back, cheering, and congratulating the pilot. So many people were smiling, Alex left them alone.

The news, when he watched it, seemed so saccharine. It made his teeth hurt. Too much sugar. Alex could remember listening to his dentist. The man had been wise and sensible and had hairs in his nose. Alex had been fascinated by those hairs when he was a boy. Now he spent every other Sunday with a pair of tweezers and a mirror, trying to stay presentable. Too much sugar, the man had said, it rots your teeth.

As he stood in front of the store, watching the flashing images, Alex heard a sound. A whimpering. A cry of pain. It came from the alley nearby.

Keep walking and let someone else deal with it. That was the attitude most people would take. Alex knew he should have turned and walked away. But he heard the sound again. Someone sounded hurt. The kind of sound which would haunt him as he lay awake in his bed, the guilt scaring off the sleep. He had to take a look.

Creeping quietly, Alex approached the entrance to the alley. It was dark inside, a dead end. Fire escapes loomed above and a pair of dumpsters meant he couldn't see all the way inside. Gang graffiti was printed all over the walls in Spanish and English. Fumbling with the light on his phone, praying the Chinese hardware would hold up, he shouted into the shadows.

"Anyone in there?"

The whimpering sound came again and then died, instantly. Someone was definitely there.

"Hello?"

No response. Plausible deniability, Alex thought to himself. He'd tried.

Taking a look up and down the street, he tried to spot a cop. They bustled and ran about in teams, crisscrossing the streets every night. But there was never one when you needed one. Just an empty street and the painful sound.

Flicking his wrist, Alex flashed the light into the darkness and started to walk forward. He arrived at the dumpster and paused.

"Hello? Are you hurt? Who's there?"

"We're fine, man. Back off." A gruff voice. Someone bent down.

"I heard someone. They sounded hurt."

"That was me." The gruff voice had an edge to it. An implication. A threat. "Just me."

Someone whimpered even as the hidden man was speaking. He wasn't alone.

"Just you?" Alex asked, arcing his light higher. "No one else?"

"Just me." The man was standing up now. "You want to check?"

Alex inched forwards, dumping his bag quietly behind a trash can.

"I heard someone else. Are they hurt?"

"Ain't no one else here but me, friend. Leave me alone."

Alex sighed. He moved forward again. He should have dialed 911, he told himself. Fat difference it would have made. There was that whimper again. Pain. The pang of guilt. He knew he had to do something, even if it was the wrong thing. He had to try.

"I think they're hurt," Alex called out. "Just let me help them."

"People need to stop giving a damn when it's ain't your damn to give."

The man was right next to Alex. The dim light on the phone did nothing. The stranger's breathing moved around in the shadows.

Alex ducked the first punch. He knew it was coming, staggering back toward the entrance of the alley, raising his fists. The phone fell to the ground, throwing its light up on the walls.

The knife emerged from the darkness first, held in a tattooed hand. As the man stepped forward, Alex knew he was in a gang. He'd seen them all over the news. The way they painted their skin, the long black letters written across their throats.

The gang member smiled, revealing a row of golden teeth. Two blue eyes and a shaved head creased and folded as the grin spread.

"Oh, I am going to enjoy stitching you up, my friend."

The alley was a dead end. This man was going to come through him, no matter what. Watching the knife, not the eyes, Alex relaxed on his toes and raised his fists. Just like being back at the warehouse.

The knife moved, darting forward. Alex sprang back, all his weight pressed down through his toes, his fists raised in defense. All that hard work in GUNPLAY, it had raised his confidence. Time to put the practice into action.

The man laughed, swinging the knife again. He didn't have to be accurate. The alley was cramped. Slash anywhere and Alex would be cut.

"Just had to interfere, didn't you? I hate you types..."

The knife slashed through the air. Alex watched the blade. He waited.

"You're going to learn to mind your business."

The knife wasn't sharp. It didn't need to be. Alex watched it slice back and forth. This wasn't a game. This was a mistake.

"Now you're going to learn-"

The man slashed with the knife before he finished talking. Alex jumped to the side, feeling the blade cut through the air beside him.

As the gang member stumbled, Alex kicked out with a sneaker. He caught the man in the hip, knocking the knife from his hands and sending him sprawling into the trash can.

Alex picked up the knife from the ground. It was lighter than he expected. Rusty.

The man picked himself up, turning around.

"That's it, you're dead-" He turned around and saw Alex holding the knife. "Now, hold on..."

"Go." Alex jutted the knife into the empty air. "Get out of here."

The man walked backward toward the entrance of the alley.

"Now, listen, buddy. Don't do anything stupid. One word to my friends, and we come back here and-"

Alex waved the knife at him.

"Run away!" he shouted. "Now!"

The man dodged the knife, his tattooed hands flailing. He looked Alex in the eyes and bolted, sprinting around the corner and out into the street. The sound of footsteps died away.

Alex heard the whimpering sound again.

Turning around, fetching his phone from the ground, he threw the knife into the dumpster and shivered. The blade had felt wicked. A short, sharp evil. He had no business holding it.

Looking around with the light, he delved deeper into the darkness.

"Hello? He's gone. You can come out now. He might come-"

It was a girl. A teenager, most likely. She was shivering, balled up against the wall behind a dumpster. When Alex flashed the light on her, she recoiled, trying to hide herself. He turned it off.

"Hey, hey." Alex crouched down beside her. "Don't worry. I'm here to help. I…"

Something was wrong. The girl wasn't really looking at him. Her hair was stuck to her forehead with sweat. She was shivering. It wasn't that cold.

"You're scared? I'm not going to hurt you…"

Alex offered her his hand. She looked at it with a pair of big, gray eyes. They were bloodshot.

"You've been crying? Look, I'm sorry, I don't know what happened here…"

The girl was pushing herself up against the dumpster, trying to hide from Alex. He backed off, pulling his phone from his pocket.

"Okay, okay. Look. I'll call the police. It's fine."

Alex dialed the number, pressing the phone to his ear. The girl was blinking her eyes, struggling. Twitching. Sweating. Whatever the gang member had been doing, she was scared. Terrified.

"Er, yeah, hello? Is this 911? Yeah, I need the-"

The girl swatted the phone from his hand, knocking it to the ground again. She sprang to her feet, panting and heaving.

"Woah, sorry." Alex stepped back, holding up his hands. "I didn't mean to…"

Staring at her, all he could see was terror in the girl's face. Pale and sickly, she didn't look well.

"I won't call the police. Fine. How about the ambulance? They can help-"

The girl screamed, pushing Alex back into the darkness of the alley. As he regained his footing, he saw her running and teetering toward the street. He chased after her.

"Wait! I'm trying to help…"

Alex reached the opening of the alley and looked around. The girl was nowhere to be seen. She'd disappeared.

"Weird…" Alex muttered to himself as he walked back to his phone. It was still connected.

"Yeah, hi?"

"Hello, sir?" The voice on the other end sounded distant and tired.

"Okay, you're still there. No, I had an issue. There's a sick girl, I just found her in an alley. But I lost her. Do you know what I should do?"

"Where are you, sir?"

Alex didn't know. He looked around, desperately.

"Maybe halfway between Forest Park and Riverside, but I'm not sure where-"

"Thank you, sir, we've logged this information. Have a nice evening."

"Wait, what are you going to do about it?"

"We'll keep it on file. Have a nice-"

"But there's a sick girl out there, aren't you going to help me find her?"

"Sir, we have too many calls tonight to chase rumors. We have to-"

"But I saw her. She looked close to death."

The line went dead. Either they'd hung up or the phone had cut out. Alex looked up and down the empty street. She was gone. Lost into the same night as the news reports and the protests. That same sweaty fear, a pale gray terror across all the faces. At least he'd tried to help. Maybe his parents would be proud.

Screams could be heard in the distance. Shots being fired. An explosion. Alex was still hungry. He still had to get home. Collecting his bag, he began to walk again.

CHAPTER 5

*P*icking a place to eat was easy. Two blocks from his apartment, Alex knew that Al's would always be open. Hot dogs, chili fries, wings, and minimal health bylaws followed. Pretty much what you'd expect from a place that was open till just before dawn. The neon lights inside were not only on, they lit up half the street in front of the store. It was blinding.

"Hey, it's Alex. Alex Early, coming in late. Look at this guy." Al pointed toward Alex with a fork, speaking to a man in the back who was face deep in a plate of fries. "Eh, you don't listen."

Offering up his respects and his greetings, Alex looked around the room. There were a few empty seats. To call it a restaurant would give Al's too much credit. There was no space for a restaurant. There were two sides: one was Al, sitting behind his grill, watching over everything with the meanest eye for detail; the other was a flat shelf, about chest height, with a row of tall chairs which spun in half circles, ready for the customers. There was no better place to eat in the city.

There was always a TV, stuck up in the corner of the room. Al used it for sparring practice. Stuck in behind the grill for fifteen hours a day, he'd shout back and forth with the screen, with the customers, and with pretty much anyone else.

"You'll have your usual," Al announced. "You seen all this?"

Alex nodded. His usual was rarely the same meal. Sometimes it was a hotdog. Sometimes cheesesteak. Whatever, Al had a knack for picking the perfect food for any time of night. Tonight, it was a Coney dog. It filled a hole.

All the while he was cooking, Al pointed at the TV. As well as Alex and the man with a face full of fries, there were two other people in the small room. One of them was a young man, blonde and dressed up nice, in a suit and tie. The other was older, but not ancient. Middle aged, but not wearing it well. He dressed in military-store supplies, that very specific kind of green. Tags around his neck, too, Alex noticed. The same air as Freddy. There were plenty of folks like Freddy these days.

While the food cooked, Al was busy shouting about Koreans. He wasn't shouting much, just making sure everyone was watching the TV. You hearing this, he'd ask, you see what they're doing? He'd ask the room at large, waiting for a rumbling of support. Most people nodded in gentle agreement, but the younger man decided that he'd speak up.

"Turn it all to glass, that's what I say. Let's see them try to run an ash field."

The man cackled while he said it, a thin wisp of blond hair falling across his eyebrows.

"That right, huh?" Al responded, his eyes already back glued to the screen, his hands flipping meat on autopilot.

The younger man didn't stop. Encouraged, he began to chat, talking about Korea this and China that. They're taking over, he garbled, cheap products as Trojan horses, leaving the country stoney broke. Typical talk radio fodder. Alex ignored him. Lots of people talked in Al's, though often not for long.

But not everyone ignored the blond boy. Alex began to watch the other man in the room, geared up in fatigues and twitching every time this youngster ran this tongue about dropping bombs. Al offered up Alex's food and he turned back round to face the TV.

"Got to show them we mean business," the younger man snapped.

"Only one thing they understand. Boots on the ground. Bombs in the air. It'll be glorious."

And on he went, on and on as Alex chewed through the food, watching the older man's fists clench and unclench, knuckles whitening and then rushing with blood. A vein throbbed on his forehead, each boisterous syllable causing it to swell a little more.

Then, the older man snapped.

There wasn't a shout, there wasn't a warning.

He simply got to his feet, walked across the room, and grabbed the back of the blond kid's neck and smashed his face into the counter.

As the younger man writhed on the ground, Al shouted over his grill, the older man dared his opponent to his feet, and the man with the plateful of fries just watched. Alex got up. This had all happened before. Not just in this diner, but everywhere. The same scenes playing on different stages, up and down the nation.

Alex stuck a ten-dollar bill by the door, making sure Al saw it. He stepped out into the night again. Someone else could deal with the fallout. Al would sweep up the debris, making the most of whatever was left.

The sounds of the fight spilled onto the street. The light from Al's diner was interrupted by the shadows, the men moving fast behind them. People on the other side of the road were stopping to watch. Alex left them be. He walked home.

THE LAST TWO blocks were the hardest. It was cold now and nearly midnight, the last warmth of the day having risen up into the sky, and the wind off the lake blowing in low and hard. Alex had his bag slung over his shoulder, the sleeves of his T-shirt billowing about his arms. Just two blocks to walk, though, and then he'd be home.

Across the flat side of a concrete tower block, a person had crawled up to the gutter with a spray can and written the words APOCALPYSE NOW SEPTEMBER 2027. Alex had no idea what they were worried about now, the unseen graffiti men. Kids, probably. They'd crossed out the month regularly, different dribbles of paint poking out from beneath the month. It had been January, then March, then May. Always worried about something.

At least it was up to date.

At least it was better than all the gang tags.

Alex walked in silence. He was quiet, at least, but the city offered no such option. There were sounds everywhere. The ambulances, the squad cars, the freeway–it all came together in one chaotic din, mixing together along the length of the street and emerging as a single, untidy racket.

It was the sound of the city, as Alex had come to understand it. Different than life on the farm, for sure, but not worse. Just different. If the sounds were out there, he thought, it meant people were busy living. Going about their business.

Even now, Alex could remember the shroud of silence which settled over his parents' farmhouse every night. Nothing for miles, nothing but rustling corn and calling birds. It was never quiet but it was silent. Anything could have happened on the other sides of the fields and no one would know any better.

Instead, the hum, the drone, and the noise of the city was reassuring.

One street from his house, a cop car pulled up alongside Alex, siren blaring.

The officer stepped out. Tapping his pockets, searching for his documents, Alex began to worry. They weren't in his front pockets, or the back of his jeans. Had he left them in his car? These regular stops weren't too tricky to navigate but if you were one piece of plastic short, you'd be spending a night in the cells.

"Sorry, officer," Alex said. "I just need to search my bag. Is that all right? I just want to reach inside."

Bending double over the bag, Alex watched the cop's face for permission. The man said nothing. His uniform was crisp and his dark trousers had a crease which could cut cold butter. Alex took the silence as agreement and began to unzip the bag. The cop's hand moved to his hip, unclipping the button beside the gun.

Alex continued, slowly.

The bag was full of junk. Not stuff he ever needed but stuff he'd regret not having. Cables for this or that device. Old work for the office. Pens. Paper. Keys. But not the documents he needed right now. They were buried somewhere, underneath the dirty laundry. Alex kept fishing around.

The cop's radio crackled into life. Still rummaging, Alex couldn't hear all the words. They were drowned in static, lost to the ether. But the cop seemed to understand. He called in his position, told them that he was waiting on a "possible perp."

"Gangs out tonight?" Alex tried a hollow laugh. "I saw a guy earlier that-"

The officer kicked the bag, cutting the conversation short, and folded his arms.

Alex dug harder down into the bag. The radio continued. The words were scattered. Hospital kept coming up. Doctors. Ambulances. A siren sounded in the distance. Gunshots, too. Disease, Alex was sure the radio said. Back-up. Roadblock.

He stopped, looming over his bag, listening to the radio. Bag searches happened enough times that he knew how to handle himself. It didn't take a genius to work it out.

The cop kicked the closest pocket, jerking Alex back to attention. With frequent apologies, the search began again, fingers finally falling against something laminated and hidden in a corner of the bag. That had to be it. Looking up, making eye contact with the cop, he began to remove his hand unhurriedly from the bag.

"It's my ID. I'm just taking it out now," Alex said. "Is that all right?"

The cop didn't say a word. Alex pulled out the object and, without looking down to check, pulled it up and presented it. It was his ID card. It would suffice. The cop ran his eyes over the picture for half a second, turned around, and walked away to his patrol car.

As he left, he began to mutter something into his radio. There was no way to hear what he was saying, but it didn't matter now. The ambulances were crying again, closer this time. Something was brewing up inside of people. Even though Alex wasn't far from home, the journey had taken far longer than he'd expected.

THERE WERE three locks on the door but only two really worked. The third, the biggest, was mostly for show. But, even when standing at the door, Alex made a spectacle of unlocking it. It was all theater. The entire world was a stage, even this boring, bland Detroit street where Alex happened to live.

Once inside the building, Alex began to walk to the second floor. It was an older building, built in the seventies. But it had been built well back then. There were three floors. He lived in the middle. His apartment was four rooms, sandwiched between two neighbors he barely knew. It was good. Their homes provided insulation.

Not just the heat–though that was welcome during the Michigan winter–but the sound. The fury of the city life was blocked off well inside Alex's apartment. It was why he loved the place.

Alex undid the final lock on his door and entered the dark rooms beyond. He didn't turn on a light. He didn't need to. There wasn't much furniture and he knew the layout. There was the sofa, the book shelf, and the cabinet with the broken television.

He'd never gotten around to getting it fixed. Back when it had worked, he'd only used it to watch old movies. They didn't make anything good anymore. Besides, he appreciated the quiet inside the apartment. It made a nice change.

Throwing his bag beside the door with an annoyed grunt, Alex showered and readied himself for bed. Walking home had taken an age. It was already so late. So many interruptions. No time at all to think. He'd have to take the bus to work the next day, have to get Timmy to drive him out to his car. The chores just piled up, one after another. As he prepared himself for bed, he opened a window. It was cold out. No wonder people were sick.

Through the open gap, he listened to Detroit singing its song one last time, reveled for a moment, and then shut the window and went to sleep. He didn't dream.

There was something happening in Detroit. In America. The country was far beyond dreaming now.

CHAPTER 6

*A*lex sat at his desk and tried not to think about anything. The cubicle was small. The computer in front of him was loud and cheap. All around the office, the sounds of a hundred fingers hitting a thousand plastic keys sounded like a million drops of rain against a tin roof. A thunderstorm, really.

There was a coffee cup, now empty, and a selection of pens. Papers were stacked in trays. Certain pieces had to be stamped. Certain forms had to be signed. The name above the office door was an acronym. No one seemed to know what the words stood for.

Alex stared at numbers in a spreadsheet, as he did every day. If he stared long and hard enough, they became shapes. If he stared even longer, he might be fired.

Alex had his phone balanced on his lap. The computer had been gutted, locked down and prevented from accessing the outside world. A security risk. But Alex could still read on his phone, when the device decided to work. Today, it was well behaved.

The cubicle was very open. Only three walls. Anyone walking past could look right in. But Alex had found a position, leaning slightly on his right arm, where he would hide most of his body from passers-by. To them, he might seem as though he was concentrating incredibly hard. But, in actual fact, he was reading articles, news, books, and everything else on the small screen on his knees.

But it wasn't enjoyable. It was worse than actually working, in a way. Flicking between stories, reading only headlines and isolated sentences. Every time he started to read, Alex felt his attention snapping to something else. There was always a more important matter, a more deserving way in which to waste his time. In the end, he tried to read everything and eventually read nothing. A Teflon attention span. Nothing stuck.

At this moment, Alex found himself determined to read. *Korea*, the headline began, *has today announced…* As he read through the opening paragraphs, he could feel his attention slipping. Trade wars, troop movements. Always the same stores, rehashed and re-released. Alex resolved to read the rest. What had they announced? It was buried in the text somewhere. But his eyes were darting over the lines, picking out random words.

China. Boat. Airborne. Injection. Warning. Alex was drawn in, determined to read properly. This seemed important, he told himself. He had a duty to know more. The work be damned; they weren't paying him to think. He squinted harder at the phone balanced in his lap, his mind tracing lines between these stories and the pilot on the news and the girl in the alley and -

"Hey."

Alex snapped to attention, dropping his phone to the floor.

"What's up?"

It was Timmy, his flustered red hair moving into view. Alex bent down and retrieved the device. It had turned itself off. The reboot sound chimed around the cubicle.

"Not much," said Alex. "Shoulder's still a bit sore."

"Sure thing, shooter," Timmy replied. "You get used to it. How about that beer tonight? Don't tell me you got your car already?"

"Nah, I still need to collect it. Once I'm free, I can pick up whatever."

Timmy looked around the cubicle, eyes lingering over the stacks of paper that still demanded Alex's signature.

"Great. Hey, weird question. That girl. With all the... blue. Works two cubicles down. Seen her lately?"

"Tan?" Alex said, rubbing his head. "I think that was her name."

"Yeah, her. You seen her around lately?"

Standing up, head poking up above the cubicles, Alex looked out across the sea of bobbing heads. Tan had a shock of blue hair, which was easy to spot from pretty much anywhere in the office. That could be an advantage, when sailing an ocean of anonymous, damn-near-antonymous workers. Easier for a superior to pick out.

But that could be a bad thing. For the same reason. Alex would never had risked it. Safety in numbers. Herd immunity. Better to keep plugging away. Tan's blue hair was missing from the crowd of cubicles. He slumped back into his chair.

"Haven't seen her in a few days, actually," Alex thought aloud. "Though I'm sure there's less people working here than before."

"Fewer. Who raised you?" Timmy said. "Shame about Tan. Probably canned her. Thought we had a spark, though."

Sitting back in his chair, Alex realized that the office was quieter than usual. The stacks of paperwork were shorter than normal. He'd been having too many emails bouncing back. Out of office. Sick day. Leave me a message. A break in the routine. It might be worrying, he thought, but at least it was different. Play the same song a thousand times and a bum note starts to sound good.

"This company's going belly up, I guess. Hiring freeze? Wouldn't surprise me."

"Hey, people hear you two talking like that, they'll start asking questions."

It was Eddie, who'd wandered up to the cubicle, coffee cup in hand. Eddie had worked at the company for years. Back when it had been an entirely different acronym. He had the nicest chair in the office, a holdover from the good old days. A man devoid of any sort of hustle. A worker. A drone. A nice guy with a funny tie. Eddie was clean shaven and at least ten years older than everyone else. Alex liked him.

"Hey, Eddie. Working hard?"

"Or hardly working," Eddie replied, apparently hoping that such a statement might contain some trace vestigial humor. He beat the funny out of the line with a bat, an old slugger who'd overstayed his retirement. Second base was Eddie's world. Nothing more, nothing less. Steady Eddie, no one called him. Not to his face, anyway.

"Watching the Tigers tonight, Eddie?" asked Timmy.

Eddie patted the pocket on his shirt. Two tickets were conspicuously placed, visible behind a row of three pens.

"Got an extra if you want one. Always room for one more."

"Nah, I'll watch it at home," said Timmy. "Got a trick to get around the blackout. You get a screwdriver, you see, and then…"

Timmy talked Eddie through how to take the plate off the back of his television, how to fiddle with a few screws, and solder this and that. Alex tuned out. Eddie seemed to do the same, but he was politer.

Eddie nodded and smiled. Alex looked down at his phone. Alive again. He restarted the article.

At least, he started looking at the pictures. It was easier to focus on the photos. Images of American military ships, patrolling the high seas. They were shot like an action movie, placed near the top of the article. All those clean-cut men, it seemed to say, ready to defend the country. Probably more men like Freddy than you'd expect, Alex thought, not quite so slim and bountiful as they'd once been. Probably an army of computer geeks buffing up the men and whitening their teeth in some government sub-basement.

Scrolling down through the pictures, the images of the military ships and men vanished. They were replaced by pictures of different ships. Cobbled together boats, made from plastic oil containers and railroad ties. Rope lashed across anything buoyant. These photos were not shot as dramatically. They were seen from afar, flotsam and jetsam bobbing on the water. Alex crouched his head down by the phone.

There were faces on the boats, all of them lined up on the edge. Alex had never met a Korean person. Not that he could remember, anyway. In the article, in the photo, these faces peering over the side of the boat almost didn't look like people. They weren't happy. They weren't smiling.

But they didn't look sad, either. It was like they'd never known that either end of the emotional spectrum was available as an option. Alex knew how they felt. The article captioned the images. A boat of Korean refugees, it said. These people probably had families. Maybe they were there with them. Each one probably had a story. Couldn't tell that from the article.

Next was a group of American fishermen. They'd been dressed up in their thick knit sweaters, their beards bustling and rustling in the sea breeze. They were posing with a group of ten stragglers. People who'd been afloat for days in the ocean. Picked up somewhere in the Pacific. Brought back to harbor. Catch of the day, the caption read. The quiet eyes of the boat people were half-closed in the sunlight. Too close to the sun.

It was dawning on Alex, slowly, how little he knew of the world. How the cogs turned and twisted, their teeth locking together, and driving the big machine forward. How this piece connected to that, how interwoven and entwined everything had become. From tower block fires to traffic stops, GUNPLAY leaflets to refugee ships, sinking in the China sea. All that information was out there and he was immune. Inert. Passive. Maybe, he wondered, it was time to switch himself back on.

The screen shut down. Clapping the phone against the heel of his hand, Alex tried to bring it back to life. He hadn't finished looking at the pictures. He hadn't even started reading the article properly. He wouldn't be able to find the same piece again later. The news moved too fast. Cursing, he threw the phone across his cubicle.

"Those Chinese ones," Eddie announced, "they always were unreliable. I buy American. Only the best, they say."

Eddie had reached into his pants pocket and produced his own device. Even from his chair, Alex could see that it was more polished. More cared for. Probably cost Eddie two month's wages, he wondered. And now it was just covered in fingerprints and coffee dust. What was the point?

"Did they get a new coffee started?" Alex asked Eddie.

"Oh, yeah," Eddie replied. "We got that new blend in, as well. Javan, I think. Rich and aromatic. I'd get down there before it's all snapped up."

Standing up, leaving his phone behind, Alex emerged from his cubicle. "I'm going to the break room. Anything I can get you?"

"Just your John Hancock." Eddie motioned to the paperwork on the desk. "Time's a tickin', Mr. Early."

Timmy just shook his head. He knew how Alex felt about puns on his name. The same tired jokes. Just noise, now.

"You're on drinks," Timmy told Alex. "Do we need to sync our watches?"

Looking down at his bare wrists, Alex shrugged.

"Time is a cruel mistress," Timmy agreed. "She comes for the best of us. Don't be late."

He turned back to Eddie and the two delved deep into some technical mess. Turning away, Alex stretched his legs out and went looking for coffee. He hardly needed the kick. But a change in scenery can often do a world of good.

He'd heard that on some travel TV show. Why travel, thought Alex, when there's bits of Detroit still unexplored. Parts of Virginia that he'd never seen. Whole swathes of the states where he'd never set foot.

Wouldn't have to spend money on gas, either. Alex remembered the clamp stuck on the wheel of his car and groaned. Better pay up. They'd caught him, fair and square. There was still an hour to go before he was allowed to leave. Maybe the coffee would help. It came from Java.

CHAPTER 7

"*Y*ou want anything else?"

The beer cans clunking down on the checkout had made the owner sit up and take notice. Alex looked around the store.

"You got anything left?" he asked.

The shelves were as empty as the streets. There were pockets of products. No one had wanted the cat food, it seemed, or the washing detergent. But the canned foods were plundered. Entire shelves held nothing but dust.

The shopkeeper started shaking his head, ringing the cans through the register. He looked like he'd been running for miles, running hard with something chasing him. As he reached for the second six-pack, the scanner shut down. The entire machine crackled and sighed. It was a sound familiar to everyone. The reboot loop. Alex knew he'd be waiting here for a few minutes yet. A cost of doing business.

"Driver was late." The shopkeeper gestured at the empty shelves, making conversation to cover up the faulty register. "Haven't had any deliveries in days."

"That so?"

"Sick. I ring up, say I got nothing to sell, they say they got no one to drive. They ain't sick."

"You know how it goes," said Alex. "Bugs spread pretty quickly. Same thing happens in my office."

"Half the trucks are automated, though," the man replied. "But they don't send those ones down here. It's the gangs, really."

"Yeah?"

"They won't tell you about it on the news, but I've been reading on the internet. Whole gangs, taking over towns out in the country. Law enforcement won't go after them, don't have the resources."

Alex listened to the register rebooting, hoping it would hurry.

"Yeah, whole lot of them gangs," the shopkeeper continued. "MS-13. Triads. I know the names. News won't tell you about them. That's what's stopping the trucks getting through."

"Think they'll be back by the end of the week?" Alex asked, watching the computer screen as it reset.

"Doesn't matter. You miss one delivery, the whole thing messes up. One thing, two things go wrong? It all comes down. 'Cause a supplier couldn't send stuff out, it's there rotting in some warehouse. Then the truck won't load up anything that's in that condition. Then I can't get a delivery because the truck won't travel when it ain't full. It all comes down, you know?"

The man was animated, tapping the flat of his hand against the table with every mistake he described.

"Used to be so simple," he went on. "Field to table and all that. Now? Now we don't know what the hell."

Alex had tried corn from the field in Virginia. It had come right in from their farm, through the door, through his mom's hands, and on to the plate. He'd been sick of corn by the time he was twelve.

"All the stores like this?" Alex asked.

"All the stores down here. You need something, you get in your car and you drive over to Windsor. They got it good over there. Hell of a time to get there though. They take that border seriously. They don't let just anyone across. No gangs up north."

Surveying the shelves where the food used to be, Alex wondered whether Timmy would have something to eat. Maybe he should get something. Maybe Timmy wanted to eat cat food. *Whatever*, he thought. *We'll just order pizza*. Thirty minutes or less. The one constant in an ever-changing universe.

The register was back online. The owner cursed at the machine, slapping the side of it. He rang up the beer cans and waved Alex out of the store. The Chevy had remained resolutely unstolen. Everything was a Chevy these days. They'd bought up every other brand, absorbing them all like a feasting monster.

Getting the clamp off had been a hassle. A long, boring hassle. Calling through various local government departments, trying to read out his bank details, waiting for the phone to reboot every ten minutes. They didn't make it easy to pay. Alex sighed and fumbled with his keys in his free hand.

"Hands up!" a voice shouted over Alex's shoulder. "Now!"

The bodega door slammed shut. Alex could sense someone standing behind him.

"I don't have any cash on me. Car's worth nothing."

Would someone mug him for a couple of six packs? Hardly the organized gang violence the store owner had warned him about.

"I said put your hands up!"

There were nerves in the voice. A frailty. Alex obeyed the order, lifting up his arms, still holding on to the beer and the keys.

No one would want his car. A clapped-out old Chevy, not even one of the new electric models. Everyone wanted electric these days. Alex preferred the primal nature of internal combustion. A bit of fire in the belly. Finding an electric outlet was tough, especially in this part of the world. Why would anyone want to steal his ride?

"Good, now face the car!"

"Listen, man, I can-"

"Do it!" the mugger screamed, pushing Alex's shoulder, knocking him into the car door.

The cans fell onto the roof of the Chevy.

A weak push, Alex thought, his throat tightening. *This guy's an opportunist.* All around, he could hear doors locking and windows opening. People were paying attention. Why weren't they helping?

The mugger reached out for Alex's arm and spun him around. The keys fell to the ground.

The man had a knife. Not a sharp one. It looked rusty. Alex followed the hand, up the arm, and found himself face to face with a toothless old man, whippet-thin and toothless. He looked like a bum. Not an unfamiliar sight on the streets of Detroit. Not in this part of town.

"Listen, I just want to help you. Let's all relax, now…" Alex tried to keep eye contact, talking softly.

Everyone he knew had a story like this. Most of them ended up with a police report which went nowhere.

"No!" the mugger shouted. "Hand it over!"

"Hand what over?" Alex kept his hands in the air, his voice gentle. His heart was beating at a hundred miles an hour. He hoped it didn't show.

"The money!" the mugger yelled. "The drugs!"

"Like I said," Alex continued, "I don't have any money. I don't have any dr-"

The mugger jumped forward, throwing his whole body and knocking Alex into his car. The door rattled and Alex fell to the ground.

"I don't have time for this," the mugger said, leaning down beside Alex. "I have to get my medicine now."

The man's hot breath seeped into Alex's ear. Rolling over, trying to get to his feet, he could see the bloodied spiderwebs spreading out from the mugger's irises. He looked like he hadn't slept for days.

A sound behind made the mugger spin around. Alex looked. The bodega door had swung open. Standing in the doorway was the store keeper, swinging an old shotgun around the street. He fired it up into the air, rattling the windows in the nearby houses.

"Get out of here!"

The mugger ducked down, hiding behind the hood of the Chevy.

Alex searched around for his keys. The store keeper strolled into the street, gun pointing up in the air.

"Both of you, get gone. And you, don't come back!"

"I was just-" the mugger tried to protest before another shotgun blast cut him short.

As the store keeper reloaded, the mugger turned on his heels and ran. A shuffling, shambling run which didn't take him far. The shells in place, the bodega owner gave chase.

The street fell quiet as the two men ran away. Alex found his keys on the ground and opened up the door, collecting his beer from the roof.

The engine spluttered into life and Alex began to drive. It didn't used to be like this in Detroit. Things were changing. People were changing. He thought about calling the police. They already had too much on their hands. Better to call for food instead. Timmy would be wondering what had happened.

With the cans on the passenger's seat, he began to dial the pizza number. It was a dead line. The phone reset again. Throwing it into the foot well, the reboot loop called out again. Reliably unreliable. Another universal constant. He started the car and made straight for Timmy's house.

Quiet roads, quiet streets, and a quiet drive. The road out to Grosse Pointe was easy. All Alex wanted was for the things in his life to work. For the complicated structures and machinations to ease off and allow him to settle into a nice rhythm. For it all to make sense.

At least the car was on his side. The old gas engine rumbled out in front, the exhaust rattled out behind. It was a calm moment. Alex enjoyed it while he could.

CHAPTER 8

This was the suburbs. Grosse Pointe. How Timmy lived out here, Alex would never know. This was a whole different kind of quiet. He found the house easily. The huge SUV outside acted like a lighthouse, steering the Chevy to shore.

Parking in the street, Alex could almost feel the curtains twitching in the windows of the other houses on the row. Collecting the beer from the seat, he walked up to his friend's house and knocked on the door.

Waiting on the step, he looked around. The house was simple. Just the one floor, probably a basement below. Other houses in the area had pools and white picket fences. Timmy barely had a lawn. He'd concreted most of the space in front of the house, the SUV parked in front of the garage and the ground flecked with oil stains all over. No quarter shown to the homeowners' association.

Timmy was taking his time to answer the door. Alex knocked again. There was movement on the other side. A mechanical sound. A deadbolt shifting. A lock being turned. Another. And another. There must have been five different ways this door had been sealed shut. Finally, it swung inward and there was Timmy, grinning his lopsided grin.

"Glad you made it."

"Expecting trouble?"

"Always be prepared, Alexander. Always be prepared."

"Never had you pegged for a boy scout."

"Never had you pegged for an Alexander. But here we are."

Waving his friend into his home, Timmy took a quick look through the door and then sealed it up. They left the suburbs behind them.

This was the first time Alex had actually been to Timmy's house in a long time. For a while now, he'd been hearing about all the crazy additions and grand plans that his friend had been pondering. If he'd been invited into the home, then it meant the project was nearing completion. Castle Ratz was almost online.

For weeks and months, Alex had been wondering what kind of nuclear fallout bunker Timmy had built in his basement. Thoughts of lead-lined roofs and potable water tanks. All the excitement was beginning to fizzle – just a little – as Castle Ratz seemed like a fairly normal house.

That meant taking the tour. They started in the hallway, which seemed innocuous enough. Step through the front door and there was a simple, straight corridor which carried through to the kitchen. There was another door, fitted with thick steel plates, which presumably led to the basement. There were pictures in frames lining the walls. It was remarkably unlike what Alex had expected. He said as much.

"Look closer, man," said Timmy, taking the beers and making a beeline for the kitchen.

Alex leaned in on the pictures. Whereas most families had photos of kids, cousins, pets, and friends, that wasn't right for Timmy. Instead, Timmy seemed to have printed photos from the most famous moments in American history. And there, casually and artificially inserted, was Timmy. He was watching Nixon board the impeachment chopper. Sitting alongside a stressed Kennedy in the Oval Office. He stood behind Roosevelt during the Pearl Harbor address. He was watching Johnson get sworn in on the plane.

There was Timmy, dressed for the period, a part of history.

As they stepped into the kitchen, things did not get easier. The freezer had a padlock. The floor tiles were gun metal blue. Timmy seemed to have enough kitchen gadgets to feed a small army, including a vacuum packer. Alex was shown the various experiments, including carrots, kiwis, and watermelon, all of it sealed shut from the world.

Once the beer was in the fridge, the tour began in the garage. The heartbeat, as Timmy called it. The SUV outside, Timmy had a ditch dug out of the concrete floor. It was lined with bright bulbs, all pointing upwards. It was for working on the car, but Timmy called it his punji pit.

Along the wall was every tool imaginable. Each one had a place. Around the tool, Timmy had drawn a thick chalk outline. Take the tool off the rack and there was the empty shape, ready and waiting. It was spotless. Alex wondered whether Timmy ever actually worked in there or whether it was all for show.

The question was answered when they took a look at the basement. Unlike the rest of the house, which still had lingering traces of a regular family home, Timmy had worked hard on the basement. As they eased down the stairs, Alex could see the immaculate strip lighting. There were no shadows. The floor was perfectly flat, brilliantly clean. Alex joked about eating his dinner off it. Timmy was happy to try.

The basement was split into set areas. Not outlined with cubicle walls, like their office. That would have been too obvious. Instead, the linoleum floor was marked with corridors and areas, distinct spots for distinct jobs. It was very organized.

They reached the bottom of the stairs and the wall immediately facing the pair was twenty feet long and lined with guns. The real meat and potatoes. There must have been two dozen of them, at least. All shapes and sizes.

With the guns hanging carefully from the walls, behind a locked cage, Timmy had created a set of cabinets below. These were welded together and decorated with varnished hard wood. A real artisanal job. This was where the bullets lived. Each bullet, carefully organized by caliber and sitting beneath its parent, waiting for action.

The first thing which struck Alex was the sheer quantity. Timmy had a real arsenal down in the basement. Once he was over that, the organization was a level above and beyond anything he'd come to expect from his friend.

Timmy beamed like a proud parent.

Though Alex had grown up on a farm, he knew he'd struggle with the technical details. To his dad, the guns were just the twelve-gauge, the rifle, the twenty-two. Stock names, but Alex knew what the old man was talking about. For Timmy, it was a whole other world. It had its own language.

Alex watched his friend take a pistol down from the rack. A small lecture followed. It was ten years old, Timmy said, a classic.

It wasn't vintage, he assured Alex; that was a whole other thing. The vintage guns are on the other end of the wall. One of the smallest was called a SIG Sauer. Timmy took it apart.

The carefully machined pieces glided together, satisfying clicks and clacks as Timmy showed off the magazine and the action. Short reset trigger, Alex heard, just an utter pleasure. Em eleven A one. double stack. Alloy frame. Night sights.

As the gun came apart, Timmy handed the pieces to his friend to hold.

The words washed over Alex. He just held the disassembled pistol parts in the palm of his hand. There was a heaviness to them. Reassuring.

Once Timmy had reassembled the SIG, he handed over the entire piece. Alex began to lift up the gun, feeling the texture of the trigger. Timmy grabbed his wrist.

"Don't point unless you're gonna kill, man. Definitely not down here, either."

"What, the bullet bounces around in the basement?"

"Nah, you'll hit my plumbing. You want me to have a cold shower? I didn't think so."

He took the gun and placed it back on the rack. They walked

through the rest. German this, Italian that. Some of them were historical, stretching back as far as the Second World War. Those came with a short lecture and a detailed itinerary of how the gun had come into Timmy's hands.

"You don't take dates down here, Timmy?"

"They should be so lucky."

"Just me then?"

"Just you, my friend."

"What an honor…"

As well as guns and ammo, the basement brimmed with toys and tech. Cellular jammers, lock picks, and GPS units. Timmy had taken most of them out of the box for a cursory inspection. Alex approached a sealed black box, about as big as the containers which hung from pizza delivery bikes. When he pointed it out, Timmy scuttled over excitedly.

Inside were three pairs of night vision goggles. They fitted them up and turned off the lights. The whole basement glowed in a green hue. They must have cost a fortune, Alex half-asked. Timmy waved it away.

In one corner was a wooden pallet, piled high with cardboard boxes and sealed up with plastic tape. MREs, Timmy said, beside himself with excitement, meals ready to eat. Clunky name, thought Alex. The pallet sat beneath a row of four TV screens, each tuned to a different news network. One of them was the weather channel.

"What they taste like?"

"Like crap. Want to try one? Impossible to get a good taste and be nutritionally functional or whatever."

"Some people might call you paranoid, Timmy," Alex suggested. "You got a bomb shelter down here, too?"

"Don't be ridiculous," Timmy wagged a finger from side to side.

Alex laughed, looking around the basement. The guns on one wall, the MRE pallet on the other side. The TVs, now silently playing through the news. There was even a sofa, a tatty three-seater, which looked as though it had seen better days.

"Bomb shelter in the basement is against regulations," Timmy continued, smiling with half his mouth.

But Alex wasn't listening. Something had caught his eye. There was one corner of the room which wasn't lit at all. Alex had assumed it was storage. A place to stash all the junk used when renovating a house. Buckets of paint, plaster, that kind of thing.

But he was looking closely now. It was a huge shape, about the size of a hatchback with the top cut off. But it was covered in thick tarpaulin, from top to bottom. There was no hint at what was underneath. Above, a single strip light was fitted beneath a green shade, but not turned on.

"What's this, then? Hovercraft? Some kind of drone? Bet it's illegal if you've got it down here, wrapped up."

"What, that?" Timmy replied, turning toward the unlit corner.

He ripped away the tarpaulin in one smooth motion and flicked a switch. The strip light lit up the surface.

"That's the pool table."

The green felt was immaculate. Timmy walked to a cabinet and took out a long, thin case. It was metallic, the kind of crate Alex had seen rock bands use to cart equipment across continents.

Two clasps opened on the side. Timmy reached in and removed two separate ends of a pool cue. He pieced them together, screwing the thin end into the fat.

Fishing a chalk cube from his pocket, Timmy leaned over the light. It threw the shadows up over his chin.

"Welcome," he said, "to Castle Ratz."

CHAPTER 9

*A*lex was having a good time at Castle Ratz. Once the pool table had been set up and the beers retrieved from the fridge, Timmy brought down a battered old box. An old analog radio. A wireless, he insisted on calling it. "Thought we could hear the game on this."

"Didn't you tell Eddie that you knew how to get around the blackout? What was all that about soldering?"

"Ah, I read that online. Seemed easy enough."

"So these don't have it?" Alex motioned toward the bank of screens watching over them.

"Nope. They're just for the news. Got to keep on top of these things."

Timmy had muted all the TV sets but they played on in the background. The light above the pool table and the light from the screens was all they had. It was enough to play pool, at least. As they played, they talked.

Timmy would invariably react to some story on the news, a story neither of them could hear, while the baseball played on some ten miles away. The man announcing must have been doing it for years.

He didn't so much know the players' names, but he knew when to shut up and just let the audience hear the sound of the ball on the bat.

The sound was one of the only things which had stayed the same. It wasn't the reboot loop of a cheap Chinese phone. It wasn't the hum of an electric car creeping out of a warehouse carpark. It wasn't the screaming din of the news channels they'd silenced in the background of the basement. It was just a stiff piece of wood hitting sweetly against a square inch of tightly stitched horsehide.

No one watched baseball anymore, though. They were all at GUNPLAY. Alex listened again but didn't know the score.

But between innings, they'd get back to the news. That was Timmy's chance to evangelize. He'd bend down over his cue, lining up the white, waxing lyrical about this or that. But it wasn't just one subject and then another.

No, to Timmy, they were all interconnected. It was all butterfly wings and tornadoes, Korean biotech and San Francisco fisheries. Cartels, gangs, and the rising cost of medication. He was in his pulpit, on the other side of the pool table, and Alex was happy to listen. It was reassuring that someone was paying attention, at least.

"You really think it's all like that?" Alex asked. "You're just paranoid."

Timmy was quiet. Try and pry deeper into his mind and his surface level knowledge would thin out. Alex lined up his shot. Hit it. Caught the corner of a pocket and bounced out. He swore.

"Your hit," he said. "I shot a blank."

Timmy stayed quiet. Alex looked up. His friend was transfixed in front of the TV screens, edging closer and closer.

"Don't get too close, Timmy," Alex said. "You'll get square eyes."

Picking up a fresh beer, Alex pulled back the tab. There was that familiar hiss. But then he noticed. The baseball commentary had stopped. The sound of the bat on the ball had stopped. There were still sounds coming from the radio. But it was shuffling feet. The ambient noise of a huge group of people lumbering from foot to foot. Alex looked up again at Timmy.

"Hey," he said, "what's happened to the game?"

52

Waving a hand for silence, Timmy remained with his eyes glued to the screens. The hand turned into a pointing finger, twisted, and drew Alex's eyes up to the row of televisions. Alex watched the world change.

THERE WAS THE PRESIDENT. Terrance Fletcher himself. His face was across all five screens. Even the weather channel. They'd stopped mid-storm. There was still no sound. Alex could see the man's trademark smile. It had been plastered over every surface during the election. He'd been a handsome man in his youth. Winning easy against such an unpopular candidate, they'd made sure that everyone knew the face.

Knew which box to tick.

But that same youthful confidence wasn't there now. Alex carefully left his pool cue leant against the table. He walked around to watch with Timmy. The President was sitting behind a different desk. Not his usual oval office position. Everyone must have seen that a hundred times. This was different. Smaller. Cramped.

"It's Air Force One," Timmy said. "That's the desk they got on there."

Alex trusted his friend. When the man started to shake, along with his chair and table, they knew it to be true. Turbulence. They were hitting hot air. Which meant they were already flying. It had been serious enough for the news channels to cut straight to the President. They hadn't even updated the rolling tickers along the bottom of the screens.

As Alex watched, Timmy began digging around between the cushions on the chair. As he dug deeper and deeper, desperately looking for the remote, the radio crackled back into life. They cut to the same audio feed, the President speaking. The sound lagged slightly behind the man on the screen, the familiar words – "my fellow Americans" – arriving after the lips had already moved. It gave the entire speech a ghostly quality. A man speaking from another world.

There was too much information to process. Alex found himself studying the grain of the footage, the little beads and crackles which spoke to him from the past. This was the high definition future. The President's video fidelity was the least pressing issue, but Alex couldn't focus on anything else.

"You hear that? Eko virus."

The red mess of hair was standing still, for once, parked in front of the screens. Federal emergency and martial law. In twenty-four hours, they'd be shutting down state lines. People should get to where they needed to be. Alex had watched too many terrible action movies for this to make any sense. It shouldn't be happening.

He forced himself to concentrate, like trying to catch a waterfall in a paper cup.

"-on the advice of the FAA, FEMA, and other government departments. We have thought long and hard about this course of action and," the President's voice stuttered, "we can see no alternative. We must plan for a future, a future in which America the bold, the brave, and the free continues in the strongest possible fashion."

The man was talking, the delayed voice from the radio blathering about a national guard who had been federalized and a curfew introduced for everyone. Police leave cancelled. Don't leave your home. Lock your door. Stay inside. Don't dial the police. They're too busy. *This must be a joke*, Alex thought. *He can't be serious.* Timmy didn't move.

Walking back around the pool table and picking up the cue, Alex took another shot. He missed, again, and it didn't matter. They were playing a different game now. The radio was ancient and fickle. Most of the words were present and correct. But occasionally, the speech would fizz and hiss. In these empty pockets of dead air, Alex knew that people would be pouring in their deepest fears.

"Your shot," he told Timmy. "Looks like I'm staying here tonight. Holed up in Castle Ratz."

It was too dark in the basement. Alex went searching for a light switch. The radio broadcast was still echoing around the room, bouncing off the concrete floors.

"I implore you, my friends--" The President's voice ached, heavy with the weight of a hundred days arriving all at once. "—to stay safe. This is only temporary. We will not be defeated. This is a disease and, it seems to me, something against which we can fight.

"But we will not win this battle at the end of a sword or down the barrel of a rifle. We will triumph through our social graces, our common sense, and--" The voice snapped, catching a high note in the throat. "—our innate greatness. We must work together to stop the spread of this dreadful plague. We must deliver ourselves from the danger. We must entrust unto ourselves the power to conquer this terrible threat. Good night, and God ble-"

The lights went out. The basement was dark. Empty. Quiet. Another blackout. It felt good to be back on familiar territory. Alex heard his friend fumbling through a drawer. A match struck, lighting up Timmy's face. The sound of sirens was heard away in the distance, all over Detroit.

"You think it's real?" asked Alex, shadows catching strange shapes across his cheeks.

"I guess. I mean, it looked like him. And it was on the radio and all the TVs. What do you think happened?"

"I don't know. There's been some weird stuff happening lately. This is the weirdest bit of all."

"They're on the plane, so that's obvious. I don't know. Something seems off to me. They can't just announce that. We'd have known."

"Before now? Really?"

"They don't tell us everything. Why would they change now?"

"They've told us something."

"We'll see."

The match fizzled out, burning fingers as it went.

"Have you got any torches or whatever? You must have something that runs on batteries."

There was that familiar laugh.

"We can do one better than that, man."

Lighting another match, Timmy vanished into the darkness, taking the light with him. After a few minutes, a rumbling sound was heard. Then, a moment later, the basement sputtered into life. The gloom vanished and the screens lit up. The radio, too, was alive again. But no one was broadcasting. Instead, there was only static. Alex turned it off.

Of the five screens, only two were still broadcasting. They were running on a skeleton crew, it was clear. Gone were the complicated graphics, the glitzy animations, and the thin veneer of professional reassurance that was the newsman's stock in trade. Instead, there were two terrified people, reading falteringly from cue cards. Next to their heads, headlines rolled past with advice.

Stay at home. Don't break the curfew. Virus. Spreading. Quarantine. Cure. After just thirty seconds, the words were almost meaningless, repeated across both channels.

"The generator should be good for the night," Timmy said as he walked back into the room. "Think they're the regular rolling blackouts, but I've set it up to cut in whenever we're caught short. Might be a few wobbles."

Alex motioned to the screen.

"They're treating it seriously."

"Any of them mentioned Detroit yet? We never get any attention here. Bet it's some California thing. Or New York. They get all the new stuff."

"You're handling this very well. I thought you'd be up in arms. Gung ho."

"Look, the way I see it: either this Eko virus is unstoppable and we're all screwed. Or they're working on it and we've just got to sit tight and wait for it all to blow over. Guess we're not going in to work next week, huh?"

"Guess not."

THEY PLAYED POOL AGAIN. And again. The TV screens stayed on. The same stories. The crew seemed to dwindle, the broadcast crumbling into nothing until there were just a few people left. They stopped switching cameras, stopped cutting away from the anchor. First one fell, then the other. The news people were heading home. They were replaced by words. Warning signs. Just the same stock phrases, repeated back. Be careful. Be safe. Don't step outside. Don't panic.

The internet seemed to have ground to a halt, too. Both men checked all the devices they had available. Phones and computers. All dead. Nothing showing.

"Must be a tower down or something."

That seemed a decent enough explanation, Alex thought. But it would be nice to know what was happening outside of the house. They tried the radio. Nothing. The other TV channels. Nothing. Calling people. Nothing. So they went back to drinking beer and playing pool. There was nothing else they could do. Three beers in, Timmy began to talk.

"See, you want to stay away from the cities. Times like this, city is the worst possible place. Too many people. They all panic. We need to keep level headed. Out here in the suburbs, we're not getting looting or whatnot. Your place? Well, you're a target. You'll be staying here, though, so that's fine. Just don't get your hopes up about heading home."

Trying to call the pizza company was a dead end. No answer. They ate one of the meals from the pallet. It wasn't great. Putting it to the side, Timmy complained about a "grand wasted." But his fridge was bare, the vacuum sealed fruit tasting of plastic leakage. So they ate another meal. By the time they'd finished the second, Alex never wanted to see another readymade meal ever again.

By the time the small hours of the morning arrived, they were out of beer and out of energy. Timmy began to yawn and announced that he was heading up to bed.

"Fortunately for you," he told Alex, "I've been preparing my whole life for this kind of thing. My old man was sure the world was going to end. Beats me why he had kids. Still, that kind of thinking is in the blood."

Hidden in one of the cabinets under the guns, behind all the ammunition, was a leather bag, four feet long and half a foot wide. It was pulled out and placed on the floor.

"See, between the generator, the guns, and the night vision goggles, you've got to be ready for anything."

He pulled out poles, thin metal sticks which he clicked together. Threading them through a piecemeal slip of cotton, Timmy assembled the pieces and threw them on to the floor. It was a cot, barely wide enough for one. It rocked slightly on uneven feet.

"All this end of the world crap," said Alex, "and you don't even have a pull-out couch?"

Timmy grinned as he presented the rickety camp bed.

"Waterproof, light as a feather, and ready for anything." He was too happy as he said it.

Alex slept on the couch. After his host went to bed and the lights went off, the house rumbled on. At least three times in the night, the generator purred into action. It seemed like the electricity was cutting in and out around the town.

It was times like this that the imagination began to stir. No, Alex realized, there were no times like this. At least, it didn't seem like there could be. They'd have to find out more tomorrow. They needed information.

But that was on the other side of a long sleep. Uncomfortable on the couch, Alex twisted and turned throughout the night. Tomorrow, he assured himself, everything would be fine.

CHAPTER 10

*T*he door opened at the top of the basement stairs and the morning rushed in. Waking up, kitchen light falling across his face, Alex remembered everything that had happened. It all came back at once. The news. The images. The implications. A strange smell wafted down from above. Timmy was cooking something.

"Wake up!" he shouted down. "We're moving out."

The smell crept down from the kitchen, strong enough to stand up on its own two feet. It did not smell good. Wandering up in spite of his nose, Alex reached the top and found himself confronted by a hectic scene.

All across the kitchen counters lay a collection of handguns and ammunition. These items were arranged carefully, lined up in their rank and file. But around them, Timmy had tried to cook breakfast. He had hauled a couple of MRE packets up the stairs from the basement and thrown the contents into a pan. From there, he'd added salt, pepper, and an inestimable number of spices. That explained the smell.

"I thought the power was off," Alex said, running a finger along a line of something powdered and brown.

"About that," Timmy responded, turning back to his kitchen.

"Turns out one of my wiring jobs wasn't up to much. The power was on and off all night."

"I heard the generator kick in."

"Exactly. Exactly. Probably just some rats chewing through it or something. Bet they're smarting this morning."

"You get in contact with anyone?"

"Nope. Comms seem down. Tried it all. Phone. Internet. Radio. TV. The lot. Ended up just sticking my head out the front door. Saw some guy running past. Shouted at him and he told me that they've got rations or vaccines or something someplace in the city. They'll be handing them out."

The MRE packets lay on the kitchen counter, ripped apart. Timmy picked up a handgun and holstered it on his hip.

"But we're not waiting for that, are we?" Timmy said, the confidence in his voice disconcertingly palpable.

Eyes widening, Alex took a seat on one of the barstools at the counter.

"And why would we go out into a city when we've been told not to? Why the hell would we do that?"

"Oh, come on, man. You don't think that was real, do you? Eko virus? You ever heard of the Eko virus? I have and, let me tell you, we don't have no Eko virus in America. Who knows if it's even real? Just a figment of some conspiracy theory online. They're just trying to scare you. What don't they want us to do? What don't they want us to see?"

Rocking uneasily on the chair, Alex looked at the food. That was their breakfast. It hadn't tasted good yesterday. It hadn't improved.

"You want us to walk into the center of a city, under martial law, and just look around a bit?"

"It's all probably a reality TV joke, man. They're watching us. They want us to do something."

"You're crazy, Timmy."

"Maybe." His eyes gleamed. "Maybe I'm right. Maybe my crazy old man was right."

"I hope not."

"Yeah, me too. But, still. We gotta know."

Even as he had fallen asleep, Alex had felt his certainty draining away. It was like someone had poked a tiny hole in the base of his foot. After watching the President, after seeing him deliver that address, Alex had been filled with terror, uncertainty, and every other emotion known to man. It had been overwhelming. Too much to comprehend. He'd just had a few beers instead.

But, as the evening wore on, the slow drip, drip, drip of certainty fell away, the terror leaking out of the tiny hole. Space opened up in his mind. It couldn't have been real. The emptiness was filled with questions.

Sleeping through the night and then waking up, Alex found he had even more space inside him, even more room for uncertainty and doubt. What he'd seen last night could not possibly have been real.

A mistake. A prank. A hack. A social experiment. If he sat down and thought about it, there must have been a hundred different explanations. He wasn't even sure that this wasn't all Timmy's doing. *One Night at Castle Ratz*, the title would read, *Watch One Man's Terror as The World Collapses!* And then they'd go paintballing or something.

"Listen, if it gets us away from this crappy food, then I'm on-board."

"My man!" Twirling a pistol around his finger, Timmy handed his friend the gun, grip-first. "I got this one just for you. Say after me: 'I love my Glock'."

Mumbling the words back to Timmy, Alex searched around the room.

"You really have no other food apart from these readymade things? What do you eat?"

"I got a few phone numbers. I know a few guys. Italian guys. Chinese guys. I'm a busy man."

Alex saw a pile of pizza boxes in the corner of the kitchen. At least they were being recycled. If they were going to eat, then the food wasn't going to be coming from inside the house.

Plus, he reasoned, being outside might help them figure out what the hell was going on. Taking the guns wouldn't hurt. They'd had guns on the farm. Sort of.

But there was no knowing what kind of Detroit was on the other side of the door. Holsters holding guns, the two of them ready to head out, they left Castle Ratz and went out into the real world.

IT SEEMED THE SAME. Same gardens. Same houses. Same curtains, twitching back and forth. But this was the suburbs. They needed to be somewhere more interesting.

They took the SUV. The car rolled along, eating up the Grosse Pointe asphalt. The windows were rolled up. Even if this was all a joke, it didn't hurt to keep things sealed. The roads were empty. The stop lights were still working. Not that they mattered. They ran on solar, anyway. The SUV pulled up at a junction, engine ticking under a red light. Nothing in either direction. It turned green. They were off again.

Everyone was indoors. There were signs of life, seen only when squinting. During one pause, Alex was sure that he saw a garage door opening. Next, he saw two people through a ground floor window. They were arguing. As the houses drew closer together, as they got closer and closer to the actual city, the signs grew more frequent.

People were outside, here. But not really. It was storekeepers and bar owners. They had wooden slats with them, hammers in their hands and nails between their teeth.

One man was accompanied by his young son, couldn't have been more than seven, who passed his father the slat and held a bag of nails in the other hand. Along every street, there was the sound of men hammering their homes closed.

Every other person moved like a fox under a full moon. A few steps. Stop. Look. A few steps more. Look again. Scurrying between points. From a lamppost to a mailbox. Doorway to doorway. Even more people were wearing those surgical masks now. It was a warm day but everyone wore heavy clothes. Not an inch of flesh on show.

When they were in the city proper, they noticed the cops. And the guards. People in uniform, standing on every corner. Each of them wore one of the masks, made to match the uniform. Each of them had a heavy gun. Semi-autos, Timmy whispered under his breath.

Alex pulled the Glock from the holster. It was heavy. Heavier than he had expected. That paintball gun from that warehouse game? That had a weight. It had felt real. But there was more to this than metal. The curve of the grip sat snug and secure in Alex's hand.

"I picked that one out for you, man," said Timmy, his eyes still on the road. "I get your size right?"

"Like a glove."

They sat quietly. Both were watching. Occasionally, the driver might lower one hand and fiddle with the radio dials. The passenger might try his phone. But neither of them found any signal, any communication reaching out to them from above. It was just them and the road and everyone else.

A COP FLAGGED THEM DOWN. No vehicles beyond this point. No arguments. Get out or turn around. Go back to your homes. It wasn't a conversation; it was a command.

"What's happening, man?"

Despite the open window on the driver's side, the cop stayed well away. Alex had been pulled over enough times to know that law enforcement loved an opportunity to lean into a car and take a look. The blue mask across the man's face showed that he was happy to keep a distance. It moved when he talked.

"No vehicles beyond this point. That's all I can say. Either turn around or get out."

"People are scared," Timmy continued. "Can you at least let us know about these rations?"

"No rations. That's a rumor. We can't let cars beyond this point."

"So where are people heading, you know, for more information?"

The cop was about to speak. He stopped himself and pulled the mask down, revealing a thin goatee beard.

"Listen, I don't know anything. I heard they were giving out shots four blocks down. But you didn't hear it from me."

Putting the car in gear, rolling up the window, Timmy nodded to the cop and pulled away. Alex watched his friend turn back to the car.

"Rations. Knew it'd be too early to talk about rations. Society's only ever four square meals from chaos, remember? But shots sound wise. This Eko thing sounds just like a big flu scare, you know? Seems a bit serious."

Unconvinced, Alex unbuckled his seatbelt and began to get out of the car. It seemed fine to leave it on the sidewalk. Still some way from the city center, there were cops on every corner here. People were too scared to leave the house. It was never this easy to find a parking spot.

THE WALK into the city was like stepping down into a hot, sweaty tunnel. The buildings were higher, here, the people moving. Alex and Timmy walked two blocks before they realized that there were no longer cops around. But there were people. They were everywhere, just trying to stay out of sight. These weren't rioters. They were too scared to riot. Something was wrong.

The shopkeepers were out in force. Every store front – every business – had a man in front of it with a hammer. One or two had faces pointing out from the windows above, watching over the street, no doubt with a small arsenal perched just below, ready to open fire.

"Fat chance that's keeping the germs out," Timmy chuckled as they drove past. "And they call me paranoid."

"I'd be more worried about the people. Everything's already on a knife-edge."

Further up the street, a car backfired. Alex saw everyone drop to the floor and then stand up, embarrassed. He could taste the brittle tension in the air.

As the buildings towered overhead, the streets were hot with movement. People ran into neighbors' homes. They ran between doors. Almost all of them had their faces covered. But most people had not managed to buy the small surgical masks. There were those with ripped cloths tied from ear to ear. Some in ski masks. One man was wearing a hockey mask, the old kind from the horror movies. It had great big holes in it. Not the most hygienic option.

But hygiene might not have been the man's priority, Alex noted. As they walked another block, they crunched across the glass shards of the shops which had not moved quick enough. Inside, the shelves were not just empty. They were broken and pillaged, laid out across the floor.

Gang names, curse words, and anti-government slogans were spray painted across the walls. The paint was still drying.

The sound was something else. Alex had lived in the city long enough to grow used to the sounds. The ambulances and police cars. The constant drone of a million-people moving in spite of one another. The deafening thunder of existence in a tight space. It was loud now and just, well…more. Everything was the same but everything was louder. More intense. More aggressive. Occasionally, he'd miss the quiet but it seemed more and more distant with every passing day. Another life he'd left behind.

There was an edge to the city and it was increasing every time they put a new block beneath their feet. Both men had guns, balanced conspicuously on their hips. This was an open carry state, for the most part, Timmy had announced with authority back in the SUV. It didn't seem like it mattered now.

Breaking glass in the distance. A shout. There was the smell of sweat and worry everywhere. If people were sick, they weren't showing it. They were too busy preparing themselves. One woman ran past holding a sack of rice. Two men maneuvered a jerry can full of gas up a stoop. Three teenagers pushed a shopping cart down the street, laden heavy with sneakers and cigarettes. What were they preparing for, thought Alex.

Nobody knows. Nobody knows anything.

CHAPTER 11

*I*t was barely noon but it felt like midnight. Midnight under a roaring sun. Strange. Alex walked with his friend through familiar streets, picking out places he'd stopped for a beer once, or where he'd met a friend, or had his wallet taken. The same streets but crawling, sinking, searing with uncertainty. Everyone was scared.

Even without many people on the sidewalks, it was clear, palpable. There was a fear which just crawled out of every window, seeped between the porous spaces in wooden doors. The kind of terror which could find the empty space in an oxygen atom and fill it up with dread. It was infectious, thought Alex, which was probably the wrong word to use.

"You know, I'm actually still hungry." It was the first thing Timmy had said in a half-hour.

"I think there's something up ahead," Alex replied. "Could be a shop. A bar? Could do with a drink."

Alex had seen it and he pointed it out to his friend. While the other streets had been as quiet as a beartrap, waiting to snap shut, there was obvious movement here. People weren't treading carefully or watching over their shoulder. There were at least a dozen of them.

They were all standing in front of a 7/11. It was one of the new stores. The ones without the gas pumps or parking lots. The switch to electric had really messed with their model. Car owners were on the brink of a revolution. Too early to go fully electric, too scared to give up the gas. This meant 7/11 was caught in the crossfire.

So now they were just in the middle of cities. They'd buy up a few businesses, finding the cheap spots, and knock through all the walls. Boom. Instant 7/11. Right in the middle of the city. It seemed to work.

The people had flocked to the store. Wooden slats were nailed across the windows, but it had been handled better than most. Where the mom and pop outfits had made do with any wood they could find, these seemed like proper two by fours. Arranged properly, too. A professional job.

Standing beside the door were two guards. These weren't state troopers. Not police or army or national guard. They were all in black. Body armor. Helmets without any insignia. Radios on their shoulders. Masks over their faces. At least four guns between the two of them, probably more. They were letting people in, one at a time.

The line stretched around the block. Part of this was the volume of people, part was due to the fact that none of them wanted to stand near one another. But it was moving fast. If they had food inside, there seemed to be no other choice. It was the only place open. The only game in town. Alex and Timmy joined.

Rumors and lies ran up and down the line like a wet cat. Happy to listen in, Alex and his friend smiled at the words. It was almost funny. It would have been funnier if there was no chance that the rumors might, somehow, turn out to be true.

This store is run by the government. They're only selling canned items. They're doing vaccinations inside. The vaccinations rot your brain. The guards are CIA. The guards are SEALs. The guards are from the cartel. They shut down the phones so no one would worry. The internet cables got cut by China. The gangs have taken over. The store has run out of food. The store has run out of food. They're selling at ten times the price. The store has run out of food.

That last one came back time and time again. Whenever it was aired, people shifted on their feet, looking over the shoulders of the people in front. But, slowly, the line crept forward. Soon enough, the two men were next in line.

"No guns." The guard was pointing to the pistols. "Give them up if you want to go in."

"Listen, guys, we're not giving up our guns. Would you?" said Timmy.

The masks were tinted. The glass covered the whole face. Just a flat, emotionless surface. If he stared hard enough, Alex was sure that he could just about see a pair of eyes.

"No guns inside. Easy rule."

Reaching a hand up to a guard's shoulder, Timmy adopted what Alex recognized as his familiar face. His friendly face. At least, he thought it was his friendly face. He thought he was being charming. The guard swatted away the hand.

"O...kay..." Timmy eased off. "Say we just want a couple of items. How about we show you guys how serious we are? We have quite excellent credentials."

The two guards remained unmoved.

"What if I told you my good friend Abe sent me? Sent me twice over. Impeccable reference. Nothing? How about Andrew? He knows your boss, I'm sure. Nothing? Nothing at all? Will you Grant me nothing? Ah–there! I saw you move. So now we're negotiating. What if I said I could reach out to my good friends, the two Abes and Mr. Grant?"

One guard twitched.

"I can introduce him to both of you."

The guard on the left nodded. The guard on the right watched over the line.

"Excellent," Timmy said, using his smug voice. "Alex, pay these fine men."

Timmy walked into the store and the guards allowed him. This left Alex facing the two blank masks. He reached for his wallet.

By the time he joined Timmy, Alex was worried about cash. Finding an ATM at this time would be a lot of trouble. After he'd paid off the guards, there wasn't much cash left. There wasn't much food left on the shelves, either, he noticed. It was mostly canned goods. Some rumors had a grain of truth to them.

Timmy had a basket and had grabbed anything that seemed edible. Chili in a can. Kidney beans. Corn. A few of everything. The basket got heavier.

"Hey, Timmy, you thought about how we're paying for this?"

"It's all right, I got a plan."

"Forgive me for asking," Alex began, "but what exactly is this grand plan?"

"Okay, so it's simple. I'm going to get hold of everything and then– and this is the important part—"

Timmy never finished the sentence. There were shouts from outside. The unmistakable sound of someone being hit, hard. One bang and another against the wooden boards covering the windows. Alex looked up, over the aisles, and across the store to the entrance. The space where the two guards had been standing fell dark.

People rushed into the store. They wore masks, but not the surgical kind. They were bandanas, worn low and tight around the face, which was encircled by the black cotton ring of a hooded sweater. There must have been five of them, rushing the door and bursting into the room. Immediately, they ran to the food section.

As quickly as they could, the invaders grabbed hold of any and every item. They didn't need baskets. They'd brought their own sacks. They thrust in cans. Bottles of water. Searching through every shelf, they left nothing behind.

Alex and Timmy stood, transfixed. As they watched, one of the invaders ran up to them and reached down, rooting through the basket. They grabbed the kidney beans, inspected the can, and threw it into a bag.

As Alex watched, the intruder looked up. Beneath the hood, above the bandana, there was a pair of glacial eyes. Artic ice, criminally cold. A woman's eyes. But young. Barely out of her teens.

Before either man could say a word, the young girl had sealed up her bag and rushed back toward the exit. She lagged behind her friends, who were already out. Alex ran toward the entrance. Timmy, taking the basket with him, grabbing a few other items along the way, followed.

They ran toward the exit, now unguarded.

Stepping out into the light again, Alex was met by a different scene. Gone was the orderly line. Gone were the two guards.

Instead, the public was pressed up against the wooden boards, afraid to move. They were enchanted by the scene in the middle of the street. Terrified.

The girl had run out of the store and straight into the one remaining guard. The other must have run off. Either home or chasing the invaders. But the guard had moved quicker than she did. He was standing above her, holding a gun to her head, screaming into her ear.

"We gotta do something," whispered Alex.

"What? For who?"

"Anyone. Before someone gets hurt. Come on."

Timmy was still carrying the basket. He'd carried it right out of the store. He dropped it to the ground and fumbled with the clasp which held the gun in his holster.

Alex didn't wait.

He'd already dealt with the clip, drawn his weapon, and was running toward the middle of the street. Holding out an arm, not expecting the Glock to be so heavy, he stood a foot behind the man and began to talk down the barrel of the gun.

"Let her go."

The guard didn't move. The words had felt weightless in Alex's mouth, like cotton candy melting away.

"I said let her go."

Firmer this time. More assured. But the gun was so heavy. Heavy with the threat. The man ripped off his mask, throwing it onto the street.

"You didn't see what she just did? Thieves. We should shoot her now. Zero tolerance."

In the films, this was the point where the hero would pull back the hammer. Making his point. Alex flicked his eyes to the Glock for a second. This pistol didn't have one of those, no hammer to drive home an argument.

He stepped closer and settled with prodding the guard in the base of his bald skull with the muzzle.

The man didn't move.

"I can't just-"

"Don't make me say it again," said Alex, trying to sound assured.

"Fine," the guard grunted and threw his gun to the ground.

It didn't fire, but Alex had been watching it, just in case. It skidded along the street as the crowd watched and listened.

The girl ran. She was quick, around the corner in barely a second. The guard swiveled round. He seemed surprised. Alex felt his shoulders slouch, the energy falling from him. All his authority went with it.

"The hell was that?" the guard hissed. "Who do you think you are? Robin Hood? Christ."

The man didn't wait. He snatched up his firearm from the ground and chased off after the thief. Timmy crept up beside Alex, who was still holding the Glock out in the air.

"Pretty cool, man. Pretty cool," he said. "Guess that girl gave you the eyes."

Alex lowered his hand and looked at the gun. This wasn't like back in Virginia. He remembered being taken out back one day. His dad had pointed the family shotgun at the ground. Pulled the trigger. Blown a hole in the earth a foot deep. Never point a gun at something you ain't willing to kill, he'd said.

Her eyes. Something about her eyes. They had reminded him of Sammy. They'd reminded him of home. For just a fleeting moment, he'd felt as though he was back there. The rush of emotion and memory had driven him forward without time to think.

The Glock was tiring Alex's arm. He checked the chamber. It was empty.

"Oh yeah," Timmy continued. "I didn't think we'd actually have to, like, you know, use them. Bullets are back in the car."

"What?" Alex's voice quavered now, for the first time.

"Yeah, on the back seat. You want to explain to a cop why you're carrying a loaded weapon during a curfew? Not worth it, man."

It was hot under the sun but Alex felt a chill. All the events of the day, everything that had happened to them over the last twelve hours, it crawled quickly and coldly along his skin. Down his spine. Down his legs and into the ground.

"Just… just tell me next time you do something like that."

"Sure thing, chief," said Timmy, encouraging him to walk down the street with some speed.

"I wasn't expecting… I didn't…" Alex was searching for the words.

"Yeah, yeah, I know. I froze, too, man. These things happen. Bet she thinks you're a hero though."

"It's not that… it's… Hey, why are you pushing so hard?"

Timmy had Alex by the elbow and they'd reached the end of the block. Turning down a corner, they could hear all sorts of shouts and crashes. Things were happening.

"I'm sorry you're not feeling yourself," Timmy began. "But it's probably time I told you something."

"What's that? This is a prank? This isn't even a real gun? That guy was an actor. I knew—"

"No," said Timmy, looking around, breaking them both into a run. "I didn't pay for this food."

CHAPTER 12

*O*nce they were around the corner of the block, they stopped running. There were other people, roving through the streets, chasing and shouting. The city was like a pan on a stove, filled with water and fitted with a lid. Now, the lid was rattling and fidgeting, the pressure of the boiling water inside building and building.

Once they found the SUV, Alex and Timmy drove back to Castle Ratz. They drove quicker this time. The cops who had been standing on the street corners had evaporated. Almost every window on the ground floor was boarded up. Every shop was shut. The radio was dead and the car ride was quiet without being calm.

"We can't stay here." Timmy broke the silence. "This city is going places."

Alex had been thinking something similar.

"But you heard last night. Border's shut down. No crossing state lines soon. It's like they're trying to corral people. Plus, we still don't know what the hell is actually happening."

With one hand off the wheel, Timmy reached down and began to desperately flick through the radio stations. Dead air. Dead air. All of it digital. He tried the analog stations and there was only static. Then the long wave, the AM frequencies. The numbers shimmered as fingers flicked through every possible position on the radio spectrum.

There was something. A sound. A voice. Timmy nearly leapt out of his seat when he heard it. But already he'd searched on ahead.

"Find it again, find it again."

Leaning into the dash, Alex fine-tuned the radio. He found it.

"—in your homes," the soothing female voice announced, arriving midsentence, "and wait for assistance. If you are unable to wait within your home or you wish to seek help, please leave a white cross on your door. We advise that you use chalk or any easily removable—"

The message went on, providing calm, relaxing advice for how to deal with the situation. But it was devoid of information. Stay at home. Await help. If you require food or medicine, please mark your door. Stay at home. Await help. Repeated again and again. There was no rhyme or reason or explanation. Timmy turned the radio off.

"Hey, leave it on." Alex reached for the dial. "They might say something interesting. Something helpful."

"Man, it's just the same sterile message, over and over. We're better learning about this with our own eyes. Not just believing what they tell us."

"Still…" Alex sat back in his seat, the radio off. "We should do something…"

"We can't stay in the city, man."

"There's food at your place, the generator. We're out in the suburbs. Plus, the whole arsenal you've been building up. You think we should move?"

"I'm telling you, we need to be somewhere else."

"This is your specialty, Timmy. You prep for years and now drop it all and run at the first sign of trouble?"

"I wasn't ready for this, man."

Alex watched his friend shake his head. It was afternoon, stretching into evening. They'd been driving long enough and they were almost at the right street.

"I've been reading about this Eko virus for years, man. It wasn't meant to be something real. No one ever thought..." His voice trailed off.

"Just tell me something, Timmy. Anything."

Timmy talked. He linked together theories and thoughts. Eko was like Ebola. Almost. At first, it looked like the flu and then, boom, death hits. The real nasty thing was the way it mutated. It moved quick and fast, changing every time they tried to cure it. Researchers trying to play whack-a-mole with antibiotics. Luckily, he said, it had been confined to Mongolian forests. A bogey man, a tale told by chemists to their kids to make them behave. It wasn't meant to be real.

Then, the little information Timmy had petered out, if it was reliable at all.

"Listen, Timmy," Alex said. "We should wait it out, stay here. Eat those meals, this food we have. We're better prepared than most people. We need to think calmly. We need more information."

The SUV arrived in the driveway, pulling up to the garage. The concrete garden and its oil-stains seemed to glow in the early evening light. As the sky turned chimney red, the slicks caught the top end of the colors and turned them all upwards. Little pools of glowing sky light, floating over the concrete ground. They went inside.

"THERE'S something I got to tell you, man."

Timmy talked as he unpacked the stolen food. Alex could see the blood had drained from his friend's face. Either shame or fear, he couldn't tell. The cans were placed into empty cupboards and onto empty shelves. Alex tried the light switch beside the kitchen door. Nothing. It wasn't dark. There was still enough light outside. He noticed the water swelling beneath the freezer door.

"Power's out. That generator of yours working?"

It was an innocent question, thrown out with careless abandon. But it seemed to kick start something in Timmy. He turned around with a confessional tone.

"Here's the thing," Timmy said, as Alex felt like a priest on the other side of a wooden lattice. "I'm not ready for this. This whole... everything."

Timmy wasn't smiling anymore; his red hair was hanging lank and he brushed it behind an ear and continued. "I wasn't ready, man. At the store? You saw me. Did you? It wasn't right."

"People get scared. They do bad things. They do strange things. It wasn't—"

"Not them, Alex. Me." Timmy slapped his hands on the kitchen counter. "I froze up. Watched you do it all. Everything. What if you weren't there, only me? What would have happened? That girl would have been killed."

"I didn't notice," Alex offered. "I wasn't watching you. No one was."

"Exactly. That's exactly it. You didn't skip a beat. Didn't pause. Didn't stop to evaluate the situation. Didn't have a hold of a load of tin cans. You just acted. That girl could have died."

This was the first time Alex had seen his friend without a smile. The way his lips creased and pursed, Timmy always had an angle. But now, with his hands flat and his head bowed, he had no smart answers.

"What if you weren't there, man?"

"Timmy, my gun didn't even have bullets. You said yourself. It was a dumb thing—"

"You didn't know that, though." Timmy slapped the surface, hard. "You just did it. Like it was nothing."

The whole ride home, this exact thought had been weighing on Alex's mind. It was squatting in the space that he should have been using for important thoughts. While he knew he should be thinking about the state of the world, all Alex could remember was the sensation of his finger on the trigger. Had he ever been tempted to squeeze? Still remembering that shelled-out hole in the ground back at the farm, he didn't know the answer. Never point a gun at something you ain't willing to kill. Had he been willing? Driving home, staring into the sinking sun, Alex still wasn't sure.

"Timmy, you've been training for years," he replied. "I've seen you in action down at GUNPLAY. I was there for one night. I was impressed. And all this in your house? Don't tell me you aren't prepared for exactly this."

"And where's it got me? A stack of meals in boxes we can barely eat. A load of canned beans I had to steal. A generator I can't even get to work. I got a seed bank downstairs. You want to bet it's full of nothing but daisies and weeds? You try to plan for everything and then you're unprepared for the one thing which actually happens. Come to me in the nuclear winter, I'd be fine. But this…"

Walking around the kitchen, Timmy tried the light switch again and again. Nothing happened.

"See? It's all just playing around. It was easy doing this when I only had to worry about turning up at work the next day. What's happened to that? It's been twenty-four hours. We're under curfew. This is all crazy. It's all so mad. This shouldn't be happening. But you haven't broken a sweat."

Alex checked his brow, just in case. It was dry. Timmy was right. But he was wrong, too.

"I never planned any of this. I just do things."

"Do what?"

"Survive, I guess. I just do what I think I need to do."

"Why?"

"I don't know, Timmy. I don't really want to talk about it."

It wasn't quite the truth.

For hours, there had been one consistent image in Alex's mind. It was another man's head, seen down the flat top of the Glock. Everything was fixed in place. The weight of the gun, even though Alex hadn't known there were no bullets inside. The way he'd held himself, balanced on his front foot. The way the world smelled, in that moment, like a normal city turned up to maximum. Everything, every sense, frozen in one perpetual moment.

There were other memories like this. The girl's eyes, the way they'd reminded him of home. Of Sammy, standing alone, on the front porch of her house. The parking lot outside the recruiting office, sitting in the same Chevy that was outside now. The sound of the farmhouse keys as he'd dropped them into Eames's hands. The feel of the white sheets which lay across all the furniture. There were many memories. But few managed to fix themselves to the inside of Alex's head, waiting to be called upon when he was least expecting it.

"You don't want to talk about it?" Timmy repeated. "What do you mean? This is some Sammy thing, all over again? I thought we'd got you over that."

"It's not that. It's… I don't want to talk about it."

Timmy waved his hand in front of his face, forcing a breath between unimpressed lips. Alex was starting to regret every mentioning her to his friend. It was a weird time in his life. A few too many beers had let the cat out of the bag. Timmy had barely been interested, seemed to file the thought away under 'girlfriend trouble' and had never mentioned it again.

Taking a can of chili con carne, Timmy found a pocket knife from somewhere. With both hands, he struggled to get the can open and ready to eat.

"So it's not a Sammy thing and–'cause you won't tell me–it's not a Timmy thing. So here we are. World going to hell in a handbasket and we're not talking."

There were the jokes again. At least, Alex hoped it was a joke. He laughed anyway.

"Listen, man, if you don't want to talk about things, that's cool. We can put on the radio again."

Still struggling with the can opener, Timmy adopted the calm female voice from the radio.

"Please stay in your homes and wait for assistance. Please stay in your homes and wait for assistance."

The can opened, spilling chili all over the kitchen counter.

"Success!" Timmy shouted. "At last, something good in the world. Hey, how many people you think are actually going to stay indoors? You think they'll do what the government says?"

"Sure, for like two days." Alex answered, knowing Timmy was making conversation. Covering up his nerves, acting as though he hadn't planned for this all along. "Then it'll all go to hell."

"You think? "

"You're going to pretend we can't hear sirens right now? These blackouts won't be doing any good. It's not just your wiring. I can see every house out there hasn't got any electricity."

"I noticed that. No cars in the road, either. No one walking about. So, this is real, huh?"

"You're the expert on the end of the world, you tell me."

"Expert? You're too kind." Timmy laughed and Alex heard a note of nervousness. "Eko virus, here we come. Hey, about that Sammy thing. Man, I'm sorry I keep bringing it up. I'm still not sure whether you two broke up or she died or—"

"We broke up," Alex said, firmly cutting his friend short, pushing the memory deeper. "And we don't talk about it."

A long, slow whistle. Timmy stood in the kitchen, the fork end of the pocket knife now open, and began shoveling scoops of chili between his teeth.

"She really did a number on you, man," Timmy mumbled with his mouth full.

"You're just trying to change the conversation because you don't know anything about this disease."

The two men stared at one another. *Don't call me on the Sammy thing and I won't call you on the knowledge gaps*, Alex thought. A détente.

"Anyway," Alex continued, finally giving voice to a thought which had been lingering at the back of his mind. "I was thinking. We need to get out of here. You were right. The city isn't safe anymore."

"Finally. Finally, someone agrees with me. I'm telling you, we need to focus on the less populated areas. I've got maps. These diseases feed on population density. So... what?"

"This is going to sound strange."

"Hit me."

"You're not going to like it."

"Come on. Come on, come on, come on."

"Virginia."

"You're right." Timmy stared Alex in the eye "I don't like it."

"You said we had to get out of here." Alex worriedly gesticulated toward the setting sun, his nerves rippling under his skin. "Where better than Virginia? Near the coast, away from the city, loads of natural resources. You said you've got a map?"

Say yes, Alex thought to himself. To the map and to the idea. Nervousness. Excitement. It felt good to actually do something. But first, Timmy had to get on board.

"I agree." Timmy spoke slowly, Alex waited for the moment of disagreement. "It's lovely. To visit. But it's not exactly where I had in mind. When we're not under curfew and the country's not in the midst of an epidemic. Rural's good, but there's plenty of rural a hell of a lot closer than Virginia. Tell me this isn't about Sammy."

The stare Alex gave his friend could have been used to bend steel girders.

"This is about survival, Timmy. There's a farm there. Where I grew up. It'll be empty, practically. In the middle of the fields. If you're worried about infection – there's no one there. You're worried about food—we can grow our own. You're worried about anything else, it's perfect. You saw what happened today. In the city. That was after one day of people trying to deal with this…whatever this is. That was one day. With no information. What happens when people start to really panic? When they start to get angry? What happens when they march through the streets? Your street. What happens when they start to die?"

Reaching the bottom of the can, Timmy dropped it into the sink. He opened the faucet. Nothing happened.

"That's all well and good. And I agree with you. But what were we told? Stay indoors. Definitely don't break curfew. Absolutely don't cross state lines once the deadline passes. I've got enough food and supplies here, I've been preparing for this."

"For all of this?" said Alex, pointing at the outside world. "For the Eko virus?"

"Well, no." Timmy admitted, shaking his head. "I never thought it would happen like this. I kind of expected to be able to stay here. I never knew the Eko virus was going to do something like this…"

"There's an empty farm house in Virginia, Timmy. Waiting for us."

"We'd have to break curfew. We'd have to sneak out the city."

"So, we've still got time to get there. Twelve hours, I make it. Get on the road to Virginia by then and who's going to stop us? This is only a short-term thing anyway. They're just working on some sort of vaccine, need people to stay still so they can hand it out when it's ready." Alex wasn't sure how much he believed but continued anyway. "Like I said, we'll get creative."

"I like creative. I've got the tools for creative."

Alex knew he had his friend in the right position. It was the way his eyebrow twitched. One small, slight pulse of the muscle. He was tempted. Finally, a chance to use all those wonderful toys.

"What do we need? What can we carry?" Alex asked. "What can we fit in the car?"

"We'll take your car. The Chevy. Runs quieter. Uses less gas."

"But it's so much smaller."

"We're trying to not get caught."

"But what can we take? We can hardly fit everything inside."

"The essentials."

"Which essentials?"

"They're all essential." Timmy smirked. "But we'll take a look."

The sun was setting. The last of the light crept in through the kitchen window. It didn't matter. Both men were down in the basement, poring over maps and itineraries. A gas light burned for hours above the pool table. The green felt glowed. The red pen circled Virginia. Outside, the rest of the world began to collapse.

CHAPTER 13

*A*lexander Early began sorting through his friend's possessions. There were the guns–best left to the knowledgeable parties–but there was so much more. Timmy must have gone through thousands of dollars assembling this collection.

God knew where he'd got it all from. SkyMall for survivalist types. He had tents, animal traps, more knives than Alex could count, walkie talkies, and jerry cans. But it was something smaller that turned out to be the most useful.

It was a wind-up generator. Not the huge, gas-guzzling monster which lived out back. This was a smaller affair. It was pretty much just a handle. Turn the handle, generate power. Charge whatever electrical device needed charging. With Detroit still at the mercy of the rolling blackouts, Alex breathed a bit of life into his dying, unreliable phone.

It wasn't much good for calling, though. Just like trying to order a pizza the night before, every line seemed dead. Landlines, cell connections. Nothing was getting through. Timmy thought it was just society collapsing but Alex had his own theory. In his opinion, there were just too many people trying to get through. An overload. People were scared.

It was easier to demonstrate this with internet connections. The

signal was just as spotty, just as unreliable. But every now and again–
if he kept checking and encouraging the phone–it would bring up a
web page. It was like trying to connect to a distant planet. Requests
took hours to send. But when they did, they brought back stories
from another world.

Every now and then, after cranking the handle on the charger,
Alex would check the phone. If there was a new story loaded, he'd
read it aloud. For the first time in years, his attention was focusing on
one article at a time. There wasn't much else to do. But he read it
aloud anyway.

These were the times when Timmy would fall silent. He'd stop and
listen as Alex read about illness across the west coast. San Francisco, it
said, had its hospitals overwhelmed. Portland, too. Up and down the
coast, this Eko virus had been spotted everywhere. So far, fifty people
had died, but thousands were showing symptoms.

Alex thought about the emptying office and the vacant cubicles.
The lucky pilot and the girl from the alley who'd run away into the
night. As Timmy listened, he mumbled something about incubation
periods and reached for another flashlight. Every time he pulled a
new toy out of a basement cabinet or a bedroom wardrobe, he'd walk
through the technical specs.

"P-12 tactical flashlight, by Nitecore," he'd announce to an audience of one. "A thousand lumens of the brightest light you'll see and it
can take a beating. A pure classic. Never bettered. Throws light nearly
800 feet. Got three of these, knew I'd need them one day."

They went in the bag. Alex had to intervene every now and then.
The Leatherman multi-tools were an excellent addition, but would
they really need a full tool set to accompany them? Surely there
wasn't a need for fifty different screwdriver heads on the drive
between Detroit and Virginia? Though he acquiesced, Timmy put
the screwdrivers close to the bag. Just in case there was space at
the end.

"Hey, man, you know, I've been thinking something," Timmy
announced, sorting through a collection of water purification tablets.
"If all these people are getting sick on the west coast, then why was

the President on Air Force One? Why did he look… like… like he did? You know what I mean, right?"

"You saw it, too?"

"He didn't look healthy."

"Could be stress," Alex speculated aloud. "You think he's sick?"

"I'm just saying I noticed is all."

Alex was still gleaning as much information as he could, loading up a new article every hour. But finding information seemed tougher than he'd expected. Even when he could reach out to a company or a news outlet, they didn't have any fresh stories. Nothing published in the last twelve hours.

And no one was calling him. Parents, obviously, weren't going to be an issue. But friends. Colleagues. Doctors. Government officials, maybe. Perhaps even Sammy. Nothing like a countrywide panic to reunite with an old flame.

No one seemed to have reached out. Something was broken and the data they had didn't explain the malaise.

"You said you'd heard about this virus? Eko, they called it?"

"Oh, yeah, man. It's a doozie. Not a nice thing to think about. Comes from a jungle somewhere. Can't remember where. Mongolia, maybe."

"But they'd shut down an entire country for it?"

"That's the thing. Last time I heard, it was just a couple of hospitals here and there. Like, it'd come up on the news, man, and you'd see these horrible pictures of the kids and stuff. Nasty National Geographic type stuff. But it always went away real quick."

"Didn't seem like they thought it was going to go away real quick."

"Right? That's what I've been saying. Something's going on here, man. Something they're not telling us."

"What were the symptoms? Why doesn't anyone know anything about it?"

"That's the thing, man. It was always slightly different." Timmy laughed to himself. "I looked like flu for the most part. Fever. Sweating. It always messed with your eyes, though. See, I remember reading some crazy stuff online about it. Biowarfare stuff and DNA editing. Like, they'd change it. Or it would constantly evolve."

"You believe that?"

"I don't know what to believe, man. All I know is I've read some crazy stuff on the internet. I wouldn't trust those guys too much, you know?!

Timmy was one to jump the gun on almost anything like this. The traffic cops, they gave him a ticket because of some government war against gas vehicles. The bosses at work overlooked him for a promotion because he knew too much about them. Or he worked too hard. Timmy always had his excuses. But Alex didn't have any answers. An excuse, right now, was close enough.

The longer they thought about these kinds of questions, the more they realized that they knew nothing. So they went back to packing. There was a reassurance in action. An immediate problem.

This bag has a certain volume. Inside, they could place x amount of ammunition, plus a fishing rod, a shovel, two sheets of tarpaulin, and a tourniquet. It meant they couldn't fit the crossbow or the signaling mirror. Sacrifices must be made.

But packing everything up neat and tidy–and making sure they had enough room in the trunk of the car–was a problem they could handle. Even though neither man mentioned it, there was an unspoken agreement not to dwell too much on the bigger questions. To do so only made them feel small.

LATE INTO THE NIGHT, it was time to eat again. Deciding to save the canned food for the road, they started again on the MRE. If they could learn to love them now, Timmy reasoned, then they might be able to save a lot of trouble by the time they got out on the road.

So they tried another. There was no cooking required, so Alex unpacked the contents and lay them all out across the table. They were sitting in the kitchen, the gas lamp suspended from the ceiling between them. It was almost like a restaurant. Not a nice restaurant.

The language on the individual packets was difficult to decipher.

Each was labelled by its course. Entrée. Dessert. One item was labelled 'cracker' and another was labelled 'spread for cracker'. A pale imitation of peanut butter.

Under the names were the calorie contents of each part of the meal and allergy advice. Neither man suffered an allergy, but that didn't stop the meals from turning the stomach. Mixing the packet pound cake with the apple cobbler, stirring the mixture with the plastic spoon, Alex could taste it before it even entered his mouth.

"This stuff," he said, chewing his food, "is not great."

Timmy was still eating, staring determinedly at the information emblazoned down the side of the box. He spoke up but didn't move his eyes away.

"I know. I'd always expected much better. I got it from a friend of mine. There's meals from all around the world in there. Military guy. Said they ate this kind of stuff in Iraq. He gave me a decent price."

"How long ago was this, Timmy?"

They checked the expiration date on the packaging. Three years ago. Good for another eight months. Supposedly.

LATER, the bags were packed. They'd eaten what they could and saved some for the journey. At the bottom of the MRE pallet, they found a few more recent meals which tasted better. These new meals even had flammable tablets to heat up food. Luxury.

Both men enjoyed a cold shower and changed. Alex was wearing one of Timmy's old T-shirts, taken from a gun range, and a sweater from the inside of his car. It had spent some time buried in the footwell and smelled like it. But, after airing it out, the familiarity had been more than welcome.

They sat with the map between them. It was a ten-hour trip on a good day. The deadline for crossing over the state lines was barely twelve hours away and it was the early hours of the morning already. They had to sleep but decided that they'd be able to leave at first light. It had a certain ring to it: Leave at dawn.

"We should drive in shifts," Alex said, looking over the map. "I drive, you sleep."

"Nah, man." Timmy used his slightly condescending voice. "We need both of us awake. If we hit trouble, I need you sharp and focused, not blurry eyed. We can camp. I'll find us the right spots."

Timmy spoke with authority. The theory was that, once they were on the road, any cops they encountered would just tell them to go home. If that home was in Virginia, then they would just have to keep driving. It wasn't a complicated plan. It wasn't a good plan. But it was all the plan they had. Even sticking their heads out the front door, they could hear sirens in the distance. And not just in the city. They were in the suburbs. There were helicopters overhead. It was dark and something was happening.

"There's one more thing I need to get," said Alex. "From my place."

"We got the time for that?"

"It's the keys to the farm house. We'll make time for it."

Alex wanted to collect more than just the keys. But he didn't want to tell Timmy that.

"I'll duck out, first thing. Take my car. It'll be twenty minutes there and back. I'll do it in record time. Last thing we want is to be arrested breaking into my parents' old farm."

Nodding along, happy to listen to his friend's sage advice, Timmy turned a plastic spoon around over his fingers. He twirled it, rotating the spoon as it proceeded from the first finger to the last and then back again.

"I just wanted to say," he began. "I don't know what's happening, exactly. I don't think you do either. But I'm glad you're much better at not knowing than I am. I don't know what I'd be doing right now if I'd been stuck here on my own."

At that, Alex realized that he had never asked Timmy about his family. Whether he had loved ones. A brother. A sister. An uncle, a girlfriend, or even a dog. Alex didn't really know much about his friend at all. When he asked, Timmy just sat there, shaking his head.

"Story for another time, man. But it's just me and you now. You're stuck with me, brother. Better make the most of it."

Alex laughed. Somehow, they'd managed to find a couple of unopened beers and a bottle of something which might have been rum, once. Bags packed, they drank and talked. Not about anything in particular. About nothing at all, in fact. But enough to take their minds off everything.

The hours rolled by at Castle Ratz. Tomorrow was another day. Sleeping on the couch in the basement, Alex bade goodnight to his friend. As he went to bed, he tried one more time to get any information out of his phone.

There was nothing. Not just no response, but no stories about the state of the world. It was more worrying than if there had been articles about cities on fire or decimated populations. Just a vacuum of information and, as he fell asleep, he knew that his dreams would fill in the empty space with the worst outcomes imaginable.

When he woke up, he thought, it might be to an improvement.

He would be wrong.

CHAPTER 14

awn had hardly broken before Alex was up, dressed, and in his car. He had not slept well. His dreams had been full of fire and fury. As the key entered the Chevy ignition, turned, and got the engine running, the images were still fastened to the inside of his eyelids.

The street lamps were dim. These should have been the solar-powered types. But, after long hours of darkness, they fell back on the grid. Without that, they were struggling. Keeping the beams low, keeping his speed down, and glancing occasionally across to the pistol he'd been unable to leave behind, Alex drove through the suburbs out of Grosse Pointe.

It was a simple route. On the right night, with the wind behind him, he'd make the trip in twenty minutes. That meant accounting for the traffic, the stops, the little annoyances which slowed down the drive during the day-to-day.

But this was different. The roads were empty. Not just empty. Alex had driven places on Christmas day, had worked night shifts on New Year's Eve. He knew what empty streets looked like. This was different. As he drew closer and closer to the heart of the city, it became impossible to shake the feeling of unease which crept out of every storm drain, which lurked around every corner.

There was no other car on the road. But there were people. Alex could see them, in front of their houses. Not many. Scattered from place to place. When they heard his car coming, they ducked inside their doorways. As he drove past, it was clear that they were loading up their own cars. One man was holding a crying baby. He covered the baby's mouth as the Chevy rolled past.

With the sun only just arriving over the horizon, Alex understood why the streets seemed so strange. One of the reasons, at least. Every now and then – at least once a block – the sunrise caught the edges of the glass shards which lay across the asphalt. They twinkled sharp in the morning sun. Windows smashed the night before had now been boarded up, but there was no one to sweep the streets.

Parking in front of his apartment block, Alex locked the car. He didn't want to be stranded in the city. He let himself in, through the locks, not pausing to feign the third. Practically running through the hallway, his feet hardly touched the stairs as he ran up each step. Arriving in his home, he looked around.

It was exactly as he had left it. Even if looters had got in, there wasn't much to steal. A broken television? Maybe they could do the laundry. Shoving the keys in his pocket, Alex began to search furiously through his home. Through every drawer and every box. Every place something small might hide.

The farmhouse keys were easy enough to find. He hadn't touched them in years. The other thing, though, that was… more difficult. In certain moments, he'd take it down from a shelf or out from a bag, find it hidden in his jeans pocket or stuck down the side of a couch cushion. When that happened, he'd have to pause and take a look.

It was important. It was the pivot around which his life had turned. A round, metallic object which had dictated the course of his very existence. And it was so small. Just a golden circle, empty of everything except meaning. It was always appearing around the house, in the places he'd least expect. When that happened, he'd have to sit and think about everything for a while. Even now, it was altering his life.

He found it. Beside the coffee maker in the kitchen. It was cold and lonely. Alex's searching fingers turned it in familiar circles. He knew every single atom of it. Every dimple and imperfection. No one in the universe knew anything as well as Alexander Early knew this ring. He shoved it into his pocket with the keys, grabbed a bag full of clothes, and then headed for the door. He'd be happy never seeing the apartment again. There wasn't much to leave behind.

IT WAS STILL dark and dawn struggled on to the scene. The lights in the apartment block were off, the house straining like the rest of the city to stay awake and functioning. But the creak in the stairs never slept. Every footstep called out through the hallway. Alex was worried that he was waking someone.

The stairs sang like the larks in a morning cornfield. Already, Alex was remembering the birdsong he'd heard in his youth. He hadn't thought about Virginia for years. Not since he'd handed everything over to the farmhand, Eames. But the thought had knocked him, hit him hard like a freight train, and wouldn't stop running through his mind. He had to go back. If something was happening, then Virginia was the only place in the world he needed to be. It was a place where he knew how to survive.

It just felt right in some inexplicable, dangerous way. It felt like home.

Reaching the ground floor, Alex thought he had left the singing stairs behind. But as he stepped across the entrance hall, he heard a long, high-pitched sound. A howl. It wasn't the stairs. It was a person. They were in pain.

Searching around the hallway, Alex knew there was no one else. No animal caught in a trap. No person beckoning him into a place he shouldn't go. He was alone. But the voice kept calling out.

Trying to find the source, Alex crept around the hallway. It wasn't a big space. But he pressed his ear to the wall, listened at the door down to the basement, and even tiptoed up to his neighbor's welcome mat to see if there was anyone inside. There was. The sound was coming from inside.

Glancing at the front door, Alex knew that his car was on the other side. Timmy would be waiting. The Chevy was only a few feet from the front step. He'd be out and ready to leave in no time. But there was no way to mistake the pain in the voice. The person called again, a longing, desperate howl directed at anyone passing by.

With his fingers pressed up against the door, the latch rattled. It was closed but not locked. The calling from inside grew louder, stronger. They knew someone was outside. Alex couldn't remember the last time he had seen his neighbors. They wouldn't have any idea that he'd been there. There was nothing they could hold against him if he decided to just leave. He'd be in Virginia by this time tomorrow. He'd have new neighbors.

Still, when the time came to return to Detroit, how would he be able to explain why he'd deserted a wounded person? Someone in pain. Someone calling out for help.

Turning the door handle, Alex thought it felt wet. Cold. It was brass. The condensation in the hallway was clinging to the metal. It felt sweaty. It stuck to the palms. Pushing just hard enough with his shoulder, Alex opened the door.

Inside was an apartment just like his own. The same layout. The windows in the same place, though the view slightly different. There was more furniture here, more possessions. Photographs of a familiar face lined the shelves in a cluttered unit which lined one side of the room. Approaching the picture frames, Alex recognized the face. His neighbor. A middle-aged Hispanic man, pictured in a white uniform beside an airplane. With friends and family. A man Alex must have greeted in the hallway once or twice. The two had never exchanged names.

But the sound was so much louder, unmistakably coming from the bedroom at the other end of the apartment. No words, just a closed, dry throat calling. A pained single note reaching out from the bedroom to anyone outside. Alex left the door of the apartment open and inched, cautiously, toward the bedroom.

The door was already open. Ajar. No light on inside but for the beam breaking through the window, brought in by the rising sun. A patch of light crawling across the floorboards, closer and closer toward the bed, yet to arrive. Alex pushed the door further open.

The man lay on the bed, the blankets thrown to the floor. Alex's eyes began with the feet and moved upwards toward the face. The skin was a gray color, just like in the news reports and in the alley. The toenails and the fingers turned yellow. He seemed thin. Dehydrated. Alex could see his ribs.

Upon his face, the man wore a week's worth of beard. Hairs hung from the sallow cheeks, the black below the eyes exacerbated by the piqued red bloodshot above. Eyes that looked directly at Alex. The man tried to lift a hand. A wrist trembled, raised an inch, and fell. That same, slow moan came again.

The man was a picture of pain, something conjured by a medieval painter and daubed on the wall of a rural European church. Pestilence personified, the kind of person Alex had only ever seen accompanied by scrolling phone numbers and donation pleas. A body which, in the world Alex knew, belonged on a screen in a commercial break.

But here he was, suffering. Still. Screaming in the weakest way imaginable. But already Alex's thoughts had turned selfish. Arriving at the same time as the self-loathing, the worries of contagions and the dread of infection. Such a self-serving thought in the face of such suffering. But real, all the same. Alex felt his body freeze, refusing to move closer.

The reality of the world came raining down all at once. Finally, Alex felt the same skittish anxiety that he'd seen in the President's eyes. He could see the illness, could have reached out and touched it. Felt the thickness and the closeness of the air. The struggle to breathe. The smell.

The smell was like nothing else. It had overwhelmed the senses already. Only now, Alex noticed that his nostrils had simply shut down. Refused to work. Overcome. Stunned into submission. This man, flat on his bed and desperate for help, in every amount of pain and too feeble to help himself: this was the future. This was the present. This was the now.

But this was still a person. Alex could feel every muscle in his body, reacting on some instinctual level, telling him to flee. To preserve what was left of his health. But this was still a person. One look into the man's pupils, each a tiny pinprick abyss drowning in the bloodstained whites, and Alex knew he couldn't leave. Not without trying to help.

Water. That was the first thought. Alex ran out of the room, heard the man's renewed groans calling from behind him. Whimpers. The kitchen was in the same place as Alex's own. Checking around, he saw that there were bottles on the shelves. Some were filled. Wine. Beer. Orange juice.

Emptying them all, washing them out, and filling them with water from his own bottle, Alex returned to the bedroom. There was no way to look the man in the eye. Food next. The fridge was bare. The cupboards had a few granola bars. Apples approaching their end. Alex took it all and threw them on the bed.

Lastly, he searched around the room for a phone. A computer. Something. Some line to the outside world. There was nothing. No way anyone could reach inside. Alex plunged a hand into his own pocket. That piece of crap Chinese phone. Dialing, trying to call 911, there was nothing.

The sun was all the way up. The light which had lingered on the floorboards was crawling up on to the bed. It fell across the gray flesh. This man was dying. Alex threw the phone beside him, near the food and the water. There was nothing else to be done. Almost nothing else.

Alex ran from the room and tried to ignore the sounds. There was one more thing which needed to be done. He hurried, trying and failing to forget about all the guilt and shame that swirled through his mind. Timmy would be terrified. This was well past dawn. They should have been on the road.

Stepping into the hallway and then out of the front door, Alex turned around. He'd found a piece of chalk in the man's kitchen, beside a blackboard for chores. Hastily, his fingers continually catching on the corners, Alex sketched a huge white cross on the front door of the house. There was nothing else to be done.

Getting into the Chevy, turning on the engine, and driving away into the morning, Alex tried to catch his breath. He'd heard the man calling, even as he left. Driving along the street, there was no way of knowing how many other people had fallen sick in exactly the same way.

There could be one behind every door.

CHAPTER 15

*B*lock after block went by. As he looked now, there were white crosses on many doors. It was impossible to count. No one was outside any more. Any of the families that had been packing cars before dawn had hit the road. Shattered glass still in the streets, boards over the windows. Alex was afraid for his tires and decided to drive the long way back to Castle Ratz.

This route passed Beaumont. Closer to the lake shore. At the moments when the buildings fell away, paused, along the side of the street, Alex could see the Detroit skyline. Pillars of smoke rose up everywhere. Thick, clogging pillars of black smoke, their tops scratching at the sky, trying to get into the heavens. There had been trouble all over the city.

The closer the road to Grosse Pointe, the less empty it became. It was not other people. There was a police presence. Not the cops on street corners which had briefly been seen yesterday. These were armored cars, heavy plated vehicles which labored along coughing smoke. Looking left, looking right, looking in the rear-view mirror, Alex saw them headed in every direction.

At first it had been one, spotted stopping outside a home with a white cross on the door. A rare sighting. Human life, clad in a biohazard suit and body armor. Then there had been another. And another. Soon, almost in Grosse Pointe, Alex had slowed down and seen one on every other street.

The homes they had visited were clear. There were three types of door. The plain, indifferent, and unchanged doors. These were about half. Then the doors with the white crosses, done in paint or chalk or whatever it took. These were most of the rest. But the third, smallest category, were the doors with tape. The windows, too. Sealed shut. Black and yellow. Warning. Don't enter. Quarantine, written in big letters.

The once-empty streets had filled with the police and, the closer he came to Beaumont, Alex found them thickening. Cars. Pedestrians. People with covered faces doing everything they could to get to the hospital. It strangled the roads closed.

By the time he pulled on to East Jefferson, there was actually traffic. Moving slowly, crawling toward the hospital. It made sense. This was the newest medical facility around. Millions of dollars poured into the medical center in recent years. For anyone scared of being sick, it was the obvious choice.

The cars were moving. The parking lot at the hospital was only small. But people were pulling up on the sidewalk and ditching their vehicles, walking the remaining distance. Most of them wore masks. Alex made sure his windows were sealed tight. If he could see anyone–anyone official looking–he could tell them about the man back in his apartment block. Maybe they could send someone.

The minutes ticked by. Alex was ten blocks from the hospital. Then eight. Then five. Cars were joining the line behind him. Bumper to bumper. Every time he reached an intersection, the thought of turning off and heading straight to Timmy was there. The temptation.

Three blocks away and Alex could see people walking from car to car. They wore those hazmat suits. Directing the pedestrians into the building, they knocked on the rolled-up windows and began to question those waiting in the road.

Just one block away, a person knocked against the passenger's window of Alex's car. As he pressed a button and the glass slid down, a head leaned into the vehicle. The person was wearing an orange jumpsuit made from some kind of plastic. It rustled. It was tightened at the waist, where instruments and devices were clipped. The gloved hands and booted feet were colored slightly lighter. Made from the same material. The face was covered with a curved panel of darkened glass. Or plastic. There was no way to tell. It was reflective. They could see out. Alex could not see in.

"Symptoms?" The voice came from a small black speaker box positioned on the person's shoulder.

"No, it's not me," Alex told the figure.

"If you're not sick, please leave, sir. We have plenty more people to see." The voice was detached. Reading from a script.

"It's not me," Alex continued, "it's someone in my apartment block. He's sick. Needs help."

Listing the address and the man's symptoms, Alex began to search for the nearest corner, the quickest way to pull out from the line and return to Timmy's place. And then he realized.

"Hey, why aren't you writing any of this down?"

"We have plenty of people to see, sir. We will dispatch a unit to the address as soon as possible."

"You remember the address?"

"Thank you, sir," the voice from the speaker box crackled. "Please move along and have a nice day."

There was nothing to do. No way to force this person to check up on the neighbor.

"Just tell me you're going to help him, okay?"

"Sir, we are trying our best to help everyone."

Unsatisfied and helpless, Alex resealed the window and focused on the road. He beat a hand against the dashboard, angry. This was a waste of time. Time they didn't have. All for someone he'd never talked to. But he had to help. He couldn't leave someone behind. He hadn't been able to help his parents when they needed it most and now he'd never be able to help them again.

The plastic dashboard creaked as he hit it again. Alex hated that he couldn't help himself from trying to help others. A lighthouse of self-loathing perched above a sea of cynicism. Even if everything fell apart, he had to at least try to be good. Otherwise, what was the point?

In his mirrors, he could see the figure moving on to the next vehicle and watched as they held a conversation, which ended with a gloved hand pointing toward the rear of the hospital.

Following the finger, Alex turned his gaze to Beaumont. He was close now, barely a block away. The moving parts were visible. Orange hazmat suits flickering from place to place. Kevlar and face-masks and guns accompanying them.

There was a truck, not huge but big enough. The hazmats were loading black plastic bags into the back, slapping the side of the truck and closing the doors. As it departed, another truck arrived in its place.

Breath tightening, Alex stomped down on the accelerator. There was no space. He hit the car in front, which hit the next car in line. But it made a bit of room. Wrenching the wheel to the side, the Chevy mounted the sidewalk. Driving hard and fast, he saw the corner was close. People shouted behind. Alex turned. The road was open ahead. He drove, putting as much space between the car and the Beaumont as possible.

Faster and faster, as quickly as possible back to Castle Ratz. Alex could feel his lungs pushing hard against his ribs, trying to escape. His throat was tightening. Hands shaking. There was one turn. Then another. This was the route back to Timmy's place? Probably. Another turn.

The flashing lights in the mirrors lit up and Alex heard the siren. His foot hovered over the gas pedal. He almost did it, almost stormed his way along the streets and, in his mind, he could see himself racing across Detroit, his heart thumping faster and faster and faster until it finally exploded. But he caught himself. Pulled over.

The police vehicle was one of the armored patrol units. Catching his wheel against the curb, Alex stationed the Chevy at the side of the road. They stopped, too. The lights stayed on. The noise stopped. An individual detached themselves from the patrol unit and marched toward the car.

The man was wearing military fatigues and a helmet. It covered the top of his head and the sides. Over his eyes were a pair of clear plastic glasses. Over his mouth was a bandana, printed with a skull pattern. The lower jaw. Black and white. From the neck down, that heavy police military uniform Alex had seen on news channels. SWAT gear.

The man rapped a knuckle on the window and Alex shook himself back to life. What had happened there, after he'd seen the bags loaded into the truck, it was strange. Something had taken hold of him, snatched him into a panic. Rolling down the window, Alex tried to smile.

"You going somewhere?" The voice was detached. The man's beady eyes peered through the plastic shield. He looked tired.

"Just trying to get home before the curfew, officer. Didn't want to get in people's way."

"Too fast."

"I'm sorry, just running late, you know. Got to head out to Virginia tonight." Alex could feel his tongue running away with itself. He couldn't stop talking.

"No one leaves the city."

"Sure, officer, but we heard on—"

"It's shut down. Return to your home."

Spluttering an answer, Alex couldn't figure anything out. His mind had tried to overcompensate, to make conversation, and now it had got so far ahead of itself it had tripped up. Alex was a mess and he knew it.

The officer leaned back, out of the window, and knocked three times on the roof. It was a sign. It meant get the hell out of here. As he strolled back to the patrol unit, the man paused and stared at the license plate on the Chevy. He took out a device and punched in the number. It was a marked car.

As the patrol vehicle roared into life and pulled past, it left Alex at the side of the road. That had been too much. The combination of the hospital and the officer, one after the other. A one-two punch. Smash and grab. This changed things.

Leaning down over the wheel, Alex tried to read the street signs. He'd been driving hard and fast. Forgotten where he was. Forgotten who he was. Reading the sign helped. It centered him. In actual fact, he wasn't too far from Timmy's place. A couple streets over.

With care and consideration, Alex turned the key in the ignition. A spare hand felt for the ring in his pocket. It was still there. Checking the mirrors, finding the gear, the ride back was nothing special. Blissfully uneventful. Alex wanted to bottle the feeling and keep it locked up. He knew he'd need it soon.

CHAPTER 16

*A*lex didn't knock. He walked right in. There was a crashing sound from the kitchen, the sound of boots on tiles, and then Timmy burst through into the hallway, shotgun primed to fire.

"No, no, no," Alex shouted. "It's me, it's me!"

"Oh, for f—" Timmy lowered the gun and turned back to the kitchen. "You can't be serious. Where've you been? I thought something had happened. I was freaking out."

"You nearly shot me." Alex followed his friend.

"You're damn right I nearly shot you. You're lucky I didn't. Christ."

The two of them entered the kitchen, each muttering under their breath. All of the bags were packed, stacked, and ready to go. Even breakfast had been attempted, which meant unpacking a couple of the meals and arranging them on a plate. The cracker and the spread were staring up, beguilingly. To hungry eyes, it almost seemed tempting.

They sat and ate. Alex told his friend about the trip. The man, stuck in his bed. The hospital, packed with people. The trucks, the police, and the roadside stop. It was a lot to cover. Occasionally, the conversation would pull up to a halt and they'd have to discuss some minor detail. The symptoms. The black bags. The lockdown of the city.

"So this changes everything, doesn't it?" Timmy had licked the spread off his cracker.

Nodding, Alex knew he was right. It didn't just mean that they'd struggle to get out of the city, but the police had taken his plates. They knew his car. It must be on some kind of list by now. First attempt to drive anywhere and he'd be pulled over. The Chevy was a no go.

But the SUV wasn't getting anywhere either. They'd locked down the city and anyone trying to escape was going to be stopped. In the age of electrics, there wasn't a less subtle vehicle on the road than Timmy's SUV. The vehicle demanded the attention of everyone else. That was the last thing they needed.

"You said he was gray, man? Must be weird seeing it up close. Was it like the TV? I got the chills, man."

Again, all Alex could do was agree. There was no way of knowing whether he'd been able to help. The man had water and food. He had Alex's phone now, for what that was worth. Whether the hospital would send anybody out to help, who knew? The white cross on the door might do something.

"This is no flu, man," Timmy repeated. "There's something happening. We really need to get out of here. We're so screwed."

Pushing his food around on the plate, Alex couldn't help but agree. Seeing the man, stuck in his bed, his eyes riven with blood. If that was what was coming, then he needed to be as far away as possible. Even when driving through the last few blocks, he'd seen a group of masked people ripping the wooden boards from a store. This was just the morning.

The meal had come with a cake. There was a fruit puree, too, designed to be mixed in together. Mashing one substance into the other, the plastic fork did all the work. Alex wasn't even sure whether he wanted to eat. But he went through the motions anyway.

They'd been all packed and ready to go. Right now, Virginia seemed an even better plan. The house, in the middle of the farm. There was no one there. No roving bands of people to rip boards from windows. No police patrols. No crowded hospitals. Just a few walls, a roof, and enough space to sit this whole thing out. That farm meant survival. It always had, in one shape or another. Now more than ever.

Timmy had not cleared the table properly. Under the plates, the map they'd scrutinized the previous night was still there, acting as a table cloth. Fork still playing in one hand, Alex stared at Virginia. The thick forests between here and there. The mountains. The rivers. For some people, that meant heaven on earth. Wide open spaces. No people. It might be the difference between life and death, right now.

But there was something else. The space. The empty space. Alex stared at the map. For the most part, it was just empty space. That's all it was. Sure, there were the roads, pumping people across the country like the air from a pair of lungs. But between the roads? There was nothing.

"Timmy," he said. "I think I've got something."

The map sat there. Alex took a forkful of food. He chewed.

"Get the bags."

THE DEALERSHIP WAS HALFWAY across the city. They took the SUV, bags in the back and covered with blankets, a strip of carpet, and other junk. Driving slowly, trying to avoid any patrols, it took some time. They were stopped twice, had to tell masked cops that they were heading home, heading to see family, heading to pretty much anywhere else. With everything covered in the trunk, they hoped the cops wouldn't be able to see the Kevlar body armor they were wearing. It seemed to work.

The idea had belonged to Alex but it was Timmy who provided all the detail. Trying to find a motorcycle was easy. There were plenty of those places around. But trying to find this kind of specific bike? Much harder. This was where Timmy's connections came in handy.

There was someplace out in Riverside. All Timmy's favorite places were out in Riverside. Wasn't quite near the GUNPLAY warehouse, but it was close enough. The warehouse district was massive and – more importantly – almost abandoned. The same sort of post-industrial detritus, the same old relics of the trade war. Broken businesses with new ones built on top.

Even as Alex had explained his idea, his friend was butting in with names and models. Triumph, he'd said, that's the one. They've got this Tiger, Timmy had said, she'll go over anything you throw at her. Space on the side for a couple of bags. Not many. We'll have to cut down. But, boy, we'll get there in some style. The enthusiasm was palatable.

Motorcycles seemed like a reasonable solution, Alex had told himself. He'd learned to ride on his farm, one of those gold standard memories, sugar-coated in a thick skin of nostalgia that even tragedy couldn't shatter. Dirt bikes along beaten up tracks. One hundred and twenty-five ccs of teenage adrenaline.

As they drove along, Timmy was searching through his phone for details. The company was one he knew, one he'd visited a few times. The display models, he said, they had these huge chunky tires on them. Real off-roading types. But they do a job on the streets, too. Alex had sat and listened. After his friend had pulled the address, he'd asked for him to try and look up any more information. But it was hard.

Unlike the phone that had been left behind, Timmy's phone was American. This made it more reliable, as Alex was sick of hearing. But it actually worked. Not well–most of the networks were still as slow as a creeping death–but there were none of the reboot loops which plagued his life. Driving the SUV to their destination, Timmy read what he could out loud.

But the stories told them nothing. New York Times, CNN, the Post, the rest. They all said pretty much the same thing. Stay inside, wait for further information. So, Timmy tried the foreign news networks. They just didn't work. Error messages.

Not to be perturbed, Timmy tried a workaround. It was the baseball blackout all over again. Something he'd read about once. Tunneling in from another connection, a virtual one. That was Timmy's plan. It worked. They loaded one page, some Chinese site. Neither of them could read Mandarin. Just propaganda anyway,

Timmy proclaimed. But the pictures were clear enough. The Statue of Liberty. That familiar skyline. Smoke rising. Towers burning.

They got to the next page. There was some software available, a translation on-the-fly. Timmy tried it. It was far from perfect. The sentences were disjointed, the syntax broken. But they managed to piece together bits of information. Like a jigsaw puzzle, they started with the edges. The cold, hard facts.

There were words which repeated. Aerosolized, that was one. Mortality rate was another, which kept appearing alongside a 60% figure. Virus. Lockdown. Cartels. Internet. Riots. The word cure was conspicuous by its absence. The words man made appeared, in the very last sentence. The way it was phrased, however, neither man was sure what it meant. "Americans man made plague kills." It didn't sound good.

Next, the phone uncovered pictures. Videos. Taken at street level. Shared. Overdubbed with translations into languages they didn't understand. But shouting. Screaming. Rioting. That was clear. Timmy moved through the photos, getting faster and faster. And then it stopped. Instead, a blank page appeared on the screen. The seal of the United States. An error message. Nothing else worked. They focused on the road.

THE SUV PULLED up in the right place. The only sign of life in Riverdale had been an old homeless man, wrapped in a battered American flag, singing battle hymns with a bottle in his hand. They'd given him a wide berth. Too much noise.

It was nearly noon. It was almost normal for this part of town. But there were differences. The gates in front of the dealership were closed, huge chain-link structures ten feet high, razor wire wrapped around the top.

Alex looked around. They were alone. He nodded to Timmy and they unpacked the car. The strip of old carpet was thrown on top of the wire. Alex helped his friend up and over the fence. Then, with a lot of effort, he climbed on top of the SUV and threw the bags over the fence as well. Stumbling, Timmy caught them.

Once they were both inside the compound, they crossed the parking lot. It was empty. All the bikes were inside. Alex walked to the window, a single giant pane, stretched most of the length of the building. There was no electricity inside, no lights. Cupping a hand over the eyes, pushing up against the glass, it was possible to peer into the gloom.

There were rows and rows of bikes. All shapes and sizes. Alex was trying to count them, trying to spot these Triumphs he'd been told about. His friend was trying the front door. It didn't move. Not a single millimeter. They shared a shrug.

Checking around the parking lot, at the foot of the fence, Timmy found a half-brick.

"This is it then. Alarm will be off. No one around. Up to you, man."

The half-brick was handed to Alex, the rough of the broken side placed flat on the palm of his hand and he tested the weight. It was a few pounds. It had corners, too. Get one of those against the window and there'd be no chance it'd stay up. But this wasn't a question of physics.

"You think we should?" Alex asked. "Seems like this is a moment."

"I'm with you, man, whatever you want to do."

Testing the weight again, stepping back from the glass, and stretching his shoulder, Alex searched around Riverside. They were all alone. Motioning for his friend – his accomplice, really – to step back, he checked his stance. Set his feet.

"Here goes nothing."

Alexander Early threw the half-brick through the window of the motorcycle dealership. Just right, it caught the glass with a corner. The sound of the impact lasted a split second, then there was just the rain of the glass shards, hitting against the tiled floor. It all happened in slow motion. All catching the light. It was like standing beside a shimmering waterfall. They were in.

CHAPTER 17

The beams from the flashlights cut through the darkness. The midday sun wasn't enough to penetrate into the gloom of the showroom. The two men walked across the smashed glass, which crunched and crackled with every step.

The air inside was still. Up until the moment the brick had come careening through the window, it hadn't moved for days. While the old air rushed out through the new opening, it tasted stale on the tongues of the intruders. It was not the only trying taste in the mouth.

"So, we're technically looters now?" Alex asked.

"I guess so. I mean, we're leaving them my car. That's worth something. Maybe we're not looters until we actually take something. When we cross the premises. Then we're looters. Right now, we're just curious."

Alex grinned. "Curious people smash windows?"

"Depends on the windows."

Amidst the darkness, the torchlight would catch on the chrome fixtures and fittings of the bikes. There must have been fifty of them in here, all shapes and sizes. Each one stood up and ready to show off. The walls were lined with accessories.

Timmy's idea was to find the bikes, spend five minutes fitting racks to the sides (as well as anything else that took his fancy) and then they'd be good to go. Alex didn't argue. To him, all the bikes looked the same.

The bikes they wanted were in the back, perched on a raised pedestal. The display, a foot up from the ground, involved two of the bikes hanging with a wheel in the air, as though they were ready to clamber up a mountain at a moment's notice.

The bodywork, the thickness of the tires, and the exposed intricacies of the huge engine caught the eye right away. The machines screamed barely contained power, panthers crouched with their shoulders low to the ground, about to pounce.

These bikes were nothing like the dirt bikes back on the farm. Alex's dad had taught him to ride, barreling through the corn fields, racing against each other. Those machines had been light, almost like toys. The dealership monsters were heavier, utilitarian, built for purpose. *Still*, Alex thought, *you never forget how to ride a bike*. Even then, he felt butterflies fidget in his stomach.

But they weren't ready. Timmy was performing the checks. There was no fuel inside. The keys were missing. The tires could do with some extra air. Even the racks–ready and waiting on the walls– needed to be fitted.

Getting the bikes down from the pedestal was hard. They were lighter than Alex had expected but difficult to maneuver. Between them, the men lowered the bikes on the floor and began to prepare them for travel.

The dealership had a fuel tank out back. Of all the various accessories scattered around the room, the spare fuel cans seemed to be one of the most useful. Filling first the cans, using this fuel to fill the bikes, and then topping off the spare containers, the process was easy.

Alex left his friend to handle the tools. Timmy was working hard. A wrench in one hand, screwdriver nearby, he was plucking racks and items from all around the store and bringing them back to the bikes. Tweaking seat heights and testing brakes. With barely contained glee, he began fitting it all to the Triumph motorcycles.

The bikes were beastly, even Alex could see that. There was an air of quality about them, a sense that they'd be able to tackle anything. For a moment, he considered knocking one of the panels with a screwdriver, just to see what would happen. But, anticipating a poor reaction from his friend, he refrained. Instead, he held the torch above and made sure that the light was ready and available.

It didn't take long. Once the racks and bars and everything else was fitted, it was time to fix the bags in place. Bringing them in from beside the fence, Alex dumped them next to the bikes. With bungee cords and straps, they fixed each one in place. Everything seemed to fit together well. Alex was impressed.

"I feel like you've done this before."

"Man, you ever sit around bored in work? The amount of times I've just been putting together bits and pieces of bikes in my mind. I've had these babies planned out for years."

Timmy tightened the final strap, locking it shut.

"Besides, man, we still got the best bit to come."

"What's that?"

"Follow me."

They left the bikes behind. Ignitions primed, bags locked up in place, fuel in the tank: they were ready to roll. But Timmy led them deeper into the dealership. Through the showroom, past the offices, and into the furthest, darkest corner. With the flashlights busy finding the way across the floor, Alex had no idea where they were headed.

Timmy laid a hand across his friend's chest, bringing him to a halt.

"This is it, man. The big decision. You got to get this right, otherwise everything else is screwed."

There was no way of knowing what he was talking about. Alex frantically went over the entire plan in his head, trying to find holes and gaps and points where a single wrong decision could throw their lives in jeopardy. Sickness. Government patrols. There was a lot that could go wrong. The entire country was collapsing. Timmy turned the flashlight upwards.

"Pick your poison, my friend."

There were helmets, hundreds of them. From the floor to the ceiling, across two walls, the corner was filled with nothing but motorcycle helmets. All designs and patterns. Timmy was flicking his light across the inventory, practically salivating.

"You got to have the right helmet, man. Makes the whole thing worthwhile."

"You're enjoying this far too much. It's the end of the world, remember."

Timmy chose to ignore his friend. "Here, take a look at this one."

It was an American flag, a vinyl wrap around a kind of half-helmet. It covered the crown of the head, came down behind the ears. But it left the face free and exposed. The red, white, and blue were vivid, even in the dark. Alex placed it back on the rack and began to look at more conventional options.

There were too many choices. Safety wasn't really a concern. If the country was being taken over by an airborne virus and martial law was declared, then a pull-down visor might not make too much difference in the grand scheme of things.

So the half-helmet idea seemed to offer the best option. Clearly, price was not a concern, but Alex was worried about the full facial covering. It felt restrictive. He liked the idea of the less intrusive options. Really, it was a case of picking a design, pattern, or color. In the moment, he was leaning toward a simple black option.

But Timmy was in hog heaven. Timekeeping had fallen by the wayside as he stood transfixed in front of the display.

"Hurry up, Timmy," Alex hissed.

The words fell on deaf ears. Timmy had taken at least five different helmets down off the wall and was comparing them all individually. If one didn't measure up, he dropped it to the floor. Right now, it seemed that the Old Glory design was his favorite. Nothing else was coming close. Nearly satisfied, Alex watched his friend compare the flag with another design, one with green snakes about to strike, before eventually opting for the flag.

Shaking his head at the antics, Alex began to tap a knuckle against all the boring black options. They were much the same. Choosing the one which sounded least hollow, which sounded densest, Alex plucked the half-helmet from the rack and placed it on his head. The size was right, at least.

Already, Timmy had walked away. Sorting through the other clothing selections in the store, he came back, handing Alex a face mask, a leather jacket, a pair of goggles, and gloves. With the uncovered face, the cotton mask might be a good idea. It would keep out bugs, at least. Viruses might be a different matter.

There was a sound at the rear of the store. A knocking, a hammering. Shouting. A dog barked. The two friends looked at each other. Without a word, they ran back to the bikes. Alex hadn't ridden since he was a teenager. Even then, it had been dirt bikes on the farm. Even as he ran toward the bike, he could see that this was a different monster entirely.

A door slammed open at the back of the dealership. Heavy padded paws could be heard thundering toward the front of the building.

"We're going to just have to go for it, man. That's gotta be the owner. Must have tripped some silent alarm or something."

"You said the power was out."

"I don't know how these things work, do I? We need to get out of here fast."

"The gate's locked."

"Reckon these babies won't worry about that. Just get a bit of speed up."

The barking was in the same room. The dog was huge. A Rottweiler. It ran toward them, barking, and pulled up short, ten feet away. It snarled.

Still standing beside the bikes, Alex and Timmy twisted, putting the machines between themselves and the dog.

"If I try and get on here, he's going to bite me," said Alex. "And he looks pissed."

"I got an idea." Taking his eyes away from the Rottweiler, Timmy began rummaging through one of the bags. Alex watched on. There were muffled shouts from the back. Whoever had let the dog in was coming closer. Timmy pulled out one of the ready-packed meals.

Ripping away the wrappers, he threw the food to the dog. It didn't even sniff.

"Man, even the dog doesn't want this stuff."

"That was your idea?"

"What do you want, man? I thought he'd like it."

The owner was getting closer. There was no telling what he'd do when he reached the looters. That was what they were, Alex thought. Looters. The man might have a gun. Might drag them to the police. This wasn't going to end well. They needed to get out.

He had an idea, switched the ignition, and the engine roared to life. From behind the bike, Alex reached across and grabbed the throttle. He gave it some gas while holding the brake firmly in place. He revved, again and again.

The back-wheel tore through the tiled floor. The sound of screeching rubber pierced the eardrums. While Alex and Timmy knew what was happening, the dog was terrified. It began to back off. When the other bike began to do the same, the Rottweiler edged farther and farther back into the dark. A few more feet and he'd be just far enough.

"Now," Alex shouted. "Go."

He swung a leg over the saddle and took his seat on the bike. As he released the brake, the wheel finally began to gain traction. Skimming across the surface, the Triumph tried to transfer all her power toward actually moving. Alex leaned, turning to face the broken window. And then, without warning, the tires caught and he was away.

The force of the movement snapped him back and all he could do was hang on tight. Timmy was following behind. They were out of the dealership, across the smashed glass. Crossing the parking lot. There was the gate. It loomed large. Locked.

Timmy's plan had been to hit the gate hard enough that they'd just smash through. The chain was old and rusty; they'd checked on the way in. But it was still a risk. Alex was in the lead and–if the plan didn't work–he'd bounce back from the fence and be a prime target for the dog, the owner, and anyone else.

The dirt bike days. That was what he remembered. The fence

approaching, just ten feet away and closing fast, he decided to try something. Leaning back, he let out the clutch. The throttle opened. The front tire raised up off the ground. The bike thundered forward. Alex adjusted his weight.

He hit the fence. The front wheel, two feet off the ground and falling, hit right against the spot where the rusty chain held the gate shut. It snapped. The gates flew open.

Alex could hear his friend shouting and hollering as they rode away together. They left Riverside, riding faster. With the bikes, the supplies, and the plan in action, they hit the open road.

CHAPTER 18

*O*nce they were out of Riverside, they eased off. There was no need to speed, attracting unwanted attention. In the spaces between the buildings, the columns of smoke were rising up and into the skyline, spilling into clouds. Helicopters circled over distant blocks, moving skittishly above the city like dragonflies above a swamp.

The plan had been to hit Route 75. It was the best way out of the city, at least by road. Once they were reaching the city perimeter, they could change course and cover less traditional ground. The benefit of the bikes was flexibility. They could go where they pleased, nearly.

Riding was coming back to Alex, but these Triumphs were nothing like anything he'd ridden before. The layout was the same as those old farm bikes. Throttles, clutches, brakes. It all felt familiar. But there was a smoothness to everything, as well as a danger. Like the finest silk wiping blood from a sword.

The machine was engineered to an exact degree, balanced perfectly. Alex need only adjust his weight ever so slightly and the bike did exactly as he asked. As he eased off the throttle, pulling into a deserted lot, he was in danger of enjoying himself. A brief moment before the real horror of everything else came back to him.

Stepping off the bike, Alex finally had a chance to look at himself in one of the wing mirrors. The desperation of the escape had pushed everything from his mind. As well as the faded jeans and the sneakers he was wearing, he'd added a leather jacket from the store, worn over the T-shirt and the Kevlar, as well as gloves and the helmet. The mask and goggles Timmy had handed him were still in his pocket; there hadn't been time to try them on.

As Timmy pulled in behind, Alex could see that his friend had taken much more keenly to the motorcycle theme. The helmet with the American flag stole the eye, but the white leather jacket would be dirty in no time. A pair of outsized aviator sunglasses, thick tactical-style trousers, and big biking boots completed the look. On Timmy's smaller frame, it was in danger of looking ridiculous.

Taking a moment by the side of the road, they went over the plan again. They'd go down 75, parallel to the lake. When they hit Toledo, they could double check their status. But out near Zug Island, near the city limits, that would be the problem. If they crossed close enough to the river, they'd reasoned, they could use the bikes to travel along the sand, through the yards, along the shorefront. Anything to avoid the stops.

For the moment, they were content to ride the roads. As soon as they were both ready, they mounted up and began their journey. Alex rode in front, Timmy just behind and to his side, lurking in the peripheral vision but ready to drop back or accelerate away as needed.

Among the warehouses, the streets had been empty. It was approaching afternoon, the final stretches of September coming to an end. The shadows were lengthening, thrown over empty asphalt. There were guard posts and cars, though they were deserted. They'd left in a rush, hurrying somewhere.

But beyond Riverside, it was different. They were driving closer and closer to the pillars of smoke above the city. When they turned and headed south, putting the pillars on their starboard side, they noticed the people.

They were moving. It was slow and inevitable. As the roads widened and the city thinned, the numbers of cars increased. There were people behind the wheel, going nowhere. The closer they came to Route 75, the thicker the traffic became. Everyone who had been told to stay inside the city seemed to have disagreed.

To keep moving, they kept to the side streets. The alleys. The sidewalks, even. They dipped in and around the parked cars, as the bikes allowed them. The traffic was not quite bumper to bumper this far from the freeway, but it heralded a busy road. A clogged artery of the city, shortening the lease of life. The fat of the land, congested.

As they passed the cars, Alex could see inside. Some people had everything, their entire lives piled up in the back of a station wagon. Others had nothing, perhaps a worried wife or a cat in a box. The cars were moving slowly, trying to navigate their way out of the city. But there was a problem.

The lockdown. Alex realized it before they'd travelled too far. These cars were not heading anywhere. Everyone had the same idea, to get out on the freeway and drive, but they were being turned back. Cars were circling the city blocks like sharks, looking for a point of attack. But there was none available. Instead, they were travelling in endless loops.

On one quiet street, a clear sight of Canada over the river, Alex saw a couple park their car and exit. They were staring at the river, considering the crossing. It wasn't far. For a fit, healthy person, Alex reasoned, it might be possible to swim across.

But what waited on the other bank? Relations with the northernmost neighbor had not been good in recent years. The idea of crisscrossing the border on a Detroit afternoon was a distant memory. Those bridges had been burned on the altar of free trade.

Perhaps these people didn't realize what awaited them on the other shore. Perhaps they didn't care. Alex watched as he rode past. The two were embracing. He continued to watch in his wing mirrors, slowing and wondering what they would do.

The couple didn't move. Alex was getting farther and farther away. But, as he watched, he saw figures moving in and around the car. They jumped in, drove away. The couple, their moment of quiet contemplation shattered, chased after the car, which curved and snaked away, stolen. Society was coming apart at the seams, Alex told himself.

Rouge River was approaching. Zug Island was ahead, the ghost of the steelworks cutting a clear figure against the skyline. There were rail bridges on and off the island. Lined along p West Jefferson, they were nothing but piles of rubble. Not just closed down but destroyed completely.

As they approached the bridge on West Jefferson, the traffic was thicker than ever. The cars hadn't moved in a long time. Slipping through on the bikes, there were people asleep in their vehicles. Waiting for anything to happen.

Up ahead, there was a stop. They were turning back cars. But the congestion was such that there was no way to turn. Stragglers struggled back up the road on foot, leaving their cars behind, making the problem even worse.

Still a few hundred feet from the block, Alex couldn't yet see the intricacies of the problem. He knew they'd be unlikely to find a way of sneaking past such a protected position. But it would help to get a look at the obstacle ahead. He slowed the bike beside the rows of abandoned cars, hearing Timmy do the same behind.

Now at nothing but a crawl, the bike felt more cumbersome. Alex could feel himself leaning hard to change direction, felt himself catch against the parked vehicles as he went past. But there were no shouts. The entire road was quieter than he expected. The illusion of chaos with no one inside.

There should have been the din of a hundred engines. The constant blather of horns, demanding passage through. The shouting of people leaning out of windows. But there was none of that. Everyone had left.

Alex hit another mirror. No one said anything. He looked over his shoulder. The driver of the car hadn't even looked up. She was slumped in her seat, head rolling back. Asleep? The skin was that same gray. She was still. Unstirring. Alex rode on, leaving the shattered mirror on the road beside the car.

The bridge was old but it still worked. It was a mechanical drawbridge; it split in half down the middle and could raise and lower in response to ships needing to pass. Unlike the rail bridges, there was a way of closing it down without having to destroy it completely. The cops had the bridge raised and no one was able to cross.

They stopped the bikes. The hours were dragging out. A few more and it would be dark. Together, the two discussed whether it'd be easier to cross once night fell. They might be more hidden, but overhead the helicopters were buzzing by regularly enough. The cops' triggers might be itchier when they were less sure. Immediacy had a value all its own.

Cutting the engines, they ducked low and rolled the bikes through the cars. Most of these were deserted. Those left inside were either dead, sleeping, or close to both. Even now, Alex struggled to comprehend how quickly this had all become real. A city should not have broken down this fast. If this was happening in the rest of the country, well... He couldn't even entertain the thought.

There were ten guards beside the bridge. They were all armed. Alex and Timmy had their share of guns, at Timmy's insistence, but there was no use getting into a gunfight with the law. That wasn't the point of this. This was about survival. Quietude and cunning would be far more effective. Over his shoulder, Alex heard a whisper.

"Hey, man. You saw those people back there?"

"Uh-huh."

"They were...you know. Sleeping, some of them."

"Uh-huh."

"That was like the guy you saw, your neighbor? That skin and those eyes?"

"Uh-huh."

"Man." Timmy sat down, propping up his bike with his shoulders. An idea struck him. "So, er, how close did you get?"

"Not that close."

"But, like, close enough I have to worry? How close is close?"

"You don't have to worry."

Alex watched the guard post. They weren't doing much. Standing, watching. Providing a presence. A clear signal that there was no way anyone was crossing this bridge. But the bridge was not the only thing they had to worry about. There was a small dock, down by the river. Sneaking around the side, Alex got a better look at it. There was some kind of old barge tied to a mooring. No one was paying it any attention.

From here, Alex could see across the river, too. There were open roads. There were empty streets. This was the official city limits. Beyond this, people were on their own. But inside these limits? They were just as alone. Stuck with one another. Stuck with themselves. As Alex surveyed the scene—the bored guards and the raised bridge—a plan began to kindle inside his head. He turned to Timmy.

CHAPTER 19

They moved together, working in sync. But their paths split. Timmy would sneak through the line of cars, getting as close as possible to the bridge without being seen. Alex would head to the river bank, down to the moored barge. They had to remain unseen.

Alex cut away from the road immediately. The guards, when they were not watching each other, were watching the line of cars. There wasn't much to see now. The abandoned, still vehicles presented a fine barrier for anyone trying to access the freeway. They were not paying much attention to the tree line.

After a discussion, he had been able to convince Timmy to hide his white leather jacket along with the bikes. It was hardly designed for sneaking. Alex could see his friend now, flitting between the cars, heading to the opposite side of the road. His destination, the control hut for the bridge, was drawing closer. Alex watched the movement and made sure his accomplice was in position before he reached the river bank.

There was a five-foot drop to the shoreline. He could see the river from here. A slow, ambling brown sludge, snaking through the city. On the surface, the water didn't seem to move. It crawled along, a heavy flow streaming toward the mouth, hidden by the scum which floated to the top.

So far, no one seemed to have spotted him. Alex teetered behind a tree, watching a guard taking a leak over the bridge and into the river. The man's eyeline was exactly where Alex needed to be. He waited. And waited. The man did not seem to stop.

Finally, the guard finished, stretched, and turned back to his colleagues, and Alex moved. There was no way to remain steady on the ground. The sneakers were so worn down on the soles, there was no grip. Even as he moved, Alex knew he'd be falling. And he fell, slipping and sliding down the grassy bank.

There was noise. Any noise was too much but the sound of shifting dirt and snapping twigs bellowed across the quiet river. Cursing as he slid, Alex reached the bottom and collapsed into a heap. But there was no time to lick his wounds. He was up and running, ducking behind a barrier.

With his back pressed up against the metal, Alex caught his breath. He listened, savoring the second. There was no sound, this wasn't like GUNPLAY. This was real. If they'd spotted him, they would be shouting. They would be mobilizing. There would be an indication. They hadn't heard him.

Alex sighed. This was hard. Nothing about working in an office had prepared him for this. But the barge was in front of him and, with it, the plan. It wasn't a complicated idea. A classic distraction. It depended heavily on Timmy being able to work the bridge controls and being able to time his actions to the second. The more Alex thought about it, the less sure he was that it would work.

Timmy was supposed to be the man with the plan. He was supposed to be the one figuring all this out. But here they were, chasing down one of Alex's weird ideas again. He knew Timmy loved being able to rely on a well-thought out, prepared course of action.

He didn't have the heart to tell his friend that he was making this up as he went along. But Timmy had to know. It's why Alex spent at least a minute staring at situations before acting.

In his mind, Alex was just panicking. Shouting at himself. Eventually, he'd just make something up. Anything. But Timmy seemed convinced that it was fine. So they went with it.

Like now. Alex reached into his pocket and found the fire starter sticks. This was the entire plan. He looked at the barge. It was empty, bar some ropes and a tin drum, full of something. That was it. How the hell was he meant to make a distraction with this? It had seemed so much easier before.

The first thing to do was to check the barge. It was tied to the mooring with a length of rope, as thick as Alex's wrist. There was a complicated knot. Trying at it with his thin fingers, he knew there was no way that knot was going to be untied. Alex gave up. He pulled a Leatherman from his pocket, switched out the knife, and began to saw through the strands.

It took a while. But it worked. The boat was free. But there was no current in the river. Alex had expected the river to carry the boat along, taking it just beyond the bridge and turning the heads of the guards. But it was pretty much just staying still in the water. Maybe moving slightly. That problem could be dealt with afterwards.

Next, Alex examined the rope. He had been worried that it would be wet, damp with river water or sea air or whatever it was that boat people always talked about. But it was dry. The rope that lay piled on the deck was dry too. Inside the drum was something. Alex didn't know what, but it smelled flammable. Some kind of chemical. Good.

Picking up all the rope he could find, he threw it into the drum. Scouring the shoreline, careful not to be seen, he picked up any wood, newspapers, dry grass, anything that looked like it might burst into flame. Into the drum it went. When the drum was half full, Alex tossed in half his fire starters, pushing them down to the bottom.

Then it hit him. Alex didn't have a lighter. No matches. Nothing. He looked inside the box. They'd surely packed something in there. A single match. Something. Anything. But it was empty.

Alex tried to remember back to his childhood. His father had used these kinds of magnesium sticks then, too. When they were sat out the back of the farm, marshmallows on sticks. The whole countryside idyll thing. He would have known what to do.

Half-remembering, Alex had an image of his father shaving a fire starter into slivers with a knife. So he did that. Then he remembered the man using a piece of flint on the butt of his knife. A real manly approach. But Alex didn't have a piece of flint. He did have a knife.

Jumping back on to the shore, Alex tried to find any rock. Any stone. Something that might generate a spark. The barge was moving now, slower than walking pace, but drifting toward the center of the river. Alex grabbed what he could find and jumped back across to the floating distraction.

Dropping the rocks on to the deck, he worked through them furiously. In a rush, he ran the metal edge of the Leatherman against the stones. There was nothing. Nothing. Nothing. And then–a spark. Too small. Alex scratched again. Another spark. He kept going, pointing his hands at the pile of fire starter cuttings. Finally, they caught.

The fire spread quickly. It caught among the paper and the dry grass. The other sticks went up in a flash. Alex stepped back, his nostrils filled with the thick toxic fog. His eyes watered as he watched the fire begin to rise out of the drum, crackling and snapping. Looking over his shoulder, he saw that he was drifting from the shore. He had to leave now. He had to hope it was enough.

Running, jumping, Alex was back on dry land. The barge was floating to the middle of the river. Soon, it would be heading under the bridge. But was it enough? Right now, it was just a small fire in a drum. Now, it would grow into the monumental distraction Alex had imagined. If Timmy tried to lower the bridge now, he'd be noticed immediately.

Fingers grasping at the loose dirt of the incline, Alex clambered up and away from the river. Before running back to the bikes, he turned to watch the barge. There was smoke pouring out of the drum. The fire had caught. Something chemical was burning. A thin wisp of smoke. Worry and dread began to crawl up Alex's throat. The same poisonous taste as the chemicals.

The smoke stopped for a moment and the barrel coughed a blazing billow of flames up into the air.

Alex punched the air, trying to celebrate as quietly as possible. His plan was working.

God knows what had been in that drum but it was burning. The flames were stronger now, much stronger. The smoke thicker. Even from up on the ridge, Alex could smell the chemicals. He looked to the roadblock. The guards had noticed. They were scrambling to deal with the barge as it floated toward the bridge.

With his back bent low, Alex ran straight back to the place they'd left the bikes. There was less cause for care now. The distraction was in full swing. Arriving beside the motorcycles, testing their handles, he guided them both at once toward the side of the road.

It was awkward. As he balanced a handlebar in each hand, caught between pushing and pulling, the bikes did not want to be corralled. But Alex persisted. He did not have to drag them far. As he moved, he watched the bridge closely, searching for his friend.

The fire and the smoke rising from the barge were incredible. It wasn't just the sky being blackened above the bridge. The light from the flames was adding an orange glow to the underside of the thick clouds. The whole thing must be on fire, Alex thought. The guards were panicking, running around.

Slowly, the bridge began to move. It was a mechanical sigh, an old creak as the upturned pillars of road began to ease downwards and toward one another. They moved without haste, an inevitable arc toward a flat and useable road. As they closed, the burning barge was moving beneath the bridge.

Timmy was running between the cars. He wasn't bothering to hide any more. None of the guards were watching anyway. Most of them had run down to the riverbank, while the others were scrambling back to investigate the closing bridge. Ducking and weaving between the cars, Timmy arrived back to the bikes.

There was no time for conversation. Both men mounted up, started their engines. The timing would be everything. Positioning themselves with a direct route to the bridge, they stared at the closing sections. They were eating up the degrees, starting from seventy, to sixty, to fifty. When it seemed just over halfway, Alex twisted his wrist and launched.

The bike rattled, struggling to drive all the raw power to the wheels. Alex held tight and ducked down low. He could see the run up to the bridge. He could see the path opening up before him. Leaning only slightly, dipping through the cars, he could see the bridge was almost closed.

Shouting came from the river banks. Alex was travelling too fast to understand. But he could see the bridge closing; he was almost there. Timmy was just behind. The curling smoke was gripping the iron sides of the bridge, the underside of the metal colored a chimney orange shade. The barge was burning, wholly. It was now or never.

Realization struck. The bridge was not going to close. Not completely. The lips would still be a few feet apart when the front wheel would hit the incline. There was no other option. Ducking even lower, Alex opened the throttle and dragged every last drop of power out of the engine.

The first wheel hit the bridge. The guards were screaming. Loud bangs went off all around. Driving up the incline, the bike was lost in a world of thick, black chemical smoke. Alex wished he'd fitted the mask. But it was too late. He held his breath instead.

Almost at the lip of the bridge, Alex was looking up into the sky. Something hit him in the back, hard. It had to be ignored. The bike pushed on, up and through the smoke, up and over the bridge.

And then time slowed down. The tires turned with nothing to slow them. Alex eased his grip. Closed his eyes. Flew through the air for half a second, which felt like a century.

The fuel tank of the bike hit Alex hard in the chest, jarring him back to reality. Eyes open, his hands fought desperately to keep the bike straight. The same loud cracks and bangs were now behind him. He heard Timmy's bike land. But there was no time to stop.

Together, they rode down West Jefferson. The streets were empty, the parked cars and armed guards all behind them, back within the city limits. With Virginia now more than just a dream, Alex allowed himself a smile.

With a check over his shoulder, Alex could see the wind catching the pillars of smoke he'd set atop the barge. The checkpoint had stopped the people. Had left them sitting, sleeping, or whatever else inside their cars.

But a change in the wind and the air was different. The guards were not there to stop the contagion escaping. Only the people.

The smile slipped away.

CHAPTER 20

*R*iding with the river on one side and the outskirts on the other, there was not much to see. Homes on the roadsides showed no signs of life. Evacuated, perhaps, or victims of the black-outs. People possibly cowering inside. Aside from the occasional white cross painted across doors, the homes belonged to no one but the ghosts.

They rode in parallel with Route 75. West Jefferson was empty; it seemed unnecessary to switch on to a wider road. With the shoreline so close, they could easily switch down on to the mud or the dirt and continue on their bikes if trouble presented itself. But it did not.

Eventually, after half an hour of riding, arriving toward Hennepin Point, Alex held out an arm and motioned for his friend to stop. There was a fast food restaurant overlooking a small harbor. Spotting the golden arches from far away, it seemed like a safe zone. A neutral place. Somewhere to stop.

No cars in the parking lot. No people seen through the windows. One panel of glass had been smashed, the pieces now scattered across the black and white tiles of the floor. Both men brought their bikes as close as possible to the restaurant and killed the engines.

"Fine a place as any to stop," Timmy said. "Good choice."

Plucking his fingers from the leather gloves, Alex tried to adjust his back. It was still sore. Something had hit him, hard, while they'd been crossing the bridge. At the time, he'd had no choice but to ignore it. Now, he could take a look.

"Hey, would you help me get this jacket off? Something's not right."

Walking round behind, Timmy let out a long, lingering whistle.

"They sure did a number on you, buddy."

He leaned in, scratching at something with his finger nail.

"Here, take that off." Timmy motioned to remove the jacket. "Let me show you."

When it was off, Timmy held it up to the late afternoon light, gripping a jacket shoulder in each hand. Standing between Alex and the sun, it was like a leather eclipse. One small hole, roughly the size of a bottle cap. The light was shining through on to Alex's chest.

"They must have got you square in the back, man. God, that's so badass. Let me take a look at the armor, I want to see if it worked."

In a daze, Alex obeyed, swiveling around on the motorcycle seat. Timmy picked at something.

"Yep, right here. Boy, it's got some real weight. Here."

A hand appeared over Alex's shoulder. As the fingers opened up, something fell out and begged to be caught. It was dense, there was no mistaking that. Bringing it up to eye level, looking as closely as possible, Alex could see where the slug had run up against the Kevlar, collapsing in on itself.

The armor was hardly half an inch thick. Alex felt for his chest. Any lasting exhilaration, any pride or amazement drained out of him there and then. Half an inch. And he'd almost not worn the armor at all. Only Timmy's insistence had broken him down.

"The blood's run all out of you," Timmy laughed. "Gone all pale-face on me."

Taking a moment, leaving the bikes in full view of the shattered window, the two men ventured inside the restaurant. Inside, the power was out and the freezers had thawed, spilling water over the floor. An enterprising person had hopped over the counter and raided the tills for anything of value. Even the charity donation boxes, sunk into the counter itself, had been smashed and ransacked.

"Man, it's only been a couple of days. If that."

"Time moves fast."

"Yeah, but this fast? Nah. This is too big. Too much, man. Something's happening here. Where is everyone? All at home? I don't buy it."

"Saw a lot of crosses on those doors back there."

"I wasn't even looking. High on life, you know what I mean? That fire–how'd you get that thing going so good? Looked so cool with the flames and the bikes. Those guys didn't know what hit 'em."

"There was some old chemical drum down on the barge. Got lucky I guess. How was the bridge? Seemed like they didn't know what to do."

"That?" Timmy laughed. "I had an idea when I was there. Really old controls, see, so I just snapped off the lever. Threw it in the river. Guess that's why they started shooting. They're not getting that bridge back up any time soon."

The restaurant had been emptied. The thin layer of water on the floor was a sign that there wasn't any food to be found inside. Timmy pointed to one of the milkshake machines.

"Always wanted one of these for my home, you know? That strawberry flavor? Man, that's the stuff."

Even as he said the words, their heaviness weighed hard on both men. A strawberry milkshake. A drive thru. One dollar. Two dollars. Whatever it was they charged these days. Those days. It might be a long, long time before they were drinking shakes again. A simple slice of the everyday life, ripped away with no return date set.

"Man, we're really out here, huh?" Timmy had sat down in one of the booths. "Going all the way."

"We're hardly there yet. We're barely out of Detroit."

"I don't mean Detroit, man. I mean...like...yeah. Whatever. That thing with the bridge was cool, though."

There was a smell on the air. Stale. Sour. It was catching on the breeze, which was blowing in off the dock and in through the window. It was familiar. It preyed on Alex's memories. The smell reminded him of something, but he couldn't figure out exactly what it was. From the farm, maybe? Back in Virginia, definitely.

"You smell that?" he asked his friend. "Something…rotten, I don't know."

"Could be. Could be. Probably something in the freezers. Reckon those patties won't last too long out in the open. Maybe there's something to eat though? Bread? They used to do apple pies here, those'd keep."

Leaving Timmy at the table, Alex explored the store. All of these places were basically the same. Flat pack franchises. Get a plot of land, the company sends you a store to assemble. Same bricks, same menus, same quality, coast to coast. Even though it was empty, crossing over the counter seemed like breaking a small social taboo.

The restaurant looked different from back here. The smell was stronger, though. Alex searched the shelves and the drawers. There was some salt and sugar. Ketchup and various sauces. They went into the pocket. Might help with the readymade meals. But the smell was beginning to dominate, beginning to curdle in the back of this throat.

A storeroom sat in the back of the building. Usually, it'd be sealed up with a heavy door. But the door was open. The pale wood pulp with the fake grain. The same kind of doors you always get in these places. It had two portholes, one on top of the other. The top one was vacant, only home to a few jagged glass edges. Alex moved closer.

The smell was stronger. The memory was denser, some unformed shadow passing across the consciousness. Alex struggled to pick out the edges, to give it shape and meaning. Little pieces began to come together, assembling into a picture within his mind. But it was a slow process. The store room was just ahead.

"You hear from anyone in Virginia, Alex?"

The voice came calling out from the restaurant. Timmy hadn't moved from the table. Instead, he'd sat there, considering.

"No one. Phone was down the whole time. Don't even have it any more. Not that anyone would call me. Why?"

"Just wondering, is all. You sure Sammy didn't even try and get through?"

"Where are you going with this?"

"I've just… Well, I've heard you talk about her before, man. When we're in the bar. Just wanted to make sure we weren't off on some crazy rescue mission. That's all. We're heading to your folks' old place, right?"

"Right."

"Because it's a well-positioned, easily defendable farm house with good natural resources?"

"Right."

"And because it's yours and we won't need to break in or anything."

"Right."

"Not because your ex lives nearby?"

Alex didn't answer. The farmhouse. The shadow crawled across his mind, fueled by the stench filling up inside his sinuses. It was beginning to form. It was looking just like the farm house. It was all there. The way the weeds clustered up around the side with the septic tank. The stone wall up to about a foot and then wooden slats after that. The way the dirt slid slightly when he walked.

The basement window where that possum got in one year and then died behind the boiler and Dad had to scrape it off with a shovel while Mom was screaming the whole time. That was the image that was in his mind, insisting on recognition. As he walked toward the storeroom, Alex wondered why this–of all his childhood memories–should arrive in this moment.

Then he knew. Staring through the broken porthole, into a storeroom lined with plastic cups and paper towels, Alex knew why the smell was so familiar. It was that dead possum stench. But worse. Much worse. He had to keep going, daring the world to be different, dreading the inevitable truth.

There was a man, perched up against the furthest wall. Tattered clothes, he seemed like the homeless who came up to Michigan in the summer and left before the weather turned. It didn't matter anymore.

Covering his mouth and nose, Alex couldn't look away. The man was dead. His eyes, not just red but bloody, stared up at the ceiling. The skin was cinderblock gray, with the same texture, at all the joints and under the neck. The face had sagged, had sunk from the skull.

The man could not have been dead for more than a day, must have crawled in here when feeling sick. But the body, as it was, could have been decaying for a week. Alex pulled the door closed, though it did nothing to stop the smell pouring through the broken window. It gave the man some privacy, some peace, at least.

Backing into the restaurant, Alex was quiet. Timmy noticed.

"Hey man, that stuff about Sammy, I know you don't like to-"

"We got to go. Like, now."

"What's up? You look like you seen a ghost. Didn't think they could drain any more blood out of you, but here we are."

Already, Alex had begun walking back to the bikes. Timmy went to check the storeroom for himself.

Alex barely had the key in the ignition before his friend was running out of the restaurant and onto the bike.

"Let's just go, man. Just ride for a bit."

It was late afternoon and they rode onto Route 75 and into the night. The bikes were fitted with headlamps and they cut through the dusk, growing stronger with every hour. There was no need to talk any more. Only the need to put some road beneath them. With the sunset behind them, they let the highway do the work.

CHAPTER 21

For two days, the sun rising and falling, they rode along Route 75. They were not alone but they looked back over their shoulders. There were cars, some heading in the other direction, some pulled onto the side. But there were no words shared with anyone else. Every city, every town, every village seemed to be in lockdown.

The journey should have taken ten hours but congested roads, littered with abandoned and crashed cars, slowed them down. Every time they saw another vehicle, they dropped their speed to a crawl. Every sudden movement, every glimmer of light in the distance and they halted. Wary, paranoid progress.

As the miles rolled by beneath the wheels, Alex could see the license plates changing. State to state. He'd pick them off, marking them like baseball cards. Got Florida. Michigan. Iowa. Kansas. People were travelling far.

These were the stragglers. By now, they knew better than to look inside any of the vehicles. It was a lesson they had to learn the hard way.

On the way out of Detroit, they had pulled up in La Salle. All the roads went through the town, there was no way to avoid it. Cutting their engines, rolling the bikes along, they snuck through the alley ways.

There was a military presence in La Salle. Soldiers in tactical gear, their skin and faces hidden, moved from home to home. All the time, a recording blared from their vehicle as it rolled slowly down the streets.

"The curfew is in effect. Stay in your home. Keep your pets inside. Any gang activity will be punished. Present yourself for inspection when asked. The use of deadly force has been authorized."

The same words, again and again. Alex felt a lump in his throat, as though he was reading his own death sentence. Looking closely at the men, there was something strange about their uniforms. The camouflage wasn't patterned with leaves and shapes and khaki colors.

Instead, each soldier wore gear coated in jagged brown shapes, squared and overlapping. Alex mentioned it to his friend.

"Yeah," Timmy sighed, leaning back against a wall. "That's the new style. It's meant to look like low resolution video. Like it's been edited."

Alex peered out across the street, examining the patterns. Timmy was right: if he squinted, the outfits – and the soldiers themselves – looked like corrupted computer files, moving in and out of focus.

"But why?" he asked. "How does it keep them hidden?"

"Oh, they aren't hiding from us." Timmy tapped Alex on the shoulder, bringing him back into the shadows. "They're hiding from anyone filming them. Think about it, man. You see that on video, you think it's been edited. There's no one round here who can hurt them. It protects them from being filmed and broadcast. They're fighting a global war now, man. Public opinion matters. Plausible deniability is better than body armor."

As they hid from the soldiers, who seemed focused only on those inside the houses, Alex and Timmy discovered the town to be split into sectors. Each sector would be patrolled by a different military unit, all under the guidance of a man they referred to as the syndic.

The syndic, in his hazmat suit and loud breathing apparatus, would stalk from house to house. When he appeared in front of a home, he would hammer on the door. Then, the occupants would line up beside their window and present themselves for inspection. If deemed healthy, they would be dismissed and the Syndic would move on to the next home, reapplying the white cross to the door, marking it with a date.

"Look," Timmy whispered as they crouched in an alleyway. "The doors. They're locked from the outside."

He was right. Each door was held closed with a heavy padlock. As they walked past windows, they discovered them sealed shut with liquid cement. People were locked up inside their homes. Only soldiers and syndics were allowed in the streets.

"It must be like this in every town," Alex mumbled as they approached the far side of La Salle. "We should avoid them."

"You're telling me, man. Looks crazy. We got out just in time."

As they were almost free from La Salle, they heard the rumble of an engine and a collection of shouts. Diving back into the shadows, Alex leaned around the corner.

On the other side of the street was a syndic. His orange hazmat suit marked him out from a mile away. There he stood, pointing through the window at a person. Around him, the soldiers were shouting.

"Present yourself!"

Alex couldn't see through the window. But, as the soldiers' anger increased, he figured the person was not co-operating. Guns began to point at the glass.

From the vehicle, one soldier emerged and went to the door. Taking a key, he undid the padlock and the rest of his team ran inside. Seconds later, they dragged a young man into the street, kicked out his knees and dropped him to the floor in front of the syndic.

There, the heavy plastic gloves groped and explored the man's body. Medical tools were used, temperatures taking. Looking to a soldier, the syndic shook his head.

They pounced. The soldiers snatched the man up from the road and carried him to the rear of the vehicle, opening up a hidden caged door and throwing him inside.

At the door of the house, a family screamed and wept. They were held at gunpoint, not allowed to move. A box of rations was dumped beside their door.

"Keep calm." The syndic spoke through a radio speaker perched on his shoulder, the volume loud enough to be heard above the tears. "This is for your good and ours."

The family – a woman and two teenage children – could not gather themselves. Emotion poured off them, flowing out into the street, the sound of the crying failing to drown out the syndic's words or the condemned man's yells.

"Please co-operate." The syndic spoke flatly. "It is better to be here than out of the town. You would not last a minute with the gangs and cartels. This is for your own good, I assure you."

Already, he was moving on to the next home. The soldiers drove the family back and locked their door. Alex and Timmy crouched into the shadows and waited for the vehicle to pull around the bloke. Mounting their bikes, they exited La Salle.

"It's got to be propaganda, man." Timmy had said as they watched the screaming man being driven away. "All that about the gangs. They just want to control everything."

As they rode on through the countryside, the thought wasn't much comfort.

LATER THAT DAY, they pulled up alongside a parked station wagon. An old woman had flagged Alex down. After she'd encouraged him to look inside the window, he'd come up face to face with a revolver.

"You one of Roque's boys?" came a question from far behind the gun. "Tell me!"

"What?" Alex stammered, seeing the shape of an elderly man in the gloom.

"If you ain't, hand it over!"

Alex raised his hands, equal parts confused, scared, and shocked.

The grandfather wielding the gun wanted everything he had. Only Timmy pulling up alongside and unfurling one of the AR-15s had resolved the situation. They left the couple on the side of the road, ready to rob again.

Out of the towns, life seemed just as cheap.

It had been a similar story the next morning. They'd slept in a field, on a spit of land north of Toledo. When the sun rose, they unzipped the tent to find another car had drawn up alongside them. Looking in the window, the dawn sun above, the bodies were still as windless days. A couple, huddled together on the back seat. Nothing they could do.

The final time they'd stopped, Timmy had spotted something in one of the deserted vehicles. It had Maryland plates. A familiar sight in a sea of strange states. It had been abandoned. No sign of bodies. Leaning in through an open window, Timmy had tried to take an aftermarket GPS unit that was fastened to the dash.

"All's fair in love and war," he'd reasoned.

The unit had crapped out in five seconds. Already low on battery, running through the familiar reboot loops, Timmy cursed out the Chinese manufacturer and threw the unit into the dirt by the side of the highway. The gray plastic, the imported kind, cracked as it hit the ground. Nothing but empty cars and worries on the road to Toledo.

There should have been more people. That was all Alex could think. There should have been more. People were locked up in the cities, Timmy had reasoned, probably in the towns, too. The last thing the government would want would be people travelling around. People like us, he'd said, smiling.

Then there should have been an army presence. The military. Something. Alex had spent years reading articles about the wondrous toys and gadgets the armed forces could deploy at a moment's notice. They couldn't use these things in their own back yard? There was something up with that. Something they weren't being told.

Occasionally, when they found the right kind of abandoned car, they'd check the radio. Certain older vehicles were still fitted with analog aerials. The digital stations ruled the roost these days but they were done and dusted as things stood. Nothing on them for days. But they'd search through the static when they could.

One day, in a turn-of-the-century Cadillac they found by Luna Pier, the twist of the dial had almost uncovered something. It had sounded like voices. Almost. Like the way people could see all kinds of shapes in clouds. Crouching kings and sickly parrots. Whatever the mind wanted to see. It was gone in an instant, already a memory.

They never again found anything like it buried in the dead static.

IT TOOK TIME, at night, to find a place to camp. They needed somewhere hidden. Away from the road, but not too far. Somewhere the bikes could be arranged into an arc. Circling the wagons, Timmy called it, as he set up the tent. They didn't need fires, the autumn air not biting enough to warrant such an extravagant display. Their extra sweaters, gloves, and hats did the hard work. There was enough smoke over the cities. They didn't need more.

And it meant they saw the sky. Not that blue canvas, the clotted cream clouds tumbling over it every day. Not the day time, not the same old, same old. This was the sky at night. Darker than anything Alex had ever seen and so, so bright.

It wasn't just the stars. But there were so many of them, Alex had lost every point of reference he had. Even on the farm, there had been some light sources around to dim the distant stars just enough. Out here, at midnight, everything was on show.

There was the Milky Way, an effervescent crease folded into the firmament. And then, all around, were the pointillist pinpricks of every other sun in the galaxy, in the universe, burning all at once. The light was ancient, Alex knew, but out here it was so fresh and filled with energy. He could feel it in his bones.

Never before had Alex felt so small. From his pocket, he fished out the ring. Lying in the tent, door open, and watching the sky, he closed one eye and held the ring over the other. He traced out the brightest stars, drawing lines between them like a jeweler inspecting the edges of a diamond.

Of all the world, of everyone who had worn this ring, of everyone who had been meant to wear this ring, it was empty now but for the stars. They were so far away. And they meant nothing. Not really. The only reason Alex could see all the way up into the atmosphere was the same reason those cars were deserted by the side of the road. It was all gray skin and bloody eyes. Exhausting.

CHAPTER 22

*T*he sunrise was the same. It arrived while Alex was still awake. At first, the stars simply shone a little less bright. And then an orange seal began to break up over the horizon. The darkness began to fade. That heavy sun of the fall, heaving itself over the distant hills. That was west.

When Timmy woke up, they ate and planned their day. An hour outside of Toledo, they decided to skirt around the city. If Detroit was on lock down, then it made sense to stick to the highways. The aim was to get somewhere safe. To escape. To figure out what the hell was going on. Pointless to swap one city for another.

Taking the side roads, following the map, they followed the sunrise to the west, riding straight into the light along the barren freeway. When they hit the I-475 and began to head south, they ran close to the city. It was on the other side of the tree line. But the smoke was rising up, all the same.

An hour later, they were back on 75 and heading south, taking occasional dirt tracks and sideroads. Anything to avoid civilization.

On those occasions did they have to drive close to a built-up area, they could hear gunshots and explosions. Cars backfiring, they told one another. Alex didn't believe it. But he agreed anyway.

Again, there were abandoned cars. They seemed to grow more common closer to the urban areas. As though people set out from the cities and slowly fell away. Only the strongest were able to drive far. When the cars became more frequent it was a sign they were approaching civilization again.

Near Bowling Green, as the empty cars and bodies began to pile up beside the road, Alex slowed down to talk to his friend. They were heading too far south, he felt. Better splitting the difference between Cleveland and Pittsburgh. When they came across a pool of dried blood stretching all the way across the freeway between two burned out cars, they took the first turnoff to the east. No need to linger.

AT NOON, the bikes slowed down to a crawl. They'd passed Freemont, stuck only to the smaller roads. There was no one around. They didn't pass many houses. The road seemed free and empty until they turned a bend and found themselves amidst a bumper-to-bumper chain of cars stretching out for at least a half mile.

Riding out front, Timmy held up a hand with a balled fist. Between the two of them, this had commonly come to mean slow down. A flat hand meant stop. A waving hand meant overtake. They'd picked up the signals organically and had been chatting, over their food, how to make these signals more complex.

Right now, however, slowing down was enough. Under the helmet, it was hot. Alex could barely feel his thighs. The bike rattled and rumbled, shaking him at all times like an exercise machine from the forties. He was still wearing the leather jacket and the body armor.

With the heat from the engine, Alex had to wipe his brow every minute. Life on the road was more tiring than he had imagined. He'd had to switch to a shoulder holster because the saddle had pushed the pistol into his hip. The gun was now tucked up underneath Alex's arm. The entire arrangement was uncomfortable.

The slowdown was a welcome chance to catch the breath, to cool off. But the chain of cars was a concern. There had been nothing like it on any road, as of yet. Timmy stopped, displaying another hand signal. Their universal sign for taking a leak.

"I'm going on ahead for a look," Alex shouted. "Catch up with me."

The bike crept forward at less than walking speed. At first, the cars were packed together tightly and Alex had to bob and weave, turning the handlebars this way and that to get them through the space. He could see inside. There were no sleeping drivers here and no gray-skinned bodies. Every car was alone in the line, discarded.

Passing by, Alex looked in through the windows and saw the spaces where the car owners would sit. One Honda had an ashtray packed with crushed-up butts. A rusty old Ford was fitted with two different GPS tracking units. They were both Chinese, Alex could tell.

There was something about the way they made plastic over there. Gave it this really cheap shine. Something to do with tariffs, he'd read once, we don't send them some particular chemical anymore. Timmy would know more about that. The Ford owner had two of them, best way to guard against a reboot loop. Still cheaper than getting an American version.

As Alex stared hard into the Ford, wondering whether he should liberate one of the units, he heard a rustle behind him. Then a crack. It took a moment. Then it came. The pain. Right across the back. Already falling, Alex could feel the muscles and flesh of his back hurtling against his lungs, pushing all the air up and out of his mouth. With that, he crashed into the asphalt.

Cheek rubbing rough against the road, Alex rushed. He had to get up. Whatever had hit him had hit him hard. Before he was upright, a fist smashed into his jaw. Stumbling back, he hit a parked car. Raised his arms. Defense. Shield the head.

The sound of footsteps coming closer told Alex he had a moment. Dazed, he peeked through his forearms. A man was walking toward him, a baseball bat hanging from his right hand. A beard, long and plaited, hung from his chin. The man was wearing denim jeans with split knees. Big motorcycle boots. A white vest covered a tattooed chest. Gang marks. No mask. No hat. Just a bald head. He was already swinging the bat again.

This time, Alex dodged. Sidestepped. The man swung again. It smashed into the roof of a nearby car. The taste of blood was there. Rusty.

Rubbing his face, Alex watched again for the swing as the man circled round. Two hands on the handle, he swung the bat in a horizontal arc. It broke a window. Alex was elsewhere.

Stepping to the side, Alex threw a hopeful fist. It caught the man on the arm, just above the bicep. Nothing happened. He was strong. But slow.

Backtracking, steadying his feet, Alex tried to shake off the daze.

The man motioned to swing again, Alex stepped, and the man's free hand caught him right in the gut. The attacker was enjoying himself.

Alex tried for his gun. First, he reached for his hip. Wasn't there. Stupid. He should have known that. Nauseated, hands shaking, he was grasping around under his arm. The gun was there, but it was buckled into place. The man was circling around now, shrugging his shoulders and stretching his neck like he was in a batting cage.

The man started to run. There was about ten feet between them now. He wasn't quick, but he was picking up speed. The bat was raising up above his head. Alex's finger fumbled. A button. A catch. Holding the pistol in place. Could only reach it with one hand.

The man was closer, the bat higher. Five feet between them. Alex's fingers were sweaty, slipping. The leather of the holster offered no purchase, Alex realized. There wasn't enough ground between them. The man was almost here. Three steps away. Two now.

The bat was already curling round, aiming to hit him square in the chin. Should have got the helmet with the face protection. Should have done a lot of things. Should have called Sammy. Should have said all those things to Mom and Dad. Should have put the gun in a better place. Should have checked between the cars. Should have done plenty else.

There was a crack. Sounded like a whiplash at a rodeo. It came again.

The man was stumbling.

Rocking to the side.

Tripping.

Falling.

Alex looked around. Timmy was there. He had a shotgun in his hand. Staring. A cartridge rolled around beside his foot. Timmy closed his eyes. Alex too.

There was silence.

CHAPTER 23

Feeling the pain in his back, Alex had given up on his gun. Even reaching for it hurt. There was no need for it now. Timmy had already run across to the attacker, was checking his neck and feeling for a breath. The man was dead.

Alex struggled upright, the body armor–broken and bullet-holed as it was–had saved the spine from any real damage. But it still hurt like all hell.

"Thanks," Alex began, staggering toward his friend, ribs burning with pain. "You saved me there. Really."

The shotgun was still warm. Alex took it. Timmy didn't resist. His eyes had glazed over, his mess of red hair standing almost upright.

"Timmy, listen. He was going to kill me. You saw him with that bat."

The only sound was the autumn wind, blowing softly between the cars. They were standing in an open stretch of road. On one side, two trucks had been parked at angles, acting as a blockade. The line of cars stretched back half a mile but here, they'd been split open, creating an arena or sorts. A trap.

"I... I just saw you in trouble." There was a quiver in his voice, a falter.

"Yeah, Timmy. I was. Real trouble. You saved me."

The pain was still shooting up Alex's spine. This body armor needed to come off. It was already broken inside, the bullet tearing through the Kevlar layers. It wouldn't stop another bullet. A bat, maybe. But how many more bats would they be facing on the road to Virginia?

"Here, come and help me get this jacket off, would you?" Alex asked, attempting to distract his friend.

Still silent, Timmy obeyed. Holding the shoulder of the leather biking jacket, Alex squeezed himself out. Moving the arms too much in any direction hurt. A lot. Together, they unclipped the fastenings of the armor and inspected the damage.

"He really hit you, man."

"Yeah, and you saved me. I gotta say, you did amazing."

Inspecting the armor, examining the impact marks and the damage, Timmy didn't talk. Then he dropped it all to the ground. Ran back to the man's body. Jumped down next to him. Grabbed the edge of the vest and pulled up. The man was bleeding out, the pool of blood spreading and staining Timmy's knees. He didn't care.

"What the hell?" he screamed in the dead man's face. "Why'd you do that? Why did you do that?"

Rushing over to his friend, Alex tried to wrestle Timmy away. With each movement, his back cried out in agony. Finally, he managed to pull his friend free, prying him off the body. Together, they fell backwards.

"Why, man?" Timmy was shouting at nothing now. "Why'd you make me do it? We just wanted to get past. Why?"

Timmy arched his back and shouted at the sky. Long, empty syllables. Not shouting anything, no words Alex could understand, anyway. Just raw, primal sounds screamed up at the heavens.

"Timmy," Alex hissed, "we've got to keep the noise down!"

Looking around, Alex couldn't see anyone else. The dead man was wearing gang colors. He might have back up. He might be a sentry, posted on the edge of the gang's territory. Screaming would only bring others closer. But Timmy was struggling. Shouting.

Running back to the bike, Alex found a water container. Taking it back to the makeshift arena, he found his friend sitting in the same place, head tucked between his knees. Encouraging Timmy away from the body, leaning him up against the nearest car, Alex passed him the water.

"Drink. Just drink it up. Breathe. Don't think about it for a moment. You did good, Timmy."

Doing as he was told, Timmy drank. Knocking his head back against the crumpled door of the abandoned car, he let out a long, hard breath. Alex let him have a moment. The man's body was still there, still with blood pooling around him.

He'd been shot in the back. The pellets were spread out in a crimson constellation. Alex wondered whether the strays could have caught him by accident. *Don't mention that*, he thought, *it won't do any good*.

Crouching down beside the body, Alex could get a look at the man. He wasn't sick. Not like the others. Body peppered with shot, bleeding out. Dead already, really. But there was none of that gray skin which had marked out the others. Everybody so far had been marked by that skin and the eyes, the whites marked by that intricate web of bloodied lines.

But this man's eyes were open. It was disconcerting, the way they just stared upward, as though they were watching the heavens for any sign of life. This was a different kind of illness. A man prepared to do anything. A sickness of the soul. Alex stretched out a hand. He'd seen it in the movies, where they closed the eyes with one motion. This was why.

No one wants to be watched by a dead man.

Just as his hand was above the forehead, Alex felt his attention twinge. There was something different. Something not right. Looking closely, he tried to figure out what it was. Not the beard. Not the short scar just to the side of his nose. Not any of the tattoos. Not the ring which sat in his eyebrow. It was the irises.

One green, one gray, like all the color had been drained out. Odd. Alex had seen people in magazines and on TV with a similar condition. Hell, there'd been one of the cats on the farm who'd had non-matching eyes. It was cool back then. A bit different. Something to stand out.

But here, in the middle of the road, with a pool of blood at his feet, his friend still struggling for breath just a few feet away, it was almost inhuman. His hand closed the eyes.

"Look at him," Alex muttered. "He looks sick. Same as the others. This skin, the sweat. These eyes. It's got to be the Eko virus."

Timmy wasn't listening. Leaving the man alone, Alex returned to his friend.

"Listen, Timmy. I don't know about you, but I think this guy might not be alone. We should get moving. Not too far though. I need to rest my back; we need to eat. Can you help me get back on the bike and we'll stop in the next town?"

There was a trickle of water running down Timmy's chin where he'd glugged heavily. Too heavily.

"You want to stop?"

"There could be more people, you know. I'm worried about these gangs." Alex grasped his shoulder. "And I need to rest. You'd be doing me a huge favor, man. We need to get out of this place. We need shelter"

"And what about the military patrols?"

"We'll avoid them. Wait for somewhere deserted. They can't be in every town. I think this guy's a lookout."

Wiping away the water, getting up on his feet, Timmy nodded.

"Makes sense. Which means we're heading into gang land."

"Got any better ideas?"

"No. We need to move quickly." Timmy panted, sipping at the water, his thoughts returning. "We'll be better moving quickly through this area. Try to remain unseen. Otherwise, we'd have to track miles around. It could take weeks. We've got fuel and food, but not that much."

"What if we meet more people though?" Alex looked at the dead man. "We can't take them all."

"Same as the military patrols." Timmy's breath was slowing down.

His voice became more measured. "They won't have the manpower to cover everything. We just need to find somewhere nice and quiet. Deserted."

Alex nodded. Timmy's plan seemed sensible. Almost.

Mounting the bikes, they squeezed through the blockade and found an empty freeway on the other side. Alex let his friend ride in front. There would be somewhere up ahead but he had no idea where.

There were nothing towns all along these roads. They just had to find an empty one. Any port in a storm, he muttered, somewhere safe to rest.

A nothing town with no one in it. That would be ideal. They passed a road sign but didn't catch the name. It didn't matter.

CHAPTER 24

Three days ago, they had left Detroit behind. What should have been a ten-hour trip had been stretched and twisted beyond all recognition. Thundering through the third afternoon, the setting sun not quite ready to quit the sky, Alex Early and Timmy Ratz rode into a town.

It was barely a town. A street cutting through the middle, a tectonic crack between two uninhabited planes. On either side of the street were stores, a bar, a diner, and the other kinds of public spaces found in dead end settlements. Unessential essentials. Nothing of consequence.

The bikes purred. Rolling over pot holes along empty streets, these machines found it all too easy. Alex parked at one end of the main street, Timmy rode to the other. It took all of two minutes, even at a leisurely pace. No face poked through a door, no windows cracked open. They were alone.

At least, they were alone for now.

By the side of the road was the smoldering wreck of a vehicle. One of the military units. The same as those which had patrolled the streets of La Salle. Half on fire and forgotten. Left behind.

They stopped to look. Dead bodies littered the ground. Old corpses, the skin starting to tighten around the eyes.

Looking up and down the street, worried about an ambush, Alex asked Timmy to keep watch while he inspected what was left.

There were no guns there. No bullets or ammo. The soldiers had been searched. Any weapons had been taken. Even the body armor had been peeled off the bodies.

Inside the vehicle, in the part which wasn't burning, there was at least something of value. A collection of MRE packs, enough for a week or two, at least. Alex shoveled them out of the wreckage and onto the road. That was all that had been left behind.

"Who the hell did this?" Alex asked, filling up any empty space in his bags with the food packages.

"Look," Timmy said in his quiet voice, gesturing to the street.

Alex looked down. There, all across the asphalt, was writing. Spray paint. The sign of a cartel, scrawled ten feet wide. And words:

WELCOME TO ROCKTON

"Well," Alex responded. "At least we know where we are."

A week ago, this would have been a small community. Just last Sunday, Alex could see in his mind's eye, people might be walking up to the ramshackle chapel that stood at the north end of the street. Wearing their best. He'd seen folks in Virginia do exactly that. Might be rags all week, but there were no creases come Sunday.

The entire town was too similar to Virginia. Every main street in small town America was the same and each one was different in its own unhappy way. Smiles and suits for Sunday and when there were other folks around. But behind the closed doors? There was always something else.

It happened in circles. The smallest circle, the family units, had their own little secrets. But they made sure that those on the outside saw nothing but niceties. Then there was the next circle, perhaps a community or a workplace. Bickering on the inside, but showing a good face.

Then it went up to the town itself. People inside were happy in their misery but there was no way they'd let people from the outside know. Whether they were arguing over property lines or someone's drunk son had got himself into an accident and was up in the courts, they'd be telling everyone from outside the same old stories.

We're all happy here. Picture perfect, pretty lives.

Alex remembered the tiny town near his old farm. Athena. Much of nothing but, when he was a kid, it was the center of civilization. School. The store. Where Sammy lived. It had been one of the easiest things to leave behind. In comparison, Detroit had felt overwhelming. A more than capable distraction.

Now, this new place was the same town as every other and Alex was a stranger. The engine cut out at the turn of a key. It was good enough.

A ghost town haunted by other people's pasts.

TOGETHER, Alex and Timmy inspected the buildings. Every door was open along the main street. The bar was there, the stools knocked to the floor. The local store had its shelves cleared out and the 'open' placard still twisted in the window.

Only one store, with its thick frosted windows and heavy lock, was sealed shut. There was no sign outside, just the place where a sign used to be. Someone must have taken it down, Alex thought. Or stolen it.

But there was no one around to stop them entering anywhere else. No sign of the gangs or the guards or the military. No locals. People had left in a hurry. At least, it seemed that way.

No one actually lived on the main street, Alex knew that. If people lived in this town, they'd have bigger plots, anything up to a few miles away. Names would hang around the area for a hundred years, passed about like a trade. People would apprentice in their families' reputation,

learning how they fitted into the community as a whole. But most would live in the middle of fields and along secluded streets. Everything in the center of town was a bit loud. A bit too obvious. Better to have some privacy. Behind the main street, a twisted tumble of alleys, shortcuts, and dirt roads connected everything together.

There was no need to check every building. It was clear that there was no one around. Besides, Alex was feeling his back and Timmy still had a tremble about his fingers when he had to do anything with a delicate touch. It was better to get some rest.

In the bar, they'd found an unopened crate of beers. These people really must have left in a hurry. Packing the crate onto one of the racks, they pushed the bikes out along the street at the opposite end of the chapel. There was nothing at this end. Just a slow river, ambling around an oxbow island.

It wasn't a proper island. There was water on three sides, roughly twenty feet from bank to bank. But the other side was a grassy stretch of ground. It sunk slightly, in the middle, a concave impression in the earth which must have dropped some ten feet at the center with trees lined up all above. There was a picnic area in the middle with a barbeque pit.

They had to hold tight as they rolled the bikes down the hill into the belly of the island. Down in here, they'd be invisible from up above. The halo of trees up above stretched together and almost touched, a canopy above them. There was a hole left in the middle for escaping smoke or demons. It was perfectly secluded.

Setting up the tent had become a ritual. It was easy enough. Designed to hold three people, it slept the two of them more than comfortably. Timmy had invested in a fold-out model, which meant it could be erected with little more than a flick of the wrist. Pulling it down and putting it back in the bag was more difficult, as was fixing the guidelines and pegs in place. After a few days on the road, however, they had the method down to a fine art.

Each time Alex hammered a peg into place, he felt his back protest. That bat had done some damage, even through the Kevlar. But he didn't want to complain, didn't want to leave too much to Timmy. The one-time Lord of Castle Ratz, who rarely had trouble finding any words, had gone quiet. Even the discovery of the beer crate hadn't been enough to shake him into a smile.

For the first time on the journey, they started a fire. It wasn't big. Barely larger than a manhole cover. It wasn't warm. It was hardly enough to heat up the meals they pulled off the bikes. But it was welcome nonetheless. Starting a fire made this seem like a road trip. Something from the movies. A different kind of escape.

There was no power in this town, whatever it was called. No lights came on in the dark. No gentle hum of an electronic device droning in the distance. Occasionally, one of the men climbed the incline to the top of the island and looked out. There was never anyone there.

So they sat and drank beer. The conversation was stilted. Alex had hung his leather jacket from the handlebars of his bike, the bullet hole flashing the chrome piping through the black leather. Occasionally, he'd reach up and rub his finger on the metal, hearing the slight squeak.

The body armor hung next to it. The material inside was self-healing, said Timmy. It repaired itself. Feeling the bruise on his back, Alex hoped the armor healed faster than he did. He looked at the bullet hole in the jacket again, obsessing.

"That was close."

"Uh-huh." Timmy was on his third beer already. "Pretty close."

They had checked the bruising on Alex's back. There was one blooming purple rose, the size of on apple, right where the bullet would have hit. Almost exactly on top of that, there was a thick line of darkened flesh, right where the bat had caught him. It had been up to Timmy to describe the injuries to his friend.

"You ever seen anything like this bruising? MMA or whatever? I've never had anything this bad. Hurts like hell, still."

"Nothing like that. Paintballs can be sore if they get you. Not like this, though."

"You okay, Timmy?"

"I'm fine. Just feeling a bit…you know, not quite with it. Bit sick."

"It's been a long day. A long couple of days."

"Yeah."

"You want another beer?"

"I might. Think I'm going to have to turn in soon. I'm exhausted."

"Sure thing. Hey, again. Thanks. For today. For everything. You saved me, Timmy."

For the first time in hours, Timmy raised his head up from the ground and locked gazes with Alex. His eyes were bloodshot, bags beneath beginning to sag with all the weight in the world. He'd never looked so rough and weary.

"It's nothing, man. We gotta stick together. Who knows what's happening in the world?"

"I know, I know. Wasn't too long ago we were running about in that warehouse, you know?"

"Yeah, man."

"And there was that guy – what's his name, guy with the belly?"

"Freddy."

"Yeah, Freddy. Had me in that arm lock. Remember that?"

"Yeah, I remember. You got him."

"I got him." Alex nodded. "But then you got me out of a jam afterwards. Another one. Where would I be without you?"

"Detroit, probably."

"Was that a joke?"

Finally, Timmy stole a smile. "Not as much of a joke as you with Freddy. He was going to beat the crap out of you. All seven shades."

"He's a big guy."

"He's a pussycat."

More beers were opened. The fire began to die. Trips up the hill to check on the town became less frequent. Trips to the tree line for a water break became more common. As the glass bottles piled up beside the tent, the atmosphere began to unwind.

They talked about the sick people but not the dead. They discussed the symptoms they'd seen and marveled at the way in which everything had fallen apart so quickly. When you're balanced on a knife edge, Timmy had said, even the slightest breeze can knock you off. Alex could feel the winds picking up. Summer was ending. The nights were drawing out.

They'd learned, slowly. How to pitch the tent, where to make camp. How to play with the engine throttle to keep the sound low and how to glide along on the bikes without being heard. But, as Alex leaned to his side to pick up another bottle of beer, the bruise sent shiver of pain through his body. They still had plenty to learn.

It was tiring, being so long on the road. Alex couldn't remember a point in his life where he'd wanted so much to just collapse onto his sofa and do absolutely nothing for an entire weekend. Just tune everything out. But the world was turning. The night was becoming the day. There was no rest for the wicked.

Finally, the tent seemed too appealing. Allowing themselves to fall to their exhaustions, the men crawled inside. As ever, they left the door open and let the stars inside. They'd be woken up at dawn when the sun rolled across their faces.

Perhaps it was the beer, but Alex found it hard to sleep. Staring upwards, imagining the people for thousands of years who'd done exactly the same, he was restless. Toes itching. Mind racing. Falling asleep wasn't easy anymore.

It seemed easier for Timmy. Alex lay there, counting the heavenly bodies over and over and losing count. His friend had his eyes closed tight, his head turning this way and that, living out his dreams.

Like oil in water, the dreams rose to the surface. Timmy would sit bolt upright, flustered and sweating. Speaking something only his dreams knew how to translate. Whimpering. Thrashing around. It was a lot to share a tent with but it calmed down each time.

Alex watched his friend a while longer. Sometimes shivering, sometimes still. The fight earlier had affected him. Why hadn't it affected Alex in the same way? As Timmy's sleeping mind continued to torture itself, Alex tried to solve the riddle. But it was impossible.

Eventually, he fell asleep without an answer. There were no dreams for him, nothing to soothe his sleeping mind. Only the stars and their empty space.

CHAPTER 25

*T*he next morning, Alex woke with the warmth of the sun inching up his face. There were no clouds in the sky, nothing to hold back the light. Trying his eyes, Alex could see up through the chimney hole in the circle of trees and remembered where he was. This happened every morning. The sudden awareness of everything that had happened.

Turning over, preparing to pick himself up out of the sleeping bag, Alex reached out to his friend. Timmy would sleep through the end of days, he was discovering. They had been friends for a few years, but it was the tiny details that they were beginning to discover about one another that only became clear when spending every waking second together.

Timmy had been shocked when Alex brushed his teeth before eating, for example. It was a ritual, the way Alex knew it, the way he'd done it for years. Timmy thought it was weird. One of them was an early riser, one was not. These miniscule discoveries about one another went on and on, occurring at the strangest times.

Shaking his friend's leg, yawning as he did so, Alex began to rise.

"Come on, buddy, time to get up and going. About halfway there, I reckon. Few more days and we'll be sipping cold ones on the porch."

The sleeping bag was damp. Wet and heavy. Timmy didn't answer. Looking out of the tent, searching for rain clouds, Alex wondered how they'd been caught with water. But the material was warm as well. Alex was bone dry.

Still no sound from the sleeping man. Turning into the tent, Alex rattled the leg again. Then an arm. Timmy wasn't waking up. Crawling back inside, perched upon his elbows, Alex got a good look at his friend's face. It was pale. Coated in a fine film of sweat. The whole body shivered.

Sick.

Straight away, Alex leapt from the tent. Outside, by the bikes, he searched for water. They had the bottles. Cannisters. Metal and filled with spring water. He took it back to the tent and dribbled a drop on Timmy's forehead. No reaction.

Taking hold of the feet, of the ankles, Alex tried to pull Timmy out of the tent. In the open, with a great deal of effort, he propped the unconscious man up against one of the bikes. With the other sleeping bag, he covered him up. And then uncovered him. Should he be cold or warm in this situation? What kind of sick was he?

The water again. Nothing. With a lot of labor, Timmy breathed, at least. Could be food poisoning, Alex thought—hoped, something in those beers we drank. But that would have affected both of them. They'd done everything together for the last few days. If Timmy was falling ill, then Alex couldn't be far behind.

Racking his brains, Alex tried to uncover any kind of medical training he'd ever received. He'd learnt CPR for a factory job. Didn't really help here. He'd spent many lonely weekends watching medical shows on a couch in a crappy apartment. They hadn't covered this kind of situation.

When he'd had the flu as a kid, his mother had worked her magic. But it had been exactly that: magic. She'd been a miracle worker. The best nurse a boy could hope for. That wasn't the kind of care Timmy needed. Had she done anything specific? Alex had been burning up one day, running a fever. She'd put a cold compress on his head. That might work.

From inside one of the bags, Alex found one of his T-shirts. He crunched it up into a ball and poured water out over it. That was about as cold as he could get anything. It was a warm September morning. It would have to do.

Taking the wet cloth, he applied it to Timmy's forehead. The shoulders sagged, satisfied. At least, that was what Alex thought. The eyes tremored. So cold worked better. He was suffering a fever. Tugging at the sleeping bag, removing Timmy's shirt, Alex tried to lower his friend's temperature.

Every move seemed to bring Timmy back closer to the land of the living. Alex re-wet the compress, reapplied to the forehead. A pair of eyes opened up, bloodshot and in pain.

"What's happening?" said a voice, arriving from three worlds away.

"You're burning up. I have to cool you down."

"Something don't feel right." Timmy was shivering but still sweating.

"It doesn't look right, either. You're sick, Timmy, we've got to fix it."

Alex knew they had to fix it. Travelling to Virginia alone wasn't good enough. Timmy had taken him this far, had poked him hard enough in the side that he'd rumbled awake from a five-year slumber. There was no way he could be sick. Without him, Alex would probably still be lying on his couch, waiting for the mob or the police or the germs to rush up through his windows and take him away.

All the emotions arrived at once. They'd been bottled up, Alex had been acting on instinct. Fear. Terror. Worry.

Timmy was sick. Alex didn't know what to do. How the hell would he save his friend? How the hell would they get to Virginia? How the hell had this happened? Was he next?

Alex heard himself breathing, could feel the world closing in around him. He could sense everything, the touch of his clothes against his flesh, the taste of the oxygen on his tongue. He could almost hear the blood whistling through the ventricles in his heart. Pumping like mad.

This doesn't help anybody, he told himself, slowing his breathing. *I need to be calm. I need to act.* He looked across at Timmy.

"We got to get you some medicine. Something. Anything."

A mumbled response. Nothing specific. There was nothing packed on the bikes for this. They had medical kits, sure. But they were for dressing wounds. Stitches. Maybe some painkillers at a push. Alex checked anyway. Taking the tablets, he handed them to his friend.

"These things, Timmy. I don't know what they are. But I don't know what you have. So, they're probably just going to ease the pain a bit. Does it hurt?"

"Every…. Everything hurts, man. The whole l-l-lot. Give them to me."

The pills washed down the throat, got caught halfway, and it took three big gulps of water to get them to shift.

"Timmy, do you know anything about this? What should I do?"

Another mumble. A hand raised up, just above a sitting leg, and then fell back down. Timmy was unconscious again, shivering again. There would be no help from the victim. Alex would have to handle this himself.

The drug store. There had to be one in the town. Every place in America had somewhere to buy the little medical bits and pieces. Cough syrup and all the other drugs which propelled people along through modern life. Anti-depressants and opioids. Anything to take the edge off living.

But he hadn't seen one. Just rows of barren doors. A bar. Houses. A church. Then Alex remembered. The store without a sign. That had to be it. Someone had wanted to keep it hidden. And locked.

It had been practically the only door in town which hadn't been opened. Maybe there was something inside. Flu medicine. Something for temperatures. At the very least, more painkillers. Maybe they had a pamphlet on what to do in situations like this. There are no situations like this, Alex knew, but they had pamphlets for everything.

In a rush, Alex folded up the tent. He took the keys from both motorcycles, found the lockpicks in the bags, and propped up Timmy in a safe place, right next to the campsite. He placed plenty of water around his friend, right next to the two sleeping bags. If he woke up hot or cold, he could deal with it. It wouldn't take long to rush to the drug store.

Picking the right gun was always Timmy's job. They had pistols, rifles, and some bigger pieces with them. It was time to go big. No fooling around. The AR-15 might even help with the break in. It was going to have to be a break in, Alex knew by now. That medicine was essential.

It hurt to leave Timmy behind like this. Standing at the base of the slope, about to run up the hill and make his way into the town, Alex could see his friend. Still asleep. Better that way. That pale skin was the worry. Pale, not gray. For now. And those eyes. Bloodshot. But not as bad as the others. Please, Alex prayed, not like the others. This was just some bug, something they'd picked up on the road.

It had to be.

ONCE AT THE top of the slope, Alex began to walk toward the town. The rifle slung across his back, he ducked low. It was five minutes to the bottom end of the high street when walking on foot. But it took longer. Ducking, weaving, pausing behind every available barricade, Alex worried. There had been no one in the town yesterday. Didn't mean it was empty today.

On foot, the world was different. Perched up on the bike, pistol at his hip and cohort by his side, riding through the town had felt intriguing. There were fewer threats, more opportunities. Without the bike, without his friend, the town seemed a very different place.

The southernmost point of the main street stared directly north, right up to the chapel positioned at the end. The drug store was the biggest building at the far end of the street, which was perhaps half a mile long. That meant having to get to the other end of the road without encountering anyone.

From this position, Alex found it easier to get a better reading of the geography. From the bike, everything had passed by fast, without much time for inspection. Now, looking, Alex could see that there were more stores than he remembered. More doorways. A few of them were fitted with the white crosses.

There were still no people. They might be inside the buildings. If he had been crouched inside a home and a pair of heavy motorcycles ambled down a street, Alex appreciated that he might not have sprung out and introduced himself. The ghosts of this town might still be around.

Checking the rifle, Alex crept from one doorway to the next. A slow process. Standing in the shadows, listening intently. Watching everything along the street. Trying every handle, seeing that a few gave way. No time to go inside. The only ones Alex did not touch were the homes with the white crosses.

It took twenty minutes. About halfway down the street, Alex noticed something. There were no birds. No dawn chorus or steady songs throughout the day. No flapping of wings or gatherings of crows on gutters, cackling to themselves. It's why the town seemed so strange, he thought, it sounded different.

A noise. A rustle. Alex raised the gun. Aimed it at an alley. Closed one eye. Held his breath. A rat ran out into the street. The gun lowered. The lungs relaxed. Alex continued up the street.

There was an age old human sense, the feeling of being watched. Alex knew it well. Anyone in a city whose waited for buses on cold nights has felt it. But this was an opposite sensation. A longing for another person's gaze. The feeling of wanting to be watched, if only because it would be a sign of humanity in an increasingly alien world. He considered the idea as the rat ran away down the street.

At last, Alex found himself outside the drug store. The sign was still missing but he'd cracked the code. He knew what was inside.

It wasn't just the door, as they'd tried yesterday, or the frosted glass. There was something else about this place which stirred the senses. Every other building had been broken into. Not this place. It was off limits. Sacred.

Or dangerous. Someone had taken down the sign. Someone had locked the door. Someone had protected this one store when all the others had been looted. That same someone probably wouldn't want him inside. They might be there, guarding it. Alex thought back to his sick friend at the camp site. There was no other choice. He had to get inside.

The door had stayed locked. Looking closer, Alex tried to stare through the keyhole. It was too tight to see anything. But the picks might be able to open it up. They belonged to Timmy, wrapped up in a leather case lined with velvet. Expensive, apparently. A collection of thin crooked hooks cast in steel.

Selecting one which seemed the right size, Alex inserted it into the lock. He had no idea what he was doing. When they had packed the bags, Timmy had tried to explain the procedure. Now he was burning up, propped against a bike with an unexplained fever. The picks did nothing.

Using his shoulder, Alex hit hard against the door. Again, and a third time. It didn't budge. He tried to kick it. There was a sound from behind, something moving. Maybe it was having an effect. Twisting to face the door of the drug store, he tried again with his shoulder. This time, he took a run up.

Only four steps. Picking up a bit of speed, Alex ran, aiming his shoulder for the spot just above the lock. He focused, staring intently at the target. Before he reached the door, he jumped, lifting himself up off the ground and transforming into a flying battering ram.

Just as he was about to make contact, Alex closed his eyes. It was going to hit hard. It might even break the wood. He had to watch out for splinters. Scrunching up his face, he anticipated the contact. But it never came. Instead, Alex flew through an empty space, plunging deeper into the darkness. The door was not there.

Even before it hit him, Alex knew the floor was next. It wasn't an easy fall. Tumbling, he scuffed and rode along a tiled surface. As he opened his eyes, trying to discover what had gone wrong, Alex heard footsteps. There was a sharp edge pressed up against his neck.

At last, he opened his eyes. It was a woman. She wasn't happy.

CHAPTER 26

"Who the hell are you?"

A pair of eyes stared at Alex, full of wrath. They were different colors. One gray, one blue. Both beneath a pair of thin-rimmed office glasses. Same difference as the dead man. But this woman was very much alive. Pushing himself back, away from the broken bottle under his chin, Alex tried to take everything in.

He'd sailed straight through the open door. She must have watched him, waited. The anger in her eyes was exacerbated by her hair, pulled back into a stiff knot and stretching the skin of her forehead tight against the bone. Nostrils flared. This time, she stamped down on his foot. It hurt.

"I said who the hell are you? Answer me now."

It wasn't a shout. It didn't need to be a shout. It didn't even need to be an order.

"I-I'm Alex Early. I'm just a guy."

"Who the hell is Alex Early and what does he want with me?"

"I don't want anything with you, I just want drugs. Medicine, I mean. My friend is very sick."

Relentless as she was, Alex couldn't escape. Trying to move right or left, down or up, she caught him on the prick of her weapon, balancing his skull at her pleasure.

"Well, then, Alex Early, why did you try and break into my store?"

"It's a drug store. It's where I hoped the drugs were."

"You're in a gang?"

"No!" Alex waved his hands in desperation.

"Military, then?"

"No," he shook his head. "I'm nobody. Just visiting."

"So, you're just a petty thief?"

"No. I mean, I can pay. My friend is very sick. Can't you help me?"

"I don't help thieves. What good would that do me? If a thief be found breaking up, and be smitten that he die, there shall no blood be shed for him. I know where I spent my Sundays as a child."

"I'm not a thief. Not yet. I didn't steal anything from you."

"How about from other people?"

Right then, she almost smiled. She almost smirked.

"Please," Alex said, blood thumping in his veins. "Can I just talk to you? Can't you get this thing from my neck?"

The woman motioned at the rifle, still slung across Alex's back, drooping now onto the floor, forgotten. Carefully, Alex took the gun in one hand, fingers far from the trigger, and slid it across the floor.

"Is that better?" he said, bottle still up against his neck.

"Hmpf. Perhaps."

Relenting, she lowered her weapon. As she stood up to her full height, Alex could see her properly. The hair was a light sandy blonde, falling across the shoulders of a lab coat. The coat had seen better days. Once white, it now had a number of stains. She stood silhouetted against the light from outside. Now, Alex could see that she was pregnant. Quite pregnant. She placed the broken bottle on the counter of the store.

"Well then, Alex Early, you're going to have to impress me."

THE STORE WAS TIDIER than Alex had expected. The shelves were still stacked with drugs, boxes, and everything else normally found in such

166

places. In one corner, an old set of scales was rusting away, offering to weigh people for a dime. It still seemed expensive.

The woman was closing the door. It wasn't a short process. From inside, Alex could see why it had resisted his efforts at breaking and entering. As well as the glass being incredibly thick, the door was bolstered with three heavy duty locks and a dead bolt. He could have been tenderizing his shoulder for hours against the wood without moving it a millimeter.

As well as the shop floor and the counter, a space smaller than the inside of Timmy's SUV, there was a door heading into the back. It was dark in there. No windows, Alex thought. No weak points of entry. There was no way of knowing how far the building went back. But it could be quite a distance. Then he noticed the smell.

"Hey, erm... I don't know your name. What's that smell?"

"Joan. My name is Joan."

"Joan?"

The soles of her shoes slapped against the tiles as she snapped around.

"Yes," she said, accompanied by a stern stare. "Do I need to repeat myself?"

"No, no."

Getting to his feet, Alex looked around the room. It seemed the same from up here.

"So, you guys don't have any power either, then?"

"Guys? What exactly do you mean by 'you guys'?"

"Listen, I wasn't trying to insinuate-"

"I don't much care for what you were saying, insinuation or not, Mr. Early. I said you were going to have to impress me and so far, I am left wanting."

"I was just trying to-"

"Trying to what? Make conversation? I'll have you know that I'm here all alone. Yes, poor defenseless me."

Still standing in front of the light from outside, all the better to mask her expressions, Joan had folded her arms.

"I don't know-"

"That's right, Alex, you do not know. Now, you say your friend is sick? What possibly could I do to help this situation?"

"We're in the drug store. I thought there might be something here. Please. He's burning up. Pale. Getting sicker and sicker."

Ever so slightly, she lowered her shoulders. The firm, pressing tone which had pressed Alex up against the ledge eased off.

"How do his eyes look?"

"A bit bloodshot. But we've been sleeping late. I think he's just tired."

"He's not tired, Mr. Early. You would have to be an idiot to not know what is happening."

"Enlighten me."

An eyebrow arched.

"Enlighten me, please?" Alex reiterated.

"Fine. Your friend is sick. He has the Eko virus. I am not a doctor. I am not an expert. But neither am I an idiot. I trust you have been following the news lately?"

"I've watched what I can. I've-"

"Then you will know, Mr. Early, that we are in the throes of a pandemic. An epidemic. A cruel joke played on us by God. We are in the midst of a reckoning, Alex, and your friend has been found wanting."

"He's not sick. Not like that. I've seen the bodies. He doesn't look like-"

"Oh, none of them do. None of them do. That's how it started here. Fever. Flu. That's what they told me. Came up to the counter, asking for the usual remedies. And I gave them out. They didn't come back. At least, not upright they didn't. You asked what that smell was? Where do you think they keep the morgue in this town? Where do you think they pile up the bodies when no one can drive the fifty miles to civilization? Here. That's where they keep them. In a big room. A big, cold room. But people don't die here. Not very often. So we ran out of room. We have plenty of bodies and no real morgue, Mr. Early. And now we have no electricity. Do I need to paint you a picture of what happens?"

"But you're still here?"

"Very astute. Yes, I am still here."

"But... why?"

"Where else will I go? I can't drive away. I damn sure can't walk dozens of miles. Not in these shoes."

Alex looked down at her feet.

"That was a joke, Mr. Early. Must I constantly lower my expectations of you?"

"Look, Joan. Please. My friend is very sick. I just want to help him. I can help you too, if you want. Just tell me what you need."

"Need? You think I need something? This is the most secure place in town. I have food, I have medicine. I have my baby. There is nowhere else for me to go. Nothing I need."

"So you won't help me?"

"I never said that."

"You have something, some kind of medicine?"

Unfolding herself, Joan walked around to the other side of the counter. To get there, she had to raise a wooden slat. She left it open, waiting for Alex to follow.

He hesitated, lifting his foot and holding it in the air. The entire conversation had been a nightmare. Alex had flown through without thinking, the shock and awe of his entrance, and the sudden appearance of this woman, throwing his mind into a tailspin. Now she wanted him to follow her, deep into the back of the store. He put his foot down and followed it with another. She might have the medicine. He had to take that chance.

Once he joined her, they began walking into the belly of the building, talking as they went.

"As I tried to tell you, Alex, your friend is not sick. He has the Eko virus. Flu-like symptoms at first, with the sweating and so on. Then the eyes blooden and the skin grays. This is where it gets worse." Joan paused in her walk, turning to look at Alex. "If you had seen the news any time recently, a good deal of the country believed they had the flu. They did not. And now they are dead. The best I can offer is a selection of high powered painkillers and then space in the back of this building with the rest of the bodies."

Keeping up with Joan, matching her step by step, Alex could feel the smell overpowering him. It was leaking out of every room. With a hand, he tried to cover his nose.

"How can you breathe this air? It's disgusting."

"After a while, I assure you, the smell of death can be quite reassuring."

"What, how?"

"Because, Mr. Alex Early, it means that you are alive, at least."

They stopped in front of a door. It was plain, not even fixed with a small sign informing passers-by of the contents. The only people who needed to enter would know exactly what was inside.

"In here is everything you need. At least, everything you need to ease your friend's pain. I can tell you what to take. But you will need to fetch it yourself."

"You can't come with me?" Alex could feel himself getting angry. He needed all the help he could get. Timmy's life might depend on it.

"Alex," she said, leaning hard against the wall, "I was the first person in this town to fall sick. I thought I was at death's door. So did everyone else. But I survived. I survived long enough to watch every other person in this town fall to the same sickness. One by one, I watched my friends and my neighbors die. Now they are all on the other side of this door. And you want me to go inside?"

"Oh," Alex couldn't think of anything clever to say. Guilt and regret piled up in his mind. "Sorry, I..."

"Forget it." Joan's voice was sharp, drawn short. "I have."

Dragging the flat of her palm along the paint, Joan tried to stand up straight. It was still dark in the corridor, but Alex could feel his eyes adjusting. Now he could see her, could see how tired she looked.

"What do I need?" he asked, his voice softening. "Just tell me."

"I'll call it out. I'll guide you through. Just... Prepare yourself. Your friend will be joining these people soon. It is best you learn that now."

Sucking in a deep lungful of rotten flesh, Alex took hold of the door handle.

"I'm going to save Timmy. We're going to be fine. We'll be in Virginia before the end of the week. You'll see."

"Whatever you need to tell yourself, Mr. Early. I am only trying to help."

With a curt nod of the head, she squeezed the latch and pushed open the door. At once, the putrid air poured out from within. Joan sighed. Holding on to the same breath, Alex took a step forward. It was dark. And another. With great care, he stepped into the makeshift mausoleum and found himself surrounded by the dead.

CHAPTER 27

*E*yes adjusting, Alex looked around. The room was large. Much larger than the store. Joan had been correct: this place doubled as a crude medical facility. Drug store didn't cover the half of it. This place had been the morgue. One wall was plated in metal, five hatches positioned at waist-height for the bodies.

They'd run out of room. Alex knew all too well from his childhood in Virginia that communities like this could drive out to the big cities for serious problems. A person dying was a problem. Two people dying was an incredibly serious problem. Five or more? That meant calling in outside help. In a small town, more than five people dying wasn't just a tragedy.

It was a population adjustment.

But there was no outside help these days. No power, either. Whatever was behind the metal plating, whatever was in those five doors, it wasn't being refrigerated. And they were not alone. Along the edges of the room were black bags, zipped up tight.

No dignity here. There must have been twenty bodies, counting those behind the doors, piled up and left to rot. What else was there to do? Already, Alex knew why he hadn't seen anyone else in the town. Those who were not already in this room were those who had been too sick to make it out of the house. Their homes had become their coffins.

The quaint ranch houses, the white picket fences: the American dream. The rose growing in the garden. The vegetable patch down the side of the house, beneath the kitchen window. The finest coffins money could buy. They'd passed them all on the road into town.

"What do I need? Tell me what to take," Alex shouted through the walls, calling out to the woman.

When the voice came back, it was muffled. The door had been pulled shut, the air kept inside.

"An IV drip. They should be on your right. Bags of clear fluid. Sectral, too, because you'll need to lower his blood pressure. I can't remember which shelf they're on. There should also be a crate of sports drinks. And, if you like your friend, if you don't want him to suffer, try to find the Tramadol. Though we might be out of that."

A long shopping list. Fixed against the wall opposite the metal plating were row upon row of shelves. They were homemade, constructed and painted by someone's hand many years ago. For as long as the drug store had been standing, Alex guessed, these shelves had been sitting in this room.

The wood was thick and heavy, cumbersome to move. When they'd started turning the room into a morgue, it would have been impossible to drag the shelves out. When the bodies had started piling up over the past week, Alex wondered, would they even have had time to grab all the medical supplies from inside?

Apparently not.

It was dark, but the boxes were labelled with large, stark words. The IV drips were easiest to find. An entire box of them hid on the bottom shelf. Joan had been right about the placement. Shouting back and forth through the slightly ajar door, she helped Alex search.

The blood pressure tablets were on a top shelf. Not many of them. Bumex did a similar job, apparently. Everything seemed easy to find. Apart from the Tramadol. Alex couldn't find it on the shelves. Outside, racking her mind, Joan shouted out suggestions. It should have been there, she said, it was in the store room.

She stopped, mid-sentence. Alex half-climbed up one of the shelving units, pushing past boxes with complicated names he didn't know.

"Any help, Joan? We're so close. I don't want to be in here a second longer than I have to."

The air was utterly putrid. Every time Alex breathed, it felt as though a thin trail of slime was slipping down the back of his throat and into his lungs, only to be huffed back up and dribbled through his sinuses and out through his nose. The bodies in this room had turned. From solid to liquid, they were in a mixed state.

For a while, Alex wondered about the risk of infection. But he had already found himself exposed to the sick. In his apartment, in the various cars along the road, and here, in this room. So far, it was only Timmy who had displayed any symptoms. And now Timmy needed help. There was no choice.

"I-I... I remember where it is. But you're not going to like it."

"Just tell me," Alex shouted. "I need to get out of here quickly."

"The last person who had it was the pharmacist. He works here. Worked here."

Right then, Alex knew exactly what the problem was going to be.

"Joan, please don't tell me what I think you're going to tell me."

The door creaked open. Standing there, one hand held on her hip, one on her belly, she stared into the room. It brought in a new flood of light, which reflected on the surfaces of the black plastic body bags.

"He was one of the first. He's in the drawer furthest from you. They were in his jacket pocket, I remember it so clearly. By the time he died, I couldn't bare looking at another body for more than a few seconds, especially not..."

From where he stood, Alex could see the door in question. As high as his waist. Sealed shut. Shiny in a way only metal can shine. For years, someone must have been polishing that surface. It must have been easier without any bodies inside.

The floor between the metallic wall and Alex was not empty. It was fifteen feet, at least, to the other side. Crossing that was not a problem. The issue was the black bags which lined every wall. They were under the drawer, too.

Each person had been laid perpendicular to the wall on that side of the room. The bags were a foot or so high; some were lower and some were higher. A fleeting reminder of what lay inside. All shapes and sizes; all creatures great and small. The farthest from this part of the room, she'd said. Alex could see the hatch now.

"Joan, how long has this person been inside?"

No answer. Just the deliberate footsteps of a man caught between a hurry and a hard place. Trying to reach a destination, dreading what he would find when he arrived. Alex tried not to look down. Almost there, he caught sight of one of the bags. It was barely three feet long, the loose end tucked back under the body to save space.

"Joan?"

"Two weeks. But only a few days since we lost power. It's in his pocket. There should be at least fifty pills in there."

Though the door was open, she'd turned her back on the room. Two weeks. What could happen to a person in two weeks? If he'd been on ice for long enough, maybe he'd still be thawing out. Even as the thought crossed his mind, Alex knew it was nonsense.

Arriving next to the hatch, he looked for the handle. It was not hard to find. It was ten inches long, a thick stainless-steel bar pointing down toward the ground. As he wrapped his hand around the grip, preparing to heave it up and open, he heard Joan's nail scratching the paint off the outside wall.

There was no time to waste. Alex turned the handle to his right, upward ninety degrees. Taking its time, the hatch swung out. It moved with a slow creak, the banshee hinge complaining all the way. The sound of nails against a wall, that worried scrape, came again.

Inside, it was dark. Alex held his breath. He knew he'd not be able to hold it long. Fishing around in the murk, he found a flat metal surface and tugged. The sound of oiled wheels on ruts came from inside and a tray slid out and into the room. With it came the body.

Lungs trembling as his throat retched, Alex tried to tame his impulses. But the body was horrific. It was not the bodies of the infected he'd seen already. It was older. The virus, Eko or whatever it was, had been here earlier. Two weeks of the illness, Joan had said, kicking around a quiet country town. None of the folks in the cities would listen, he imagined.

Probably had a lot on their plate.

No one had undressed the pharmacist. He was still wearing his lab coat. Slacks and a woolen vest. Glasses on a gold chain around his neck. Even the brogues.

The clothes were still present. But the skin was sagging. Sinking. Whereas the other victims had been gray in color and bloodshot around the eyes, this man was already fading from existence. Soon he would be gone entirely, just bones in a bag of mush.

Where the skin was most visible, on the cheeks, the face, and at the wrist, the bones thrust upwards, like the poles holding up a circus tent. In patches, the pharmacist had sprouted sores. Like small cigarette burns in the arm of an old couch, a darkened black dot in the center and spreading out, eating up all the gray skin as it went.

Post-mortem, they must be. None of the others had these. Perhaps they were inevitable. The bodies collapsing in on themselves, chewed up and eaten by the illness, even after they passed.

"The pocket," Joan called. "The pocket."

Alex heard a despondency in her voice. He reached across the body. The pharmacist had been locked up, sealed away in the drawer and kept from the rot of the air. Every second he spent outside, he seemed to be collapsing in on himself a little more. Alex noticed how the nose was collapsing, how the hair was growing, how the lips curled back and revealed two rows of milk-white teeth.

At least his eyes were closed.

The hand hovered above the body, eyes searching for the pocket of the lab coat. It was by his hip, barely emerged from the hatch. To get closer, Alex pushed up against the body at his feet. His ankles pressed into the plastic bag. It held firm, for a second, then gave way. Something crumpling inside. A new wave of fetid air rose up from below.

The outline of the box in the pocket. Alex could see it. Ignoring the smell, imploring his nostrils to fail, he moved his hips and swiveled his body sideways, adding an extra inch to his reach. The tips of the fingers found the pocket. The material was dry.

The lab coat had been white once. Now, along the edges, wherever the cloth touched up against the skin, that white was discolored. Muddy browns, like the coffee colors creeping up over the pale foam of a cappuccino. Alex imagined the coffee. Kept the coffee in mind. It made it easier to deal with.

As the fingers entered the pocket, they found the cardboard box. Stretching that little bit further, he pressed his entire self into the drawer that held the dead man. The steel marked a red strip across his hip; Alex felt it already. And his toes, against whatever was left in that bag by his feet, found the tiniest amount of extra room.

Finally, he had it. The box. A whole hold of it. Alex pulled, trying to turn his entire body at the same time, to better extricate himself. To get away. The smell still overpowered. It worked. Taking the box in a firm grip, Alex almost ran from the room.

Joan stepped aside, nearly had to be pushed. Alex doubled over in the hallway, heaving dry mouthfuls of air, motioning for her to stand back. In one hand, he held up the box.

Recovering, steadying himself, Alex stood up straight. Joan was watching him, half with pity, half with annoyance. She looked at the box in his hand.

"What's that?"

Between gulps of air, Alex offered her the pills.

"It's the Tramadol, the stuff you told me to get. Out of his pocket. Please, stand back."

"No, you fool. Wrapped around it. There's something else there."

Alex looked down. Wrapped around the cardboard box were a number of sheets of colored paper. Not the usual health warnings and advice. A printed-out pamphlet. Joan plucked it from his fingers, leaving the box behind. Her eyes widened as she scanned across the page.

"We need to get back to your friend. Now."

CHAPTER 28

*A*s they left the drug store, Joan collected a small bag with various medical instruments. Outside, the air was fresh. The nearly-noon sun teetered over the town. After being inside, in the unlit halls and store rooms, the brightness bit into the eyes. Joan locked the door as they exited, taking the key with her. Alex had retrieved his gun, slung across his shoulder as he carried a box filled up with medicine and supplies. He walked with a slight limp, Joan's welcoming stamp beginning to make itself felt.

At first, Alex wanted to stalk back, pausing in the shadows, exactly as he had done earlier. But Joan waved his suggestions away. Anyone who might have spotted them walking along the street was already in a black bag, lining the walls of the store room.

Instead, they walked together down the sidewalk of the main street. When Alex told her where they were staying, where they had pitched their tent, Joan shook her head. A terrible place, she said, far too exposed in case anyone came looking.

Their pace quickened.

As they reached the end of the main street, not too far from the oxbow island and the copse of trees where Timmy was waiting, suffering, Joan began to read the pamphlet. It had been wrapped around the Tramadol tablets like gift paper, sealed with sweaty hands. As she read, she swore.

"So, what is it?" Alex asked, struggling to balance the crate of medicine and the gun on his back.

"Hmm? Oh. It's just a medical pamphlet. The government makes them. Sends them out, usually around flu season. We print them and put them in our offices. People take them. Standard fare."

The bored explanation contrasted with her occasional curses.

"It's just a flu pamphlet?"

"Yes. Boring."

"Then why the rush? You seemed pretty shocked-"

"That's my concern, not yours. And yes: we're in a rush."

She swiped the paper quickly from the air and slid it into one of her pockets. Before they left the drug store, Joan had collected together her coat, her bag, and a collection of medical instruments which worried Alex. Needles and other sharp objects. Too sharp for his tastes.

"Why did he have it with him?"

"Your friend, how sick did he seem?" Joan asked, glancing sideways at Alex.

"Very sick. Sicker than I've ever seen him. Shivering. Sweating. Can you help him?"

"The chances are very slim." She rubbed her face. "The Eko virus is ravenous and he has next to no chance."

"But you said you were sick? How did you get better?"

"I... I don't know. I was the first person to fall ill in this town. Look what happened to the rest of them. I was the sole survivor. If this is a numbers game, you will not like the odds. It might as well have been a miracle."

Alex could feel the buoyancy and the hope that had come with finding the drugs begin to fade away. Joan had read the pamphlet and her tone had turned sour. He could detect a renewed sense of pessimism in her voice. But he still needed her help.

"If you don't want to help us, just tell me what to do and leave. You don't need to be here."

"Excuse me," Joan replied, her anger rising. "But you tried to break into my store. You took my medicine. You stole from the pocket of my dead boss. And you're telling me to leave? I don't think so. I'll tell you what to do, thank you very much."

They arrived at the tree line, the bend of the river on either side. Alex eased his way down the steep, grassy hill, carrying the heavy box and the gun. As he reached the bottom, he turned. Joan had stayed still, considering the slope.

"Come on," Alex called up at her, trying to keep quiet. "You said we need to hurry."

Even from the bottom of the basin, Alex could see her face contort. With speed, she began to walk down the hill, moving quicker as she went. By the time Joan was almost upon him, she was nearly running. She stopped.

"Don't shout. You don't know who's around. I can't believe I have to tell you that. I can't believe how careless you are. And don't tell me we need to hurry, I-"

"Did you just run down that hill to shout at me?"

"I am not shouting," she said through her teeth. "That is the point. You don't know who's listening."

Alex turned and walked toward Timmy. Even before he reached the two bikes, he could see the mess of red hair, poking up above the saddle. Exactly where he'd left him. Placing the box down right next to his friend, Alex knelt down.

"Hey, Timmy. How's it going?"

Barely awake, Timmy lifted his head, flickered an eye.

"I've brought someone along, someone who's going to help."

Joan was stalking around their crude campsite. Her stare crept along the trees at the top of the hill, then found the empty beer bottles beside the bikes. Finally, she looked at Timmy. All the anger which steamed from her shoulders fell to a soft simmer.

As Alex watched her, he could see lessening the anger and annoyance which bubbled along beneath the surface of Joan's personality. This was a familiar situation: doctor and patient. She was relying on her instinct, her training. And with it came a feeling of anxiety and pity.

Noting the emotions, Alex hoped it meant she was going to help.

"Oh. Oh my," she said, approaching the sick man. "This isn't right. How do you feel? How long have you been like… this?"

"I woke up and he was-" Alex began.

"I was talking to… What was your name, sorry?"

"Timothy… Timmy Ratz," the patient managed, in danger of smiling. "At your service."

"Well, Mr. Ratz, you are not healthy. Can you talk?"

He nodded. As Alex watched, Joan became a flurry of hands. Digging into the box of medical supplies, tapping against Timmy's wrists and neck, she began to evaluate every inch of him. With nothing to do, Alex settled for fetching. Obeying commands. He found her a chair—a couple of bags stacked on top of one another next to the patient—so she could rest her legs.

The crack of a grin across Timmy's sweating face, spotted over Joan's shoulders, was infectious. Alex knew his friend found it hilarious to see him demoted to down to lackey. The bedside manner—more the motorcycle-side manner—of the nurse emanated outwards. It brought with it a modicum of calm to a complicated situation. There was an expert involved.

And she did seem to be an expert, at least to the untrained eye. The questions came thick and fast, even with Timmy struggling to answer. She checked everything. From inside her bag came a stethoscope and a thermometer, two of the tools Alex knew. There were others. When she fitted an IV drip, for instance, she punctured a vein with a short, sharp needle and hung the bag from one of the handlebars.

As Joan worked, Alex found the needle, picking it up from where she'd thrown it to the ground. It didn't seem right to just leave it behind. A ticking chemical time bomb. He collected together all the waste and junk as it appeared, everything she threw away, and put it all in a plastic bag to be burned later. That sounded like a scientific solution.

"Who are you?" Timmy managed.

"Joan. My name is Joan. Your friend here tried to break into my drug store. He isn't very good at it."

Timmy laughed and it turned into a coughing fit. The IV plugged into his arm, Joan passed him a cocktail of pills.

"You're pregnant," Timmy said, taking the pills in his hand. "How come you're not worried about catching anything?"

"Thanks for noticing," came the reply as Joan leaned over her patient and pointed to her gray-colored eye. "See this? This means I had what you have. This means I survived. Do you know how they cure smallpox? They give you a tiny dose of smallpox. When you fight it off once, your body knows how to do it again in the future."

"What about him?" Timmy motioned toward Alex, who was watching from the sidelines.

"I don't know about him but he doesn't seem to care about getting sick. Perhaps he should."

"We all should," said Timmy, throwing the pills down his throat. "He wouldn't handle this nearly as well as me."

Spluttering, coughing, and forcing down a drink of water, Timmy leaned back against the motorcycle. Joan stood up and stretched. Massaging her own shoulders, she stepped toward Alex.

"We should let him rest. Those pills are strong. He's going to be cruising along on an opiate cloud for a few hours."

"Will he live?"

"Very blunt question, Mr. Early." Joan fixed him with a stare. "I don't know. You saw the bodies in the store room. That's only a fraction of the town. Once the Eko caught hold, I was the only one who survived. Caught it first and was the only one left standing."

"Those body bags–those can't have been the only people in the town. There must have been more of you."

"Those were the ones who could get out of their homes. The ones who could somehow make it down to the drug store and get help. I was with them when they died. Once the virus takes hold, it's days if not hours."

"So, there's no one else left in this town?"

"Just the three of us. Right now, at least. We get people passing through. Gangs. Military. No one I want to talk to."

"So that's why you took down the sign outside the store?"

"Very astute, Alex. You might make detective yet. Yes, a small protective measure. Nearly one hundred percent effective."

"Nearly?"

"Until you arrived."

It was the middle of the afternoon. Alex felt his stomach rumble. He hadn't eaten all day.

"Hey, do you want something to eat?"

"Mr. Alex Early, are you asking me to dinner?"

The sentence hung over the pair like a guillotine, waiting for the chop. Fearing himself the unfortunate French noble, Alex clamored to respond.

"Oh. No. I was just. We have food. I haven't eaten. I need to eat. You can, too."

Cutting a worried figure, Alex strode across to a suitcase. He removed a MRE packet and offered it to the pregnant nurse.

"Thank you, but I brought my own food."

Alex cleared away a patch, a spot just far enough away from Timmy to give him peace and close enough that they could keep a watchful eye over his progress. Ripping over the foil topping of his readymade meal, Alex sat on the ground. He had moved the bags into position, providing Joan with a place to sit, facing the patient.

"What on earth is that?" Joan stared at the meal in Alex's lap.

"It's nutrients. Calories. It comes in cake form, some of it. You don't have to cook it. Not this one."

In truth, Alex had grown used to the taste. It no longer made him retch. From her bag, Joan produced a Tupperware container. Inside was a large portion of pasta. There was even a fork. Pricking one spindly piece of fusilli at a time, she began to eat. They watched one another.

"We'll need to move him," said Joan. "This is simply not a good place to be."

"Okay." Alex's voice was slow, tinged with shame. "But when? And where do we take him?"

"You might not like the answer. In a few hours, either that fever breaks or he begins to die. I would bet on the latter, if I were a gambling woman. Which I might be, you don't know. If–by some miracle–he is able to pull through, then I know a few places in town we can take him. He'll need time and rest to recover."

"How much time? We don't have long."

"Got a date, do you? An important deadline? I can see you haven't been keeping up with the news, Alex. Chances are, you have all the time in the world. Or what's left of the world."

"We have to get to Virginia."

"If you try and move him too soon, chances are he'll relapse. Or simply die of exhaustion. I wish we knew more about this disease but I'm not even a doctor."

"Then how do you know all this? You seem to know a lot."

"I am a nurse, I do have some training. Working in the drugstore in this godforsaken town was meant to be temporary. After I began to get better, other people got sick. I was the only one left to treat them. You learn a lot about a disease as it begins to kill all your neighbors and everyone you know."

After a moment of silence, Alex spoke up again.

"I'm sorry."

"Did you make this virus? Are you the unforeseen act of God? Then no, Mr. Early, you have nothing to apologize for."

They ate their food. Timmy slept. The wind whispered through the trees. They waited.

CHAPTER 29

"*J*ust ask."

Food long finished, Alex sat on the ground watching his friend. Timmy slept. Joan had gathered together a number of bags and laid the sleeping bags on top of them, creating a temporary couch. Laying back, she spoke again.

"Alex, if you have questions, then just ask. God knows we have nothing else to do."

There were questions. There were many questions. Too many questions. The entire world had collapsed in the space of a week and now Alex sat with a pregnant stranger, who sat on a bed of blankets and guns, while he watched his friend sweat his way through a deadly infection. The number of questions could not be counted. It might be better to keep it simple.

"You live here? Here in Rockton?"

"I lived here for three years. Worked in that store for most of the time. Boss was an ass but he was better than most. I hated it."

"Then why did you come here? Why'd you stick around?"

"We don't all get everything we want, Alex. I moved here with my husband. He grew up on a farm about two miles out of town."

There was nothing to do. No way to busy himself. Only time to sit and watch Timmy, hoping for the best.

"Just ask," Joan continued. "There's nothing else to do."

"So... Your husband... He's..."

"Dead? Maybe." Joan removed her glasses and began to clean them with a corner of her shirt. "Let him rot."

"I'm sorry."

"Again, apologizing when it's not your place to apologize. Stop being sorry, Alex."

"I just-"

"He was an ass. He's not in some black bag in the back of the drug store. Don't worry. He ran off three months ago, taking little Haley Vickery with him. At least he left me something."

"Oh."

"I mean the house, Alex."

Taking a deep breath, Alex tried to change the subject. This was a minefield. This woman seemed keen to cut off every corner of conversation. Nothing ended well.

"Where are you from?" he tried, sitting up straight. "You know, originally."

"Providence. And then other places. We travelled. What about you?"

"Virginia." Alex sank back into his chair, happier to take on an easier subject. "We didn't travel. Stayed there. Then I went to Detroit."

"So why are you heading back to Virginia? I believe that's what you told me."

"I did. Me and Timmy decided that it was the best place to be once...everything started, you know, happening."

"People started dying, global political structures began to collapse, the world's worst pandemic spreads across the United States and you and your friend decided to go on a road trip?"

Staring up at the sky for a moment, Alex took in the words. It did sound stupid. But it had all made sense at the time.

"Well, if you put it like that—"

186

"No, I'm sure it's a lovely farm." The sarcasm dripped and dropped from every single syllable.

"It's isolated." Alex gesticulated, his voice rising in pitch. "It's secure. It's somewhere you can live, off the grid. It's a good idea."

"You're pretty far from Virginia."

"Yeah, well. We weren't planning on sticking around here too long."

"You'll be here quite a while, I can tell you that for nothing."

"We need to move as soon as we can, Timmy would agree."

"Is it Timmy's decision to pack up and move across the country?" Joan looked across to her patient and clicked her tongue. "I assure you, he will not be going anywhere very quickly."

"He was part of the decision. Look, you don't know how bad it was in Detroit. We had to leave."

Joan paused for a moment, sitting up from her constructed bed. She considered Alex. That glare, again. It could slice through iron, given half a chance.

"The citizens of Rockton," she began, speaking very slowly and carefully, "noticed that I was sick. Then they noticed that *they* were sick. Who do you think they blamed? When I got better, they hoisted me up out of bed and marched me to the store, insisting that I teach them how to pull through. They didn't know what a miracle it was that I'd survived."

Looking down at her empty hands, Joan continued to talk, her voice getting quieter and quieter with each passing sentence.

"They passed food through the door, changes of clothes. One by one, they turned up. Feverish, sweating, just like your friend. Some of them came inside and died as I watched. I tried to treat them. I had to. Not just because that's what they told me, but because these were people, human beings. Idiots, every single one of them."

For a moment, her hand clenched into a fist. Alex saw her knuckles whiten.

"But they were desperate," said Joan, unclenching her fist. "Scared. They saw someone survive and thought that I would be able to help them. By the end, they were too sick to do anything. I could do nothing. They all died. And now I'm alone. So, tell me, Alex Early, how bad was Detroit?"

Beginning to shape the words in the back of his throat, Alex caught himself. Joan noticed. Letting out a dry, sardonic laugh, she returned to her couch.

"That's right, Alex, don't apologize. At least you're learning something. When it's your turn to be sorry, I'll tell you."

"You're not good with people, are you?"

"I find them lacking. In many departments."

"Have you tried drinking heavily?"

She laughed again.

"Yes. I have. But not in my current condition. Such is life."

"It's all right, we drank the beer anyway."

Joan closed her eyes. Not sleeping, but feeling the late summer sun on her face.

"You wouldn't be the first to drink beers down here. It's a tradition. Every Fourth of July. And you thought this was a good place to hide. I can't even believe you packed beer to bring on your escape. You really did plan this like a road trip, didn't you?"

"Actually," said Alex, finally happy he had a chance to correct his new companion, "we took the beers from a bar in town."

"You did?" Joan's eyes opened. "From Danny Boy's?"

"What's that?"

"The bar, up on the main street. You took the beers from there?"

"Yes. It was abandoned. Empty. Someone else had already smashed the windows."

"Idiots. No wonder your friend was sick. Half the town drank in there. The other half turned up to watch them do it. The whole place is probably teeming with infection. The gangs and the army have both stopped by. I've seen them."

Without an answer, Alex wondered. Every building along the main street had been looted. By someone. Someone else. How were they to know which places might be infectious? Desperately, he tried to remember whether it had been Timmy who first suggested taking a look. Who had found the beers? They'd both been there. Then Alex found himself facing a bigger, more pressing issue.

"So why aren't I sick? Why just Timmy?"

"How on Earth am I supposed to know? Alex, you really do not think these things through. I'm just a nurse, working in a drug store in a backwater town. This is a disease that's swept through the country in weeks. Days. No one knows anything. I don't even know how I survived."

"But I should be sick as well. I've come into far more contact with the disease."

"There could be a thousand reasons. Timmy might have a terrible immune system. You might have breathed in at the right moment. You might be immune. You might have been ill when you were young and have the right antibodies in your blood. Alex, my dear, there is no science here. Only guesswork."

Turning his attention to his feet, Alex examined the soles of his shoes. Sneakers. Just the usual rubber shapes, coated in a fair amount of grime and dirt. And germs, potentially. For the entire journey, he hadn't thought once about the way in which the virus was passing between people.

Where possible, he'd covered his face. The notion of a virus attaching itself to something as normal and as boring as a beer bottle was worrying. He'd done so much in the time since he left his apartment. Hell, even in his neighbor's place, he'd touched light switches and kitchenware. It could all have been covered in tiny, invisible germs. Even the thought turned his stomach, tying it in knots.

"Guesswork," Joan continued, ignoring Alex's introspection. "Including this."

From her pocket, she produced the pamphlet they'd found wrapped around the Tramadol. She passed it down to Alex, who stretched out and reluctantly took it from her hand. It had been locked away in a morgue with a Eko victim. If the beer bottles were liable to infect, then this pamphlet was like a death sentence.

"Don't worry, it won't kill you," Joan told him. "I don't think you need to worry."

As she offered the pamphlet to Alex, he held off. There was no knowing what kind of infection lurked on its surface. Gingerly, his fingers inched closer and closer.

Trusting her, Alex began to examine the document. It had been folded and balled up. Each crease in the paper was now a thick white line, obscuring the text where it had rubbed against the inside of the pocket. Even in the tattered condition, Alex could tell it had been printed recently.

The insignia of the Department of Health and Human Services was in the uppermost corner, right next to that of the Department of Homeland Security. NOT FOR PUBLIC CONSUMPTION, the headline text read. FOR HEALTH PROFESSIONALS ONLY. Beneath, there was a picture of a gray-skinned body and the two big, bolded words: EKO VIRUS.

"What's this?" Alex asked, turning the pamphlet over and over.

"We get government issued health packs all the time. Flu season, especially. But never something like this."

"Why did they send it to you? Why was it in that man's pocket?"

"Alex, I discovered it at the same time as you. I can't believe I missed it before. When I checked the body, I must have been in such a rush. I don't know why he didn't show me. But I can make an educated guess."

"It's a warning to doctors?"

"Something like that. It can't be older than a week. I read through it. It mentions a number of recent events. I don't know how much you keep up with that kind of thing. Anyway. It's a breakdown of everything the government knows about the Eko Virus circa two weeks ago."

"But that was before the President... Before everything... Why two weeks ago?"

"Because that man was in the morgue for the past two weeks. If I had to guess, I'd say he received it, read the information, realized that his flu symptoms weren't exactly a flu, and had decided to take as many Tramadol pills as he could muster. I found him before he could execute the plan. Already too sick to follow through. He barely lasted a day."

"So this is it? This will tell us how to treat Timmy?"

"No," said Joan, sharing again the dryness of her single syllable laugh. "There's almost nothing in here that is helpful. If this is what the government knows about the disease, then they know nothing. No treatment, no symptoms beyond what even you seem to have noticed, and no indication of any research. It's mostly just demanding that doctors keep everything quiet. Lot of good that did."

Not for the first time, Alex felt the full weight of reality pressing down on his shoulders. There was a fine line between pessimism and being realistic and it grew thinner by the day. Even in those moments where he had cause to smile, the situation could inevitably turn for the worst, like trying to spot the silver lining in a mushroom cloud.

There was nothing much to say. Cautiously, Alex turned the pamphlet over and over in his hands. Joan began to sleep. It must have been the first time she'd been outside in days. As the sun tracked across the sky, he tried to read. But the words didn't stick. Eventually, he settled in to watch Timmy, propped up against the bike. There was nothing else to do but wait.

CHAPTER 30

The fever refused to break.

Before the light faded, as Timmy's temperature rose, Joan finally agreed that he had to be moved. They waited until the IV drip was depleted, placed him on one of the motorcycles, and pushed him into the center of town. Many of the possessions, as well as one of the bikes, were left behind. Alex would have to return for it all afterwards.

As the dusk began to seam in, Joan guided them through Rockton. Alex thought about the name. It was nothing. A bland, boring name for a bland, boring town. He began to understand why Joan resented the community, at least at a base level. After living here so long, she had constructed a steady foundation of dislike for the town.

But she knew her way around.

On her advice, they found a building at the opposite end of the main street. It was a home that had been left vacant some weeks before. The family had gone on vacation and never returned. It was unlikely that they ever would, now. The home was on the upper floor, overlooking the chapel at one end of the main street and with a small, walled-in back yard to the rear.

They carried Timmy up the stairs and into a child's bed. A new

IV was attached and dangled from a book shelf. With all the painkillers, Timmy barely moved. But his forehead was hot to the touch, burning up. When he did awake, on occasion, he described nightmares to Joan. He wouldn't share them with Alex and neither would Joan. They were his own private visions, however bad they were.

From within the drug store, Joan was able to fetch more of her possessions. Food, for the most part. Once he had retrieved the motorcycle and the tent, Alex offered to drive her out to her old house. But she refused. It held nothing of any interest or value. Instead, Alex stashed the two bikes in the back yard, out of sight.

Timmy did not stir.

Locked into his dreams and his fever, there was little anyone could do. According to Joan, she had only just managed to triumph over the virus by being holed up in bed. She'd lost almost a week of her life. Most people didn't make it through a few days. The fact that Timmy was fighting, she said, was a good sign. All they could do was wait.

The chances of survival, Joan continued to state, were incredibly low. Of all the people she knew who had contracted the disease, most were now in the morgue. The rest were probably dead someplace else. She was the only person she knew who had survived. But the fact that there was living proof of life beyond the Eko virus was worth clinging on to, Alex thought, however low the chances were.

Alex was restless. They'd set off for Virginia on stolen motorcycles with a small arsenal at their side. They should have been there by now., They were wasting valuable time stuck in this dead-end town.

There might not even be a farm to get to by the time Timmy had recovered. After everything they'd already achieved, being told to wait made him feel helpless. Wasted. Lost.

Every day, he sat looking at the map. It wasn't far to Virginia. When Joan caught him staring at the roads and the forests, she'd ask him questions. Alex batted them away, avoiding the conversation. Once or twice, she'd nearly hit on something important.

He'd considered telling her about Sammy or about his parents. But there was nothing to say to her. He'd barely shared that information with Timmy. This strange woman who had stormed into his life was not about to receive the same access to information.

Time stretched out mockingly. First one day. Then another. Then another.

At least the food was better, holed up here. The family had a gas stove. Once lit with a match, it was unaffected by the energy blackout. Alex began to learn about the medicine given to Timmy. Antiretrovirals. Beta blockers. It all sounded like gibberish. But Joan, with nothing better to do, explained the importance of each drug.

In return, Alex decided to try and teach her something. They took a handgun, one of the Glocks, left Timmy sleeping for as long as they dared, and went out through the backstreets of the town, taking a small trek into the woods. Though he was hardly a fantastic shot himself, they practiced with the pistol.

"Shouldn't we worry about ammunition?" Joan asked, cleaning her glasses between shots.

"You'll waste plenty more bullets if you can't shoot straight," Alex replied, repeating something Timmy had told him once. "Think about it as an investment."

So then invested in tin cans on a tree trunk. Movie material. Joan was a better shot than expected, though she hated the smell it left on her fingers.

No one else came to Rockton. Occasionally, at night, a dog howled. Birds passed by overhead but never stopped. The analog radio picked up only static. On the third night, they heard gunshots. A series of loud cracks which pierced the silence, then went quiet. They stayed inside the next day.

After another quiet night, they decided to try the shooting practice with the Glock again. It was more important, they reasoned, though they tried to keep a closer eye on their surroundings. Once they could reliably knock most of the tin cans out of place, they wandered home. Neither Alex nor Joan asked each other too many questions. Not anymore.

Then the fever broke.

It was morning when Alex entered the child's bedroom to change the drip and administer the drugs, just as he'd been taught. When he bent down to help his friend, Timmy lay still. Waiting. Just when Alex's hand had been within reach, as he focused on the task, Timmy seized hold of his wrist.

The shock drove Alex to shouting. He bellowed in Timmy's face, first with fright and then with rage. As Joan arrived in the room, her worried face edging in through the door, the two friends had fallen back into laughter.

But Timmy was far from well. The virus, though easing off, had taken its toll. Pounds and pounds of flesh had fallen away from Timmy's already skinny frame. Water weight, most of it, sweated straight through the sheets every day. The road to recovery would be a long ride, so they stayed put.

Now that the patient was awake, the planning could begin again in earnest. Taking the maps upstairs, Alex and Timmy finally found Rockton on the page and plotted a new course. Days, they thought, until they reached Virginia. As soon as the last shackles of the illness had been shaken away, they could hit the road.

As they planned, Alex watched Timmy. Even as the worst of the virus passed, the chances of survival were still low. Any time Joan mentioned mortality rates or tried to talk about the future, Timmy waved it away. He was determined to make it through. He didn't want to leave the adventure behind. Facts and statistics only clogged up his arrangements. Inconvenient truths. There would be a time, he said, when they'd all be able to break free from the house and carry on to Virginia.

Timmy said it would be soon. Joan, Alex could see, was holding her tongue. She didn't want to burst his optimism. The odds were still against him.

Until then, they practiced. After Alex had told Timmy about the gun range he'd built in the forest out back of the house, it became an obsession. Every day, Timmy wanted to get out there, to see what it was all about, to take his own gun and finally feel the feather weight of the trigger kiss the bend of his finger. That sulphur tang, he kept reminding the others, smelt like victory.

On the fourth day after the fever broke, Joan's examination ended in an all clear. Though Timmy was not yet ready to walk alone, they helped him down the stairs, through the back yard, and out into the forest. Alex carried the guns, grinning from ear to ear. He brought a selection.

This was to be a celebration. Timmy style.

They reached the range, an old river gully that had dried up. A sycamore tree, weathered and thick, had toppled down into the gulch. It hadn't rained for a month and the ground was rigid and firm. The three stood at the top end of the gully, facing downstream. Behind the fallen trunk was nothing but a bend in the river, now riddled with bullets.

The tin cans were still there. They were bent and twisted all out of shape. But they still made for decent targets. Just harder to hit. Placing the guns carefully on the ground, Alex wandered down range–some fifty feet–and lined the cans up along the tree trunk. Timmy sat on a mossy stone and watched.

"You both been shooting from here? You're practically on top of the targets. How'd you ever miss?"

As the virus had abated, Timmy's humor had come back with a vengeance. When Alex arrived back, he looked down at the selection of guns and ammo. A couple of pistols, a rifle, and as many rounds as they'd need.

"Where do you want to start?" he asked Joan.

"I think you should lead the way. Show your friend what you've taught me."

"Okay then," Alex said, happy to demonstrate what he'd been picking up these last few days. "Let's start with the Glock."

Picking up the pistol, he checked it over. He loaded it up, feeling the familiar click of the thumb release. The slide catch caught without even looking. Timmy was grinning the whole time.

"Been practicing, man?"

"A little," Alex admitted through a sheepish grin.

The gun was far more familiar in his hands than it had ever been. Thinking back now, to that night in the warehouse, how strange he'd felt holding the paintballing gun, he was almost embarrassed. A magazine was already stacked full of rounds, slid up inside, and Alex tugged back on the slide. The sound told him everything was loaded.

"Very smooth." Timmy mocked a round of applause. "Though you could just flick the slide catch with your thumb. And always point down range, man. Joan, has he been teaching you bad habits?"

Tutting, he turned back to Alex and motioned with a sweep of the hand. The targets were lined up, ready. Alex nodded. The other two covered their ears. He rattled off ten shots, hitting seven of the tin cans. They toppled through the air, falling on the forest floor. Alex unloaded the pistol and placed it in a holster on his hip.

"Not bad, not bad at all, man. But you gotta look at your standing leg. Where's all your weight going? And don't shut one eye when you shoot; you need to keep looking around. Think about where your hips are. And—"

"I thought you said it wasn't bad? I hit seven out of ten. That's all right, no?" Alex smiled as he spoke.

"I'm just breaking your balls, man. Seven's not bad. What about the other three?"

"I hit them sometimes."

"Let's hit them every time, then."

"All right, Yoda, tell me what to do better."

Timmy licked his lips. Joan, hand over her mouth, watched quietly.

"And Joanie. Let's see what you can do. Come on, I won't bite."

From somewhere, Timmy had picked up a stick. He was using it to point, motioning all up and down the range. And it went on like this for hours. They ran out of ammo once, and Alex had to run back home for more. Tin cans, too, to replace the ones which were all shot up.

As the afternoon rolled through, Timmy sent Joan looking for a bigger stick. Everyone obliged the survivor, delighted that he had even made it this far. Alex was still in shock and happily went along with any of his friend's whims. This was his way of celebrating. Beating death by having fun.

Armed with a longer reach, he could point out people's failings and errors from his mossy stone. It suited him well, Alex thought, all talk and no having to back it up on any occasion. Timmy the teacher.

They were losing the light. Down in the gully, it was harder and harder to see the cans. One more go, Joan said, insisting that she was getting the hang of the handgun. Armed with his big stick, the self-appointed teacher poked and prodded her knees and hips, positioning her to point down range.

Ten shots, ten hits. Each tin can toppled from the tree trunk. Joan turned back to the two men, daring them to criticize. Alex took the pistol, still hot, from her hands, unloading the rounds and checking the magazine. As Timmy began to stand, leaning heavily on the stick, about to open his mouth to doll out droll praise, there was a sound.

Gunfire.

Shot after shot. Not from nearby. But close. Coming from the town.

"Maybe it's an echo?" said Joan, more hopeful than sure.

Alex was already packing up the guns. Timmy hobbled to his feet. Not an echo, they knew. They needed to hide.

CHAPTER 31

*T*he house.

From deep down in the ravine, the sound of the shots echoed overhead. They needed to be back in the house. Familiar. Safe. Secure. An unspoken agreement, Alex and Joan collected together everything while Timmy tried to stand.

Before, it had been a leisurely ten-minute stroll to the river bed, kicking the first of the autumn leaves and feeling the freshness of the morning pinching the cheeks. Not today. Nearly sunset, strangers nearby, they moved fast.

Alex carried the guns. Joan and Timmy supported one another, neither one in any condition to charge headlong through the town. This left Alex to scout ahead, pausing every thirty seconds, listening. The Glock nuzzled into his palm, the chamber loaded. The shouts and shooting was still some distance away. But they were moving.

Trudging through the back alleys of Rockton, they finally saw the steeple of the chapel. The steeple, not as grand as those which loomed over most churches, was a lighthouse, guiding them home. Still stopping on every street corner, still letting the gun lead him around every blind bend, Alex guided the others toward the house.

The gate at the rear was swinging open, just as they'd left it.

Whoever had owned the house, the bottom floor, at least, had seen fit to build a wall, higher than a man. It encircled the garden. Hid the motorcycles. As Alex watched Timmy and Joan stagger through the gate, he looked up and down the alley.

Nothing. The shots were still ringing out. The shouting grew louder.

Sliding the deadbolt into place, he put his finger to his lips and motioned for the other two to get inside. They agreed, moving as fast as they could toward the screen door separating them from the safety of the house. Once inside, they clambered up the stairs and locked themselves into the abandoned home they'd made their own.

Alex waited.

The yard was self-contained. From a street level, no one would be able to see in. But he couldn't see out. Instead, he only had the sounds: the shouts, the gunfire, the mounting rumble of heavy vehicles crawling along a street. Making the sure the lock on the gate held firm, he entered the house.

Rather than join the others on the second floor, Alex let himself into the ground-level apartment. It was equally as abandoned but far less homely. It had belonged to the man who had owned the building, Joan had told them, who let out the second floor to the family and prowled around downstairs. A shut-in, no one really knew much about his character.

There wasn't much to know, Alex thought. He'd already explored the rooms, found them empty. No pictures, no posters, barely any furniture. Not even a body. Devoid of sentimentality.

It reminded Alex of his own apartment, though he had far fewer piles of old newspapers stacked beside the door. No hint of electronics anywhere inside, the man was devotedly living in the past, left behind by a supposedly paperless society.

It was dark. The front room, empty and dry and dusty, featured a bay window facing the street. Whoever the owner had been, he had enjoyed his privacy. Net curtains hung under the heavy black drapes. The perfect place to watch over the neighbors' kids and complain about people on their way to the Sunday service.

Taking only the pistol, slipping it into the holster, Alex stepped up to the drapes and drew them in. The fading light of the day abandoned the room at once. Standing at the side of the bay, he felt his fingers slip between the drapes and the net curtains, pulling them back. Not knowing who was outside, who was watching, he moved his fingers carefully, slowly, and with the utmost precision.

"Who is it?" Joan whispered, laying a hand on a shoulder.

Alex froze. The air in his lungs dropped a hundred degrees, began coating the inside of his throat and turning his breath cold. Icicles hanging from his vocal cords, he could hardly speak. Hardly dare to squeak out what he saw.

"I don't know yet," he muttered through icy teeth. "I can't quite see."

"Police? FEMA?"

"I don't think so." Alex was already worried. He wanted to be absolutely sure before he said anything out loud. "They wouldn't be shooting."

"The gang already came here once. They took everything. They wouldn't come back. It has to be the government."

Even at a whisper, Alex could hear the hope in her voice, could hear all the misplaced desire for help.

"Go and help Timmy. Keep him safe. I'll be back soon."

"Where are you going?"

"I need to check this out."

"Don't do anything stupid, Mr. Early. I know you."

Turning with a smile, Alex considered a wink. Not something he could pull off. Not something which suited the tone of the moment. Instead, he let his smile waver and settled for bland reassurance.

"I'll be fine. Go and help him."

Pursing her lips, preparing to say something, Joan had the thought catch in her throat. Left it unsaid. With care and quiet, she turned from the window and went back toward the stairs. Alex listened to her leaving, listened to the sound of the door closing above and the locks sliding into place.

FROM INSIDE THE HOUSE, Alex could see up and down the street. The chapel, to his right, sat at one end. At the other, there was movement. The gunfire had died down but the shouting was still audible. A strange SUV was rolling up the street, flanked by men on either side. They buzzed around the vehicle, flitting this way and that, like wasps around a nest.

The SUV wasn't like Timmy's car. That had been a big, blacked-out cloud designed to crawl through city streets. Whatever was crawling up through Rockton lurked. The bull bars fitted to the front bore dents and scratches; Alex could see them from the other end of the street. The doors had been removed and the tires swapped out for larger, chunkier, grippier versions.

Gangs. Cartels. Whatever they were called. These people clearly weren't government. They were clearly enjoying themselves, too, Alex thought.

The men stomping around the car were shouting. Not shouting words or threats, just bellowing from the balls of their feet to the tops of their lungs. Screaming at the sky. Every now and then, one would shoot his gun up in the air. The first shot was met with a volley of approval, his friends echoing the sentiment. What seemed like minutes later, Alex heard the spent bullets falling on the roof of the porch. That heavy kind of rain. Or maybe he only imagined it.

Once they were close enough, Alex got a better look at the men. All men. They were ready for a fight. Torn shirts, tough boots, and tattoos. They didn't look like government. But they were tooled up like an army. Even with his spotty knowledge of heavy weapons, Alex knew they were holding enough to take down a small fort.

The SUV stopped in front of the bar and was soon joined by another and another. The same place where Alex and Timmy had found the beer. One vehicle had blood splattered down the hood, obscuring a graffitied gang sign. Another was fitted with a machine gun on the roof, the word 'Roque' spray painted along the doors.

On either side, dirt bikes buzzed around, the riders yelling and cheering and spinning their back wheels, filling the street with smoke. From the way they held their guns, the men were experienced. From the way they walked, there was no one taking command. Deserters, Alex wondered, or mercenaries? Gang members?

Some of the tattoos he'd seen on the Discovery Channel. Big bold lettering, covering the spine and the shoulders, the chest and the neck. Some men had ink over their faces. Most of them wore white T-shirts and vests, showing off their flesh. Gray flesh. Sweating. As the men poured out of the vehicles and into the bar, lighting a fire in the middle of the street, Alex tried to read the tattoos.

Too far away.

For hours, the night passing, the new arrivals sat in the street in front of Danny Boy's bar. One of them, larger than the others, seemed to be holding court. He sat his sizeable frame on the blood-splattered hood and had his beer brought to him. They all shared the same haircut: shaved skulls which caught the firelight.

After watching at the window, Alex returned up the stairs. He knocked three times and was allowed inside. There, he found Timmy and Joan in the child's bedroom. An IV drip in his arm, popped pill packets by his side, Timmy was drifting off into a dream-filled sleep.

"You know who they are?" asked Joan, keeping her voice as quiet as it could be.

"I still don't know. It doesn't look like anything official. It can't be. They're sitting in the street now."

"I've seen them before." Her voice was serious, Alex noticed. Sincere. "They rode through, a while ago. Took most of everything then got chased off."

"A gang?"

"Looks like it." Joan hid from the window. "I was lucky I got the sign from the drug store taken down before they arrived."

"They don't look like the reading type…"

"They definitely look like the 'loot a drug store' type, though. There's more of them now. They seem better equipped."

"What, they wanted medicine? They don't look healthy."

"They're not. Look at them. They're sick as everyone else."

"Then how do they keep going?" Alex stole a glimpse through the window.

The gang members, the ones which were still moving, didn't seem too afflicted. When Timmy had been at his sickest, he could barely move. If these people were carrying an infection, they weren't showing it.

"I'm not sure, but I'd be willing to bet drugs are involved."

"Like, the stuff we gave Timmy?"

"No, you fool. Narcotics. Meth. Heroin. Coke. Whatever. Enough to haul them through the sickness and keep them propped up."

Alex looked again. If he strained his eyes, he could see a few of the gang members smoking. Impossible to tell what it was from so far away.

"You think that would work?"

"Seems to."

"So we just wait here and they'll keel over when the drugs run out?"

"I don't imagine the shelf life on gang members is too long these days. They'll probably replace them. God knows there's going to be crowds of violent young men out there with nothing left to lose. No wonder the gangs are taking over parts of the country. They can offer narcotics and lawlessness."

"What good's that?" Alex asked, still watching out the window.

"Better than waiting to die, I suppose."

Turning away from the window, Alex sat down on the floor. Gangs of lawless drug addicts roaming the countryside, always on the edge of dying. Wait them out. Run past them. Try to bargain with them. None of the options looked good.

"So," Joan began, staring at Alex's sinking face. "Where does that leave us?"

"Nowhere near Virginia."

Ever since Joan had joined them in the house, Alex had assumed that she would be coming with them to the farm. The entire matter had not even been mentioned. Timmy seemed to like her, seemed to get along well with her. But he got along well with everyone. She'd even warmed to Alex, cutting down on her reproaches and thanking him for his help every now and then.

"You're still going?"

They were whispering together. Pointing at the patient, Joan signaled for them to leave the room. Timmy stirred, though he didn't wake. He was putting on some of his weight once again, buoyed by the ability to heat up food on the gas stove and not have to live on the readymade meals every day. Soon enough, Alex had thought, they'd be back on the road.

"We can't stay here forever," Alex told Joan, leading her into the hallway and then into the kitchen.

"Not forever, but... I don't know."

She sat at the table, a small round wooden piece of furniture placed in the corner of the room. The flat-pack chair creaked as she sat, cradling her belly as she eased into the seat.

"Timmy can't travel," she continued, "not yet. Not for a few days. At least. And we're running low on everything. We need to go back to the store. You can't get that in Virginia, I'm sure, you can't be certain. And you won't have me to administer everything and-"

"You're not coming?"

It was dark in the kitchen and Joan struck a match. Carefully, she guided the burning stick onto the base of a gas lantern. Shaking her wrist, turning the dial on the canister, she filled the room with light and placed the lantern in the middle of the table. It bathed the kitchen in a soft orange glow. Alex moved quick, noisily, and snapped the heavy curtains closed.

"What are you doing?" His voice was a low, urgent murmur. "Any light and they could see us from outside."

"I... I... I'm sorry." Joan was glancing around the room, searching for an answer. "I wasn't thinking. I... I... just. I don't know. I can turn it off. I spend all my time being so careful and then – in one moment – it's all undone."

"The curtains should deal with it." Alex could see the regret and fear in her face. He felt pity as he closed up all the gaps in the curtains with clothespins. "But these people, they don't look friendly. They don't look healthy. The last thing I want is them to run in here and..."

"And what?"

"You know. I don't want that."

"What do you want?" Joan's voice was becoming more assertive after her moment of raw regret.

"I don't know that either. I just want us–and you, too, the three of us–to be safe."

"We are safe. As long as we stay hidden."

"We're not safe. Not here. Not now. Look what happened today. Look who's out in the street."

"What would you have us do?"

"Virginia. We had a plan. A good plan. Well, a plan, at least. And now you're here and now you're coming."

"Alex, I really don't know. I barely know either of you. This is my home."

"You hate it here."

"But it's my home. Just because it's home, doesn't mean you can't hate it. It's still home…"

Without warning, Alex's mind flashed back to the farmhouse. The furniture under white sheets. Everything important packed away in plastic boxes. The clink of the keys as they fell into Eames's palm. The black ties and veils. The dirt road leading out. Home.

"It isn't safe here. It isn't safe anywhere. But, together, we've got a better chance."

"A better chance of what?"

"I don't know. But something tells me, something in my bones, that we need to get to that farm. Maybe not today, maybe not tomorrow. But it's the one place I know–for sure–that we can be safe."

Joan reached for the lantern and dialed down the gas until it was almost out. The orange light fell away, as low as it could go. It was hardly illuminating anything, just a softer kind of darkness.

"Okay," she said. "Maybe it's destiny. But we have to wait for Timmy. And we need to take supplies."

"We'll wait out these people, whoever they are. They won't stay long. They probably won't even live long. When they leave, I'll get the supplies from the store, and then we ride. We don't stop till we hit Virginia."

It was all that needed to be said. Without another word, Joan rose from the table and returned to Timmy's room, taking a packet of medicine with her. Alex fashioned some sort of meal, left most of it in the kitchen, and went back downstairs to watch through the gap in the curtains.

Drinking, shouting, and laughing, the men outside never slept. Alex felt his eyes grow heavy, felt himself being lulled into a slumber. He fell asleep beneath the bay window, the gathered crowd outside the bar still unaware of his presence.

It would have to stay that way.

CHAPTER 32

When he woke, Alex was in the dark. In the empty space behind the heavy drapes, the morning had yet to creep into the room. After hours of watching intently, hand hovering over his holster, he had discovered nothing. The men outside drank, shouted, and partied as though they had nothing to lose. Added to that, he was seeing new faces. New tattoos. People who weren't there yesterday. He could feel his mind changing.

Standing up and stretching, creasing the hard floorboards out of his aching back, Alex peeked again through the curtains. Soundless, the street seemed calm. But the huge cars were still there. As he looked, Alex saw the men laid across the seats, the road, and anywhere else they'd fallen. They weren't going away.

Sleeping, finally.

Taking himself back up the stairs, Alex found the door locked. His knock was familiar. Not a code, as such, but something Joan had heard before. A familiar pattern. She let him in. Already, she was up and ready for the day. Not that they could venture outside of the building. Not that she could, anyway.

"They're sleeping. I'm going out." Alex's words left no space to argue.

"You stayed down there all night?"

"How's Timmy?"

"Sleeping, I guess. Those Tramadol tablets have quite the impact. He'll be down for a while."

"Good. I'm going out. Give me a list of what we need. Please."

"Out of the house? To the drug store? Why? That's dangerous."

"I've been thinking about that." Alex had been kept awake by thoughts of the gang outside. "We can't just wait for them to leave. Or die. Someone will always be out there."

Alex had arrived at the conclusion just as his eyes welded shut. The way they moved around the bar, around the cars, around each other: they didn't care. They'd found something interesting–a bar with booze–and had camped outside. They'd probably called their friends. Whoever Roque was, his gang of dying men was getting bigger by the day. They had nothing to lose.

"How do you know that?"

"Same way I know they're not friendly. My gut, I guess."

"So, what happens?"

"So I go out now, while they sleep, and as soon as Timmy's ready, we move. We move fast. And we don't look back. I don't want to stick around to learn more about these guys."

Up and down the small kitchen, Joan was pacing. Occasionally, as she did when thinking, she rubbed her belly. She was worried. Alex barely knew her last name, he'd hardly known her two minutes, but it was easy to pick up on tics and tells when spending so much time in a confined space with another person. He knew her well and not at all.

"You can't go out with just that." Joan pointed to the pistol. "That's just asking for trouble."

"I'm not going without it."

"Obviously. What I mean is, don't go out there whirling a pistol around. Try a light touch. Hide it somewhere. On your back, perhaps? We have some tape here."

"And what good is that when I need it quick?"

"I saw at least ten people out there, Mr. Early. Do you think they're just tin cans, sitting on a tree trunk? You think you can hit seven?

What about the other three? If they see you with a gun, what do you think their first reaction will be? I'll tell you: shoot."

She was right; he knew that.

"Fine. Get that tape."

Peeling his T-shirt from his back, Alex leaned across the table and un-holstered the gun. It was loaded. Full clip. He began to practice his movement, trying to figure out the reach he had available. It wasn't much.

Finally, he settled on the base of the spine. Right in the curve of the back. He held the gun in place while Joan taped it to the skin. The tape wouldn't stick to the body armor. They made the choice. A good offence beats a good defense, Alex mumbled.

"This is going to hurt like hell when I rip it off," he half-joked.

"You'll hurt more if you don't," replied Joan, balancing a piece of tape on her lips. "There. Try that."

Alex felt behind. The handle of the Glock was ready and waiting for him. Easy to reach.

"Just make sure it's not covering the trigger. Or the barrel. Make sure it's really stuck on there."

Muttering to herself, Joan double-checked every piece of tape, strengthening the structure where she could.

"That should work. What are you going to wear?"

The thought hadn't occurred to Alex, who looked down at his familiar T-shirt. Put that back on and it'd cover the gun. No way to grab it in a rush. Same with the leather jacket: too tight in a hurry. Restrictive. Even the Kevlar would hinder his access to the gun. Plus, it'd show the gang members that maybe he meant business. Better to look innocent. Innocent and vulnerable.

"Hang on," said Joan. "I saw a rain coat in the hallway."

It was a heavy wax jacket. A Barbour, according to the label. Some kind of kilt pattern on the inside, but it felt comfortable enough. More importantly, Alex could wear it loose and open. Whoever had lived in this house must have been far bigger than him. The coat hung across his bare chest. But it left the gun within easy reach.

"I look ridiculous," said Alex, catching sight of himself in a hallway mirror.

"Hardly our chief concern," Joan responded. "Besides, if they ask, you're just lost and wandering through the countryside. Maybe they'll take pity. You certainly look quite pathetic. They don't exactly seem worried about infection."

"Thanks. Fills me with joy."

With her kindly words, Joan watched Alex prepare to leave. The drug store was a few doors down. Not too far. He could exit through the back yard, stick to the alleys. She told him about a window which gave way into the drug store basement. Smash that and he'd be in without having to enter through the front door in the cold light of day.

Armed with a list of supplies to gather, a flashlight, and the gun taped to his back, Alex considered telling Timmy where he was going. But the man was too deep in his sleep, too content. *He'll hear all about it if I get back*, thought Alex, trying to focus his mind into a positive outlook.

When. Not if.

EXITING the rear of the house was easy. Alex paused a moment, checking the motorcycles. They were as good as new. A bit dirty, perhaps, but all the better for it. Just enough fuel, ready to roll out when needed.

One day, Alex promised himself, *I'm going to get myself one of these, and maybe even pay for it.*

Leaving through the back gate was more difficult. With the high wall hiding everything, the world beyond the gate was unknown. There might be anything on the other side. Maybe a person. Alex gripped a deadbolt with careful fingers and began to slide it open. The old metal scraped and groaned. Rust was pouring off. It must have been the loudest sound in the world.

But it opened.

The alley was abandoned. If the men were sleeping in the main street, they had not just discovered the intricate network of alleyways and paths which stitched themselves in and around the buildings of the town. As well as the walled yard of the hideaway home, Alex could duck and weave between the walls and fences which lined other people's property. Even in such an empty town, people were adamant about what exactly belonged to them.

It was a quiet morning. Sneaking through the space behind the houses, Alex could hear sounds. Occasional bird song, a dog barking in a distant building. Perhaps someone had left their pet behind as they fled the town. Died, more likely, Alex admitted to himself. Scratching sounds. Footsteps. He wondered whether they were really there, whether they had always been there, or whether his ears were manufacturing noises to satisfy a paranoid mind.

The drug store was only three buildings away, just over fifty feet. Alex ran quick and low through the empty spaces between the houses. As he arrived at his destination, he found the low window into the basement, just as Joan had said. It was between two dried-out rosemary bushes, about twenty inches high and made of thin frosted glass. Just about big enough to squeeze through.

Nearby, Alex found half a brick. Raising his hand to smash the glass, he stopped. Too loud. Instead, he removed his jacket, wrapped the brick inside so that the sharpest corner was coddled in the wax coat. Next, he lay the brick beside the window, looked up and down the alley, and kicked the parceled weapon. The glass cracked. Two more firm kicks and it shattered.

Using the coat, Alex wiped away all the fragments from inside the frame. Each one tinkled and chimed as it hit the concrete floor below, the melody of notes betraying his position. Unwrapping the brick, he placed the jacket back around his shoulders. Over the gun. As quickly as he could, Alex slid in through the empty frame, feet first.

HIS SNEAKERS HIT the floor with a clap. Fumbling in the Barbour pocket, Alex found his flashlight. It clicked as the beam of light stirred and began cutting swathes through the basement gloom. There was a slow drip, drip, drip from an unseen source. Everything down here was moist, from the flat packed cardboard boxes to the bicycle leaning against the far wall without any wheels.

The way out was up the concrete steps. At the top, a flimsy door, the paint peeling off the inside. Opening gently, pulling it shut after him, Alex found himself in the familiar corridors of the drug store. The stifling smell had not improved. Only worsened.

Everything was stored in the morgue. So few people died in such as small town, Joan had explained, that they'd practically treated the place like a closet. As the bodies began to pile up, she didn't have the time, energy, or inclination to move the medicine.

Now, Alex made his way toward the morgue. Each step in that direction was a worry. The air thickened. The rotting flesh in the bags on the floor of the blacked-out medical center demanded the attention of every brain cell. It smelled like so much death roasted over an iron forge. Industrialized putridity.

Alex felt his fingers rub the paper in his pocket. The list Joan had written. The medical supplies to ease Timmy back into the world. Some for the tail end of his disease, some to protect against future infection. This and that, just names on a list, random collections of letters that he knew nothing about.

As the door opened, the air rushed out. Escaping, dragging with it the decomposing stench of diseased meat. Every taste cell on the tongue began to rust, to wither, all at once. So overwhelming it rode over every sense. Deafening. Blinding. Alex fought against his every instinct, driving his gagging stomach down and holding it in place.

Move fast, he thought. Alex emptied one box, throwing its contents on the floor. Paper towels, it seemed. He went to the racks, the shelves stocked with medicine. Working through the list, he found everything. Grabbing as much as possible, he laid it all in the box. All except one item. An unpronounceable name with an annotation.

"In the front of store," Alex read to himself.

A relief. A chance to get out of the morgue. Double checking everything in the box, terrified of having to ever come back, he packed up the loot and left. The click of the door closing behind was a reassurance. A relief. He left the dead behind and breathed freely again.

Leaving the stolen medicine next to the top of the basement stairs, Alex proceeded down the corridor and into the main public space, feeling a sense of relief. He'd gotten out alive. The air felt fresh. He closed his eyes and sucked in another lungful. One more item and then it was mission accomplished.

The front of the store was as small as he remembered it. Darker, perhaps. Shadows everywhere. A thing light entered through an open space. Before, he knew, the door had been working. Now, it hung from its hinges. Someone had been inside. He had to move fast.

Stomach beginning to turn over and over, that fresh air knotting itself into all sorts of Gordian shapes, Alex scanned the shelves for the last item on the list. It was buried in a corner, behind the counter, in the last place anyone would look. Annoying, he thought, but not an unsurmountable hurdle. All that remained now was getting back to the house in one piece and the mission would be a success.

Walking back to the top of the basement stairs, there was a spring in Alex's step. He clicked his heels against the tiles, pleased that he'd managed to prevail so quickly. Even the stench of all those bodies hadn't slowed him down, he'd be able to tell Joan, already conjuring up the lurid, wretched ways in which he'd describe the smell.

"Hey," a voice called from behind. "Who're you?"

Alex was halfway between the store front and the basement steps. But the voice was coming from over his shoulder, almost. It was deep, rough around the edges. The sound of a person spitting came next.

"Well?"

Turning around, the oversized coat hiding his hands, Alex tried to hold up the boxes of medicine. Adrenaline surged inside him, making his fingers tremble. He tried to hide his nerves.

"Hi. I'm Alex. I'm just here for my pills. Just passing by. Don't mind me. Who are you?"

The man was indistinguishable from those Alex had seen the night before. Then, they'd been wandering around a fire, drinking and shouting and shooting their guns. The tattoos were the same, except

214

for an intricately designed cross perched between the eyes. The man's T-shirt clung to a muscled frame, an unbuckled belt slipping over his wrist and clanging on the tile floor. A hand dipped into a pocket and arrived back with a flick of the wrist. A knife. The man walked forward.

"I'm Saul. Me and my friends, we own this town now. Everything in it. Hand that back over."

"It's just blood thinners," Alex told him, stepping backwards. "Just a hereditary condition."

"Sick people is sick people. You want to see how sick we are? Give it up."

That was the end of the conversation. The man lunged forward, the knife leading. Alex twisted, just enough. The knife ran through the hanging body of the wax jacket. It was sharp.

Reach for the gun, Alex thought. *Get it now.*

But the man was in too close, throwing punches and feints. It was all Alex could do to dodge. One hit to the arm, one to the ribs. They hurt. The man just seemed to laugh, not offering an opportunity to switch the hand up and behind the back, where the pistol was hidden.

Trapped in the corridor, the fight was hindered. No space to run for Alex, for room to really swing. When the man pulled back his arm or slashed with the knife, Alex drove forwards, toward him. Grappling, grabbing, trying to hug him close.

The knife flashed again, arcing past Alex's face. It cut down hard into the wax coat, catching as Alex turned. The ripping sound cut through the quiet, the force of the slash dragging him down toward the floor. Twisting, the coat took the knife out of the man's hands and it clattered along the corridor tiles.

Again, Alex tried for the gun, using one hand to cover his face while the over dived into the flaps of the coat. He could feel the tape, feel the barrel. The handle was almost in reach. The man landed a hard punch right in Alex's gut. The wind knocked out of him, the grip on the pistol abandoned, he tumbled back hard into the wall beside the basement door.

Now, the man beamed. A black space instead of a front tooth, Alex noticed. It didn't matter now.

"Oh, Roque's gonna be real pleased with you."

From two feet away, the man balanced on the balls of his feet. About to pounce. Rising, Alex could barely breathe. Sucking air, staring at the tooth, he saw the sinews in the man's muscles tense.

The man jumped, flinging himself through the small space. Alex ducked, crouching down. As the milliseconds crawled by, he could feel the weight of the man passing over him. Unbalanced, the attacker tripped, stumbled, and reached out to support himself.

He found only the basement door, still ajar, and vanished into the shadows below. Alex heard the bones snap, the blood splatter as he hit every step on the way down. And then silence. On the corridor floor, desperate for breath, Alex listened. All he could hear was the blood hissing through the veins in his ear, hurtling back to his thundering heart.

Alex was alive, just.

CHAPTER 33

*T*here was no time to breathe.

The man at the bottom of the concrete stairs had not stirred. Gathering together all of the medicine, Alex collected his box of supplies and stood at the top of the steps. Reaching underneath the coat, he removed the pistol from its hiding place and placed it on top of the IV bags and pills. More use there.

Step by step, he descended. Without a free hand to carry a flash-light, he had to continue in the dark. The light from the broken window and the open door was enough to spot the man, lying prone in a pool of blood. Unerringly still.

Staring at the body, Alex felt a way down the steps with his feet. It took a long time. Once at the bottom, he walked around the body and the expanding lake of blood. Saul, that's what he'd called himself. And then something about Roque. Unfamiliar names.

As Alex took a wide berth, the crack along the side of the man's skull glared upwards at the world. Fractured, dark. The bald head did nothing to hide the bone.

Just beneath the broken window, the fresh air seeped inside. The taste almost tickled the tongue, like an ice cube applied to an open wound. Numbing with its crispness. One item at a time, Alex lifted the drugs, the IV bags, and the pill boxes out into the alley. The gun he saved until last. Even the coat went ahead of it and the box was folded down to fit through the frame.

Clambering out into the daylight, Alex heard sounds from the street. The gang members were stirring. The same shouts, muted with their morning hangover, had begun to pick up. From here, words were decipherable. Bellows about drink, food, and half-joking threats echoed from the other side of the drug store, down the main street by the bar.

In time, they would discover that one of their number was missing. Whether they'd check down in the basement of a drug store, Alex didn't know. If they discovered the body, they might even think that he died from an accidental fall down a dark set of stairs. Which was true, in a way, Alex reassured himself.

Packing everything back into the box, volume was important. The sounds of people moving were audible now. On the street, men kicking stones as they went. Heavy boots on asphalt. Hand slapping, laughter. Alex worried as the clatter of the pills in their packets echoed through the alley.

With the box, the walk back to the hideout was short. But with people all around, Alex was worried. Rather than walking in a straight line, he crossed the alley and waited. The drug store was one of a row of houses which ran parallel to the main street.

From the rear, the yards and the buildings mixed together, the alley built up on either side with walls, hedges, and trees. It functioned like a tunnel, a secret street running analogous to the main road in the town.

Carefully, Alex moved from shadow to shadow. From behind a tree trunk to a darkened doorway. Every time he heard a noise, he found a new hiding place, moving a few steps each time. As the sound of footsteps grew louder, he shrank farther and farther away from the alley, pushing himself and his box into a shadowy porch with a waist-high wall.

It belonged to a house behind the drug store, which backed onto the same space. The footsteps were near. Alex bent down low, hiding from sight. The steps continued through the alley and then stopped.

"Where the hell are you? Saul?" an unseen man shouted.

Leaning against the porch, Alex noticed the door to the home was open. In the alley, the shouting man was scratching around, searching up and down. If he came up to the rear of this house, approached the wall, he would hear the sound of hidden breathing.

"Hey, man, your brother's looking for you. Boy, is he pissed."

Alex began to crawl toward the door, leaving the box filled with medical supplies behind. Moving along on his belly, his bare chest scratching on the floor, he reached the doorway.

It was light and airy in the home. But Alex did not have time to stop and admire the décor. There was another sound now. A scratching. A whining. He'd heard it from the street before entering the drug store. Not loud enough to worry about, but loud enough to pique the curiosity.

If the man heard the same, he'd investigate. The scratches seemed to be coming from behind a closed door, down the end of the hallway. The sounds shifted, the man moving up and down the alley. Searching for Saul. Still, there was that same scratching sound.

Alex seized the moment. As quietly as he could, he ran to the end of the corridor and laid a hand on the door. It was closed. It seemed stuck, even as he turned the handle. Locked. Fiddling, finding a small dial to turn, his fingers worked fast. Finally, it sprang open and he ran inside.

Something hit him hard in the stomach, knocking Alex backwards. He rolled to his left, his attacker rolling with him. Coming to a stop, Alex prepared to lift himself up. Ready to fight, again. A tongue licked his face. A long, excited lick which came again and again, accompanied by a whine. Two paws resting on his chest, Alex looked up.

It was a dog. One of those police dogs. But younger. Not quite a puppy. He pushed it to the side, clambering to his feet, worried about the sound. The dog continued to lick his hands. Alex shut the door. Then he noticed. It smelled awful in here.

Not like the morgue. It wasn't the smell of death. It was much more... natural. Alex looked around the room; the dog must have been in here for days, if not more. A former family room, with a couch and a TV, it had been abandoned to the dog.

A huge sack of dog food had been split open along the seam and laid at one end of the room, next to an open half barrel of water. There were scratches cut deep into the floorboards and the door. The smell, Alex realized now, was exactly what he'd expect from a dog spending a week inside a single room without an opportunity to go outside. The evidence was littered all in one corner.

Still, the creature wasn't quiet. The dog was licking any part of Alex he could find, whining with delight at the man who'd arrived to free him from his boring cage. But it needed to keep it down. There were people outside, probably searching. Finger to his lips, Alex shushed the dog.

It sat. Right away, without hesitation, the dog fell instantly silent. Stunned by this adherence to authority, Alex patted the animal on the head. The tail wagged. But quietly. After so long with Timmy and Joan, he thought, it was nice to be listened to without any disagreements.

Now, he could see the dog properly. It was about three feet long, nose to tail tip. A foot and a half high. Two ears pricked up constantly searched for any sound, moving independently of one another. It was the paws which betrayed the dog's age. Long and growing, still outsized and wrapped in puppy fat.

Growing up on the farm, there had always been dogs. Even before he thought about it, Alex knew that he wouldn't be able to leave this animal behind. It wasn't even a discussion. As long as the dog was quiet, they could get back to the house and–once they were there–Joan could tell him how terrible an idea it was.

But, for now, the dog was coming. There was no question.

The room had a window which looked out through the porch and onto the alley. Positioning himself to the side, Alex tried to spot the man who had been searching for his friend. The dog followed, sitting again beside the window, watching through the glass.

"I guess you must have seen people coming and going," Alex said under his breath. "Spotted me a few times, did you?"

The tongue left a long, wet lick on Alex's hand. There was the gang member. The man had similar tattoos to his dead friend, numerals and black ink scattered up and down his arms. This man had hair and was wearing heavier clothes. Still shouting and searching, the man was now passing the drug store, walking away down the street.

Waiting for five minutes, Alex watched him go. After the man was out of sight and there were no other sounds, he crept back out to the porch and collected the box with the medical supplies. The dog followed, bending its head down below its haunches.

It was a quick walk back to the hideout. Alex didn't stop once on the way to the gate, didn't duck into any shadows. The dog was tight on his heels, sniffing at everything they passed. Once they were behind the walls, the deadbolt back in place, Alex dropped to his knees. The dog licked his face. A sudden burst of delirious laughter punctured the silence and then stopped. This soundless world was never peaceful.

CHAPTER 34

The dog ran up the stairs and Alex followed. It needed a name. Heaving the box of medicine to the second floor, he knocked three times and waited. Movement on the other side. The shifting metal inside the locks. The door swung open and Joan stood there, staring.

"What on earth is that?" she said, pointing at the dog.

"I've got everything. I think. Can you check it?"

Placing the box on the kitchen table, Alex began to search through the various bags and boxes from Castle Ratz. Finally, he found it. One of the ready meals. This was a big test. Unwrapping the food, removing the packaging, he placed it in a pile on the floor. The dog sniffed it out in a second, trotted over, and almost inhaled it all at once.

By herself, Joan was checking through the box of medicine. First, she had to remove the pistol and she checked the bullet in the chamber, as she'd been taught.

"You didn't run into trouble, then? Just found a friend."

"Not quite. I'll tell you later. Is Timmy all right?"

Nodding, she searched through the loot. IV bags were unpacked, about fifty packets of pills. The packaging could be removed and they could be slipped into side pockets before they left. But space was becoming a problem, especially with three people. And a dog, Alex reminded himself.

"You've got everything. Everything from the list."

"Good. That's good, right?"

"You did well."

There was something in her tone. Not the complete affirmation and positivity Alex had expected. And this was before she learned about his encounters with the gang members. On the floor, the dog had finished his meal and began to desperately inspect every inch of the kitchen and the house at large.

"There's something wrong?"

"Not wrong. We should have enough medicine for Timmy. More than enough, really."

"But?"

"But what about you?"

"Me?"

"I've been sick. Timmy has been sick. But you haven't."

"I've been lucky."

"You haven't seen what this virus does to people, Alex. You haven't seen it like I have."

Immediately, the stench of the morgue raced through the mind. Everybody from the past two weeks loomed large in his imagination.

"I've seen things," Alex insisted. "I've seen plenty."

"I've seen my whole town decimated. Not even decimated. Beyond that. So many people. Do you know how lucky you've been? It's extraordinary. You haven't been paying any attention and Timmy hasn't either. By rights, you should both be dead."

"I…" Alex began. There was no real way to respond to the remark.

"Obviously I don't wish that you were dead. But you need to face the idea of what is really happening here. This isn't some adventure, some fun quirky story to tell your friends one day. They'll all be dead."

They were just words, but they hit hard. Any left-over adrenaline in Alex's body evaporated in an instant, replaced by a sudden sense of dread.

"What do you want me to do?"

"I don't want you to do anything. Just… Just acknowledge the seriousness of what's happening here. Your life has changed. Your world has changed. You can't go back. This isn't a vacation. You can't just… waltz in here with a dog and ride off into the sunset on your motorcycle."

"It's just a dog."

"No, it's not. It's everything. I sat in that morgue and tried to keep people alive. I watched them die all around me. And they blamed me! They tried to say it was my fault. Like I'd brought this plague into the town."

Joan was still sorting through the medical supplies. But she had already checked everything. Turning away from Alex, her shoulders were twitching.

"We just don't know anything," she continued. "Can't think, can't plan, can't guard ourselves. And you're bringing a dog into this? It's not the dog. I don't care about the dog. It's the cavalier approach. This is a matter of life and death, Alex. Have you even looked at Timmy's eye lately? Or you just assumed he's getting better? This disease is real and we don't know anything and you're… You're not able to admit it. This is all just fun and games for you. I wish you'd just take a moment to admit it."

Joan broke into tears. Sitting at the table, head in her hands, she waved away Alex as he stepped toward her.

"No, no. Don't. Please. Just. Sorry. It's all just… Everything has changed so quickly. Too quickly. And I see you dealing with this and I don't know *how*. It's like you don't care. Like none of this matters."

Alex joined her at the table, pushing the piles of medicine to the other side. He held her hand.

"I don't know what to say. It's not that I don't care." Plucking the words from inside his mind was difficult.

"I don't even know what I'm doing here. I guess… I'm lucky. Or not. I don't know why I'm not sick. I don't know why you or Timmy got sick. I don't know why you survived. I don't know why any of this is happening. Or what it means. I'm just trying to survive. Which is sort of the same as before."

"I know you care." Joan released his hand, her voice settling into a familiar pattern. "You just don't seem to show it. You don't show any emotion. It's unsettling. It makes me feel like I'm wrong, somehow."

"Listen, Joan. You know what happened when all of this started? Right after the President came on TV? I sat there, with Timmy, watching. And it was just the same. Same news articles. Same stories. It all just played out on the screen. And then it hit me. Virginia. That's why we had to go. To get to the farm."

"Because you watched TV?"

"Because it's the last place where I felt safe." Alex could almost taste the earnestness in his voice. "Truly safe. Where I felt happy. I don't know why I'm telling you this now, but it's true. We've got a goal. That helps."

"A goal?"

"Something to work toward. I suppose I haven't really sat down and processed all this. How I won't be going into work again or how whatever was in my bank account doesn't really matter. Because, well, what's the difference? I wasn't happy then, so why would I be now? As soon as I saw it on TV, I knew I had to go back home."

"That's really very stupid."

"But it's worked. Timmy came along, God knows why. Sometimes it helps to leave everything behind. I watched a man die today. Not from disease. He tried to kill me, fell down some stairs."

"Oh, Alex, you didn't—"

"I didn't die. I didn't catch the disease, I didn't get stabbed, I didn't want to leave the dog behind. This isn't part of some huge plan, Joan. I'm just trying to get to Virginia. And, right now, I feel pretty good about that. And I want you to come, too. And Timmy. And that dog. It just feels right."

The sound of laughter came from the other room. Together, they stood up and investigated. Timmy was in bed, the dog licking his face, tangling itself in and around the drip plugged into his forearm. As the dog crawled all over her patient, Joan leaned into Alex and whispered in his ear.

"Just promise me. It won't stop at Virginia. We'll try to find something. A reason for carrying on. Promise me."

Alex nodded. There was nothing left to say.

THE NEXT NIGHT, Alex sat again in the bay window of the abandoned home, watching the gang members. There was a difference. They were not drunk. They were not shouting. Having drunk the bar dry, they were rallying together. Every store in town had already been looted and they found nothing else to their liking. Now, they were searching through the streets, calling out for Saul.

"With any luck," Alex reasoned, "they'll think he's just holed up in some basement. Junkie stuff. Or the virus got him."

It might have been a handwave, but it was enough to settle the others' nerves.

Eventually, they packed together their possessions, hopped into their cumbersome vehicles, and drove out of town. It was quiet again in Rockton. At least, the main street was empty. In the distance, the sounds of gunfire and shouting still surrounded the town. Go out at night and they could be heard in all directions. Either them or someone else.

Their departure brought with it a moment of clarity for Alex. The bikes were not enough. With Timmy barely strong enough to stand, let alone ride, one heavily pregnant woman, and now a dog, trying to fit everything together on two motorcycles was impossible.

The solution was not simple. Joan told the others that she had a car. One they didn't have to steal. An SUV, sort of. A low-slung 4X4 with mud flaps and soft suspension. A car for soccer moms, as Timmy described it. But they could work with it. Even in bed, he demanded to be brought pencils and paper and began to sketch out his plans for Joan's car.

Alex had to execute the idea. Taking a rifle, he walked out to Joan's old house and found the vehicle. It was a blue Ford with cushioned seats and more cup holders than anyone would ever need. Slowly, watching all around, he drove it back to the hideout and hid it in a tumble-down unit behind the church, the place where the janitor kept his tools. Then they went to work.

With Timmy watching from the sides, Alex ripped out all the unnecessary weight. Bits of bodywork from outside and inside went flying, torn apart with pliers, saws, and snips.

Whoever had been working on the church had plenty of tools, it seemed, but they weren't really designed to rip apart a road car. Plus, without any power, the more serious options were limited.

Once the vehicle was lighter, Timmy insisted it needed to be stronger. That meant making a skeleton. It also meant learning how to weld. Alex found a welding kit on a construction site, heaved it onto the back of one of the bikes and rode it home. Using scaffolding poles, heavy as they were, they attached a roll cage along the roof and the delicate parts of the car.

The tires were difficult to improve. It wasn't that the current tires were good–far from it–but they didn't have access to anything better. They settled for throwing some snow chains in the trunk, just in case.

Timmy kept talking about durability. The need to keep this car going. They fitted space for extra jerry cans of fuel, tightened up the suspension, and fitted a garden light to the roof. As instructed, Alex cut holes in the hood for air flow and fitted skid plates to the under-side of the car.

None of it seemed very professional but, as the days wore on, he was surprised by how quickly he was learning. The welds were stronger, the tools feeling lighter and less clumsy in his hands. The plans grew and grew. At one point, Timmy was talking about fitting a new engine. When he worked himself up into an excited fuss, he had to be talked down from the ledge.

Where were they going to get an engine?

Even the dog found a name. Finn. He'd taken a shine to Timmy, walking everywhere with him. Still recovering, the use of a walking stick meant the dog was often in danger of knocking his new friend to the ground. But it never quite happened. Neither Alex or Joan knew why that particular name had been chosen–Timmy wasn't telling—but they didn't want to argue. It seemed to fit.

One afternoon, with the evening encroaching on the day, reminding everyone how close October had come, Alex had been sent out to find a particular type of tow bar. They'd found a trailer for the car, were planning to fit the bikes to the back and take them to Virginia.

Along with Finn, Alex had checked every abandoned car in town until he'd eventually been able to untangle one from an old truck half buried under moss in a back yard. It sat in his pocket now, rifle slung across his shoulder, as he threw a stick down the street for the dog to chase.

The sound of crows scattering made him look up. Birds were few and far between. From the far end of the street, a diminished flock burst up over the horizon and flew overhead. They were fleeing from something. Alex felt the hairs on his arms stand to attention. He whistled for the dog.

Finn ran straight to his heel and followed as they ducked into one of the alleys leading off the main street. The sound of vehicles rumbled away in the distance. People were coming. Holding the dog close, praying that he didn't make a sound, all Alex could do was watch as the heavy black vehicles rolled around the corner.

There was someone new in town.

CHAPTER 35

*T*hese cars were clean. They drove past Alex, waiting in the shadows with the dog, and he counted each vehicle as it went by. Dark tinted windows, oversized wheels, government-issue and expensive. Even the brand names were polished to perfection. Order among chaos. Seven of them, all black Cadillac Escalades.

They stopped at the halfway point of the main street, halting in a loose circle formation.

A man stepped out from the first vehicle with a metal briefcase in his hand. Kneeling, he opened it up in the middle of the street and removed a small satellite dish, adjusting it and pointing it upwards. He spoke words into the cuff of his sleeve, but Alex couldn't hear what was being said. Of its own volition, his miniature device began to twist and spin, calibrating itself.

One by one, others began exit the vehicles. A select few wore suits. Others wore combat fatigues. All wore heavy Kevlar and sunglasses. In the movies, people like this always had some Velcro strap across their chest, a three-letter agency revealing where they'd come from.

From his hiding place, Alex couldn't see any identifying marks. All he had were his assumptions, which told him the way these people moved meant they were government. Or military. Or agency. Or all three. Professionals, that much was certain.

Around the man with the satellite dish, the others began to form a circle. They were armed, some with pistols on their hips and others with an M-16 cradled in their hands. They spread out across the street, closing down the available space. One man was sweeping a device over every surface, noting down the measurements. Alex could hear the beeping and the clicking.

The dog strained against his hand. Alex stroked the fur between the ears, and Finn calmed down.

"Easy, boy." Alex had never spoken so softly. "We're just going to wait and see where they go. I bet they'll be done soon."

One by one, the new arrivals were inspecting the buildings just off the main street. Timmy and Joan, Alex hoped, were still back in the hideout. They'd not been tempted to go for a walk. As two of the men began to inspect the bar, they led with their guns.

Once inside, a shout came from one of the men. They'd found something. The news rippled through the others, each one suddenly sharp and focused. From his hiding place, Alex began to plot his escape route. He knew Rockton well now, knew which alleys he could take. But, in hardly any time, these men had begun to swamp every street and side road he had found.

An engine revved, far away. Someone yelling. One gunshot. And then another. Before Alex even knew what was happening, the men had swung open the doors of their cars and were now positioning themselves facing down the street, in the direction away from the church.

They were facing him.

Alex was in the middle. On the one side, he could see the guns being positioned, pointing. On the other, he could hear the shots and the shouting, growing ever closer. The engine again. Not a car. A dirt bike. Two of them. They were so close.

There they were, bending around the corner of the high street. Behind them, the copse where Alex and Timmy had hidden on the first night in town. They were peeling around it, making straight for the group of cars that had gathered outside the bar.

Those same gang members; Alex could see the tattoos. Their bikes were buzzing like a nest of wasps. One of them released his grip on the handle bars, pulled a gun from somewhere and opened fire. Backing into the dark corner, Alex almost felt the bullets streaming past his hiding place.

The others responded. Short, controlled bursts. They clipped the firing rider, knocking him to the ground. They didn't wait for the other one to reach for his weapon. He was dropped, instantly, by a shot to the head. The bike fell out from under him, skidded along the road, and crashed into the first of the Cadillacs.

A pause.

Alex looked around. He could hear the government men reloading. They were expecting more trouble. Then it came, the louder, lower thrum of the heavy cars. The rest of the gang, arriving after them. He needed to get back to the house, to get back to Joan and Timmy. Looking down at the dog, he took a tight hold of the collar.

"Come with me. Right next to me. Understand?"

The dog whimpered and looked blankly up at Alex. Enough of an understanding. Feeling for the strap on his shoulder, Alex dragged round his rifle. The words Smith & Wesson looked up from the metal and he rubbed his thumb over the imprinted logo. Like rubbing a coin for good luck.

Already, Alex was regretting not bringing another clip. This one was full. Beyond that, he was on his own. One more time, he peeked around the corner, watching what he could of the street. The two crowds were facing one another down.

The government men–or whoever they were–had set up positions all across the street, facing the southern end. The gang sat and watched, waiting in their trucks. The big one, the one Saul had talked about, was nowhere to be seen. But the others lurked. A real Mexican standoff.

Finn barked. Heads turned on either side. A moment to slice the tension in two. Broken.

Shots fired. The dog was forgotten and Alex crouched down next to him. Tucked into the niche, set back from the gun fight, he could feel the snapping of the air as the hail of bullets tore past. The street was being picked apart, one bullet at a time.

Alex looked down at his rifle. One magazine. One gun. One man. No way to fight through all of this. Better to just get back to the others, make sure they were safe. And then run. He had to stay hidden. Had to stay out of sight.

A hundred feet to the hideout, at least. Alex was on the wrong side of the street, sitting almost exactly in the middle of the two fighting forces. A chunk of wood exploded into a million splinters above his head. Someone had missed their shot.

The dead neon sign above Danny Boy's was shattering, each shot it caught breaking apart the colored glass in a new kaleidoscopic flare.

The professionals had set up their base. They opened the doors of their Cadillacs and leaned from behind, shooting in short controlled bursts. The cars must have been armored, Alex thought. Rolling barriers, circled and defensive.

At the other end, the gang members were trying a different approach. Their hollowed-out SUVs and dirt bikes didn't offer the same protection. The men had scattered into the alleys and the houses. They were worming their way through the back streets, turning the entire town into a battlefield.

As the professionals circled their wagons, gathered around themselves, the shots started coming from all angles.

Alex had to move. Snapping his fingers at Finn, he began to run. At the other end of the street, the steeple of the chapel rose above almost everything. Right next to the hideout. Their car was in the garage behind. The guiding light, bringing him home.

Turning right, Alex ducked down an alley, away from the main street. There was a dirt road on this side, lined with ancient sycamore trees. Their trunks were thick, their leaves hanging low over the road and about to turn a golden brown in the fall. As he tucked into the space, up against the bark, he could see long-lost lovers' initials carved into the wood.

With Finn at his heels, Alex ran again. From tree to tree, and when he was in line with the professionals and their Cadillac barricade, he switched sides.

He pressed up against the back entrance of the bar. The noise was deafening. Between the wet slaps of the automatic fire and the shimmering metal clink of the falling casings, he didn't need to worry about being quiet. Every sound he made was lost in the storm of gunfire.

Alex kicked against one of the back doors of the bar. It gave way. There was no one else inside, he could tell. The air was still, the sound from outside muffled. The gang members had ransacked the innards, turning over everything in their search for valuables and booze.

Keeping low, worried about stray bullets, Alex made the short run to the front of the bar, jumping and avoiding the obstacles, the broken furniture scattered everywhere.

From the bar, facing the street, Alex could see straight into the heart of the fight. Out from Danny Boy's into the circled Cadillacs, with professionals on either side, shooting outwards. Every pane of glass in the front of the bar was gone.

Crawling into the space below the window, every sneaker step found the shattered shards and they crunched beneath the feet.

A line of shots rattled in through the window, eating chunks of plaster out of the ceiling. The heavy thud of the bullets lodging into the building could be felt in the chest.

Finn nestled up against Alex's legs, the sheer volume almost too much. With a hand, he tried to offer the dog comfort. But it would get worse before it got better.

There was no door anymore in the bar. Probably kicked out by the gang members. It didn't matter. They had to cross the street. The safest way was to run straight through the center of the professionals.

They were facing outwards; their armored cars would provide some cover. Alex's T-shirt and jeans didn't fit with either team's uniform. This might cause confusion, at least for a moment. Enough for him to slip through to the other side of the street.

There had been a long mirror laid out behind the bar. It had been broken a long time ago. Before they pulled into Rockton on their bikes, at the very least. But there were still pieces of the mirror strewn across the floor.

Alex fetched one, retreating back to his position beside the door. Pulling Finn in close, he leaned the shard of mirror out into the empty space.

There it was. The other side of the street. A small gap between two buildings which would take him right into the alley behind the drug store. From there, it was a short run to the gate and the wall behind the hideout. Without distractions, it could be done in thirty seconds, easily. But this wasn't a clear run.

Alex looked down at the rifle in his hand. He heard round after round thumping into buildings all above his head. The dog tilted its head to the side, watching. This was the moment. They had to move. The shard of mirror chimed against the floor as Alex ran out of the door and into the fray.

CHAPTER 36

*H*e ran out through the door, into the street, straight for a gap between two hulking black Escalades. The dog ran at his side, its head held low. There was no need to shift the rifle from his back, to hold it in his hands. Any firefight would be lost before he had a chance to let loose a shot.

Instead, Alex ran deeper and deeper into the hornet's nest and listened to the bullets buzzing overheard.

From the other end of the street, the gang members were firing. Whereas the professionals were grouped together in one tactical unit, their opponents had spread out across the town. Some were climbing up buildings, others running through side streets. They were circling around him, closing in. One, Alex could see from the corner of his eye, snapped and ran straight for the ring of armored vehicles.

He was gunned down in a second, his body twitching in the street.

But no one watched Alex. Every eye focused on the enemy. No one expected a stranger to run, sprinting, from one of the abandoned buildings. It was the only free space in the town. Run through the back streets, he'd be gunned down in a second. Try to hide, they'd find him in an instant as the bullets blistered through the air. Besides, he had to act fast. He had to get back to the others. He had to take the risk. He ran.

Each footstep was lost amid the whirring gunfire, the snap of the sonic booms, and the metallic rainfall of empty casings striking the ground. One man running was not enough to be heard.

Still, Alex stayed low.

Even if he was not seen, a stray bullet could catch him in the leg or the chest. Out there, there might be one round with the name ALEX EARLY stamped along the side. He could survive a plague and die of lead poisoning.

Finn, still running on puppy legs, followed his every step. When the human stopped, the dog halted. When the human ducked or weaved to a side, the dog echoed the movement.

Running from the bar to the ring of cars, they synchronized their movement and, abruptly, Alex found himself pressed up against the cold metal of an Escalade trunk, gray bullet marks chipped away at the black paint. He ducked, salvaging his breath.

Right next to him was the portable satellite, still whirring and turning, locking into position. Casually, leaning out, Alex knocked the device to the floor. The dish still tried to turn, the internal motor struggling. All above, bullets zipped through the air.

It stopped. Broken.

No one had seen him. For a second, Alex watched. These professionals moved with a skill served only by practice. As the gun emptied, their hands worked together, flipping around the triple-stacked magazine, eyes never dipping from the targets on the horizon.

Even those in suits worked with the same, steady hands. Professionals was the right word, he knew.

Alex ran again. No time to waste.

He darted through the cars, waiting for someone to spot him.

But they focused on the gang members, still coming at them from the other end of the street. The exit was there. The gap between the last two cars, the space to run through and he'd be out on the other side, ready to run right down the alley.

There was one man, suited with a tangle of white cord wrapped up over his ear, balanced beside the gap. He was holding an M-16, swiveling his hips and aiming along the rooftops. Every few seconds, he'd release a short, sharp burst.

A red cloud might burst into life on a distant roof top. A body might crumple against the ground, weapon clattering from lifeless fingers.

Alex would have to squeeze into the space behind him. Best to take it at a run.

Clicking to Finn, he broke into a sprint.

There were ten feet between him and the gap, then seven, then five. The man turned around, spotted Alex, started shouting. The words fell on deaf ears.

The guns were too loud, Alex moving too fast. The man held up a hand, making his demands clear.

Stop.

No time to stop. Alex had the speed. Before the man could swing his gun around and aim, Alex leapt. Into the air, hurling his feet first. A messy, unpracticed kind of kick. Both legs up before him, thighs flexing at just the right moment, the soles of both sneakers landed hard on the man's chest. He fell.

Alex hit the ground too, but he'd been expecting it. Finn beside him, he rolled, got back to his feet, and ran the last few feet to the space between the cars. There it was. Someone was shouting behind him. Didn't matter. Keep running. Cross the open street. Duck to avoid any bullets. Into the alley, screeching on heels slipping in the dirt as the corner came. Run around the corner and stop.

Shoulders curled up tight, lungs caught in a vice, Alex felt like he was about to vomit. Now, he turned to grab his rifle. If all the professionals were tucked away in their circled wagons, the gang members might be anywhere.

To make it through this last distance, this short sprint to the rear of the house, he'd need to be careful. A time for stealth.

Two hands grabbed Alex by the neck and threw him to the ground. His spine caught the brunt of the fall, the pain sending shockwaves down his back and into his legs. Scrambling to his feet, he saw one of the professional men standing above him, two dusty footprints stamped across the lapels of his black suit.

He moved for the rifle, but the man was faster. He kicked the ankles out from under Alex before he could even loosen the strap from his shoulder. The rifle fell to the ground, a sound lost amid the firefight a street over. Dropping elbow first on to Alex's chest, the man grunted. It felt like a rib cracking.

There was a ripping sound; the man was distracted. Finn had his teeth wrapped around the man's ankle, a cut of cloth already torn from the trouser leg. As the man fought off the dog, Alex staggered to his knees. They were weak, could hardly hold his weight. Forming a fist, Alex fell forward and caught the man's jaw. Together, they fell into the dirt, the dog chasing after them, barking.

They were locked together, arms tucked under arms, trying to find an inch of space. As Alex tugged one way, the man's knee hit him hard in the hip. Without any limbs free, Alex jutted his head forward, breaking his opponent's nose. It only made him angrier.

The two fell apart, a foot or two between them. There was a pistol tucked under the man's arm. Every time he swung a punch or ducked out of the way, the jacket flapped loose. *Don't let him get it*, every one of Alex's instincts screamed. *Keep him close*. Lunging with a tackle, he took the man back to the ground.

Finn was struggling to find a grip. Biting, snapping, growling, he tried to take the professional's leg in his mouth and drag him away. A polished shoe jerked out, catching the dog right on the shoulder, knocking him back against the wall. The dog lay down, toiling under the blow.

As the two men tussled and tangled on the ground, neither able to find any purchase, the professional's hand reached out, searching. As Alex found himself pinned down to the ground, unable to pack any weight behind his punches, he saw the man lean back, one arm stretched up into the sky. There was a rock in his hand, a sharp one, as big as a baseball. It was aimed right at Alex's head.

The hand swung down. It stopped.

The man cried out in pain. Seizing his moment, Alex snatched the pistol from inside the holster, held it up toward the chest and fired. And fired again. And again. The rock fell from the hand, which dropped down to the man's side. The face contorted, staring at Alex. Confusion, fury. Shock. It was all there to read.

Without a word, his eyes glazed over and the man collapsed. Finn still had a huge chuck of thigh in his mouth, shaking it back and forth.

"Finn. Finn. Stop. He's dead. Come on."

The dog's ears pricked up, able to distinguish Alex's voice even in the commotion. The pistol was still in Alex's hand. Looking closely, he saw that there was no branding. No serial number. It was quite unlike every other gun Alex had ever seen. He unclipped the magazine to see that each round had a red tip. Unexplained.

"Who the hell are you guys?" Alex asked the dead man.

Throwing the pistol to the ground and fetching his own rifle, Alex was about to run. But an idea struck. Kneeling down beside the body, Alex traced the white wire as it looped out of the man's ear and down inside his jacket. It didn't seem to have an end. Checking around for signs of life–no one in sight, everyone too busy shooting one another in the main street–he grabbed hold of the wire and pulled.

A long, white worm sprang forth. Alex kept tugging, dragging a longer and longer length of wire from deep down inside. And then something caught. It wouldn't budge. Lifting the lapel of the jacket, he saw a small black box, caught beneath a button in the inside pocket. He released the button and the entire device, attached to the wire, came free.

He turned it over in one hand, and it buzzed occasionally, sharp bursts of static from the dangling earbud. Alex pocketed the device. But there was something else. Further inside the pocket, peeking out over the top, were pieces of folded paper inside a plastic wallet.

Without reading them, he slipped the papers from the dead man's pocket to his own and turned back to the alley.

Rifle perched between two hands, Finn padding at his heels, limping, Alex marched along the alley. He didn't run. It wasn't far to the gate, to the entrance to the hideout, but the route might be lined with danger.

As if to prove his point, Alex spotted a gang member crawling along the rooftop of a building above him. Raising his rifle, he positioned the man in the crosshairs, aiming just below his bald head, right at the spot where his vest met his chest. Finger on the trigger, Alex watched him move.

The gang member was young. Younger than Alex, almost certainly. A revolver in his hands, the man was firing wildly into the street below. He was laughing, a sound which was taken up by his friends in the town. But every time the gang member looked down, adjusted his feet, a moment of worry passed over his face. Even in a firefight, he was afraid of slipping.

Seen through the crosshairs, it made Alex pause. A tiny sliver of humanity at the worst possible moment. To get back to the hideout, passing under this man was essential. Readjusting his stance, holding his breath steady, he knew what he had to do.

A bullet hit the man's shoulder, knocking him off balance, and he fell from the roof. He landed right in front of Alex, the crash snapping his neck with ease; the man's death mask was fixed with that moment of panic, the worry of slipping to the street below.

A river of blood began to pour out from under him and Alex had to check the barrel of his gun for warmth, worried that he had been the one who had shot. He didn't remember pulling the trigger. The metal was cold. It had been someone else.

Turning back to the alley, Alex could see the gate at the rear of the house.

This time he ran.

CHAPTER 37

One hand held the rifle strap tight across his shoulder, the other pushed against the peeling paint of the gate into the walled garden. He'd left it open, only expecting to be out for a short spell, searching around the town. That felt like hours ago.

In reality, barely twenty minutes had passed since the cars had rolled up the street. The sun was high in the sky, sitting behind a blood-colored cloud. The fall light bled into the afternoon.

In through the gate, the dog in quickly, Alex slammed it shut. The sounds of gunfire still roared through Rockton. They grew more intermediate, more spread out. The two sides were carrying the fight farther than the main street. Pushing the bolt across and locking the world out, the garden felt more secure.

The walls were a lie. Tall enough, Joan said the original owner had been a private man, not well liked in the community. His tumble-down yard, the weeds and overgrown grass, seemed to be all that was left of him. That and the walls, designed to keep the world out. But they were only one brick thick. Symbolic more than secure. But everyone inside felt safer inside.

Alex ran through the abandoned area of the house and up the rickety stairs. His hands pounded so hard against the door of the apartment, the sound could wake the dead. Too loud. It didn't matter. Fists rained down faster, desperate to be let in. "It's me, it's me," Alex announced. "Joan, open up."

The sound of the locks moving stopped the knocking. As she inched open the door, noticing there was only one person on the other side, Joan seemed to sigh. Finn ran in through her legs, searching for Timmy. The two were inseparable, the patient and the puppy. Both hoped to grow out of the titles soon.

"What the hell is happening?" Joan motioned to the closed curtains, to the packed bags. "We heard the guns."

"That gang. They're back. Them and someone else."

"Oh my God, you're bleeding." She ran toward Alex, taking a towel from the kitchen to tend to the wounds.

"It's not my blood. I'm fine." Alex knocked her hand away. "You've put everything together?"

Joan recoiled, her hand snapping back as though she'd touched a hot stove. Alex moved to the bathroom, washed the blood off his arms and removed his scarlet-stained shirt. Why wasn't he worried about infection? If he hadn't been slowed down by anything else, surely this latest spillage wasn't going to hurt him.

"As soon as I heard the guns, I got worried." Alex shouted as he scrubbed away the blood. "Timmy told me what to pack. We've got everything, I think. The rest is already with the car."

Clean, squeezing into a fresh t-shirt, Alex entered the kitchen, holding up his hands for inspection.

"We've got to move fast. Is Timmy fine, can he move?"

Still walking with a limp, Timothy Ratz stepped into the room. He was thinner than Alex had ever known him. Now, in the dim of the apartment, the scantest of light creeping in through the blinds, the full ravages of the disease were apparent.

Whatever muscle there had once been–and it had never been much–had wasted away. The skin was drab, blotchy. The red hair, once an electric mess, was flat and plain. Rusted, rather than radiant. The one eye, the left one, was gray and drained, just like the others. A walking corpse, but walking, at least.

"I'm ready as I'll ever be. Just give me a gun."

Alex threw him the rifle. Stumbling, stepping back on a heel, Timmy caught the weapon. Tired fingers checked the rounds. He stood up tall. Ready to move.

THE BAGS WERE HEAVY, full of medicine and food. Most of the guns were already in the car, fitted to the gun racks Timmy had designed. The tow-hitch, dumped somewhere back in town, meant they would be deserting the bikes. There was no other choice. The car might just about be ready, if Alex had followed instructions to the letter, but there was no time to fit the trailer.

Together, the three of them moved down the stairs and into the garden. They went over the plan again. Timmy to lead, carrying the rifle. Joan next, with one of the bags. Alex would follow, watching the dog, with the final two bags heaved on his bag. A beast of burden. But there was no other choice. Who else was going to carry the supplies? Timmy, the sick note? The pregnant woman? The dog? This was it.

The route was simple. Run from the hideout straight to the rear of the church. They stood in the yard, between the two Triumph motor-cycles, ankle deep in overgrown grass, and the ricochets and gunshots whirled around. There was fighting in every direction. But no time to avoid it.

They ran straight through the gate. Timmy, taking the lead, already with the rifle stock up against his shoulder. Any shot, Alex wondered, and he might be knocked off his feet. Joan ran behind him, trying to hide her heavy belly from the world. The barrel of the rifle cleared a path before her and she ran on and on.

It took a minute to reach the chapel. Looking up, they could see pockmarks and bullet holes all up the wall, covering the steeple. They stole a quick look down the main street, where the professionals had taken charge of the street while the gang were roving through the back alleys, doing as they pleased.

Sprinting around the walls of the church, they reached the building where the car was stored. Not quite a garage, not quite a workshop, it had been perfect. They entered through a side door, Timmy leading with the rifle and then checking everyone in after him. Once the full complement was inside, he scanned the outside once more and tugged the door closed, slotting an axe handle through the latch.

Inside, there was the car. Painted a pale green, they'd not been able to fix the color. But they'd changed plenty else. The bull bars fitted to the front, the jerry cans clipped to the roof, and the cooling holes cut roughly into the hood transformed the soccer mom aesthetics. The style was still there, underneath, but it had mutated into an entirely new beast.

The interior of the car had been stripped. There were four seats left: the two front seats had been kept, but one of the rear seats had been ripped out. More space for supplies. As Joan clambered into the car, Finn sat on what was left of the middle seat and she held him tight.

The changes under the hood were less visible. As Alex threw the bags into the trunk, tying them in place, he fished the keys from his pocket and hoped he'd done everything right. No testing. No second chances. It had to work perfectly right now. He'd turned every screw, tightened every bolt, just as Timmy had told him. Trust in the technique. He turned the key.

The engine started. Just. It turned over but there was no monstrous roar. Alex remembered the first time he'd started up the motorcycle. It had felt like riding a thunderbolt. As Joan's old SUV ticked over, sitting behind the wheel was like teetering on top of a pile of loosely tied together junk. He had to hold it all together.

With the car alive, there was one barrier left to overcome. Clearing his throat, pausing for the ceremony, Alex reached up to click the switch which opened the garage door. Silence reigned supreme in the car, even the dog watching the finger press against the red switch.

Nothing happened. He tried the button again and again, but the door obstinately refused to raise even a millimeter.

"Chinese piece of—" Cussing to himself, Alex leapt out of the vehicle and slammed the door behind him. They'd ripped so many pieces out of the bodywork that it didn't give a satisfying thud. After he searched for and found the local switch, the garage doors began to heave upwards. In crept the sound of gunfire, of shouting and screaming. People dying.

Sliding back into the driver's seat, Alex felt his grip on the wheel. The vulcanized rubber, the way the grip had been knotted to fit into the fingers. Fine for a leisurely drive about town. In sweaty palms, it felt slippery. No time to change it now, though.

Foot hit pedal and the car lurched forward. Just as the door creaked open, the car slotted underneath. A second sooner and the roof would have scraped against the hanging metal. Instead, they slipped under the door, out of the garage, and into the yard at the rear of the chapel.

Only a small chapel, the bodies were buried on the town limits. They had a proper graveyard out there. But the back yard was still home to statues and apple trees. Alex had to wrench the wheel this way and that to keep the car on course.

The gate was shut. A wide wooden farmer's gate, it lay between two stretches of waist-high wall. The gardener could drive his mower in and out; it made repairing the chapel roof easier. Today, it meant space to charge through, the steel bull bars chewing up the rotten beams and leaving only splinters and dust behind.

Inside the car, the people bounced around. Joan held Finn tight. The bags stacked into the back acted as walls, barriers to stop the dog being hurtled around the interior. Seatbelts bit into shoulders, the stiffened suspension shaking bones and bodies as Alex hit every pot hole in the road.

They were in an alley, speeding around the corner of the chapel and on to the main street. As they reached the top of the town, the car stopped. Alex watched out through the windscreen. The battleground.

The circle of Cadillacs was still there, now riddled with bullet holes. A few of the cars had been driven away, giving chase to the gang members. In the distance, the black Escalades rumbled through thin alleys. Even from a few football fields away, the professionals were still obvious. Short, clipped movements.

But their opponents moved like scattered animals. Darting this way and that, arriving from every angle. The white shirts and bald heads they all shared stood out. Their own armored trucks crashed all over, trying to mow down the professionals and slam into their Cadillacs.

Alex spied the big man again, often at the center, directing his men. The dirt bikes whirled around like dervishes, some with two men: one steering and one shooting.

Watching the chaos, Alex tapped a hand on the wheel. A conductor before the orchestra settles. Baton beating the rhythm.

"Are we all ready?" he asked.

No answer. The silence was all the agreement he needed.

CHAPTER 38

*T*here was one route out of town and the only way out was through. Through the gunfire, through the fighting. No one had spotted them yet. The car began to move down the street, the tires warming. Hit the end of the road, take a few turns, and they'd be on the highway. It sounded so simple.

The car picked up speed. The digital needle skipped numbers as it arced upwards. Twenty miles an hour. Thirty. How fast was fast enough? If he had to ask, Alex decided, it wasn't fast enough. Out the window, the sights along the Rockton high street began to blur. Home for weeks, blurring into the background.

"Spot the gap, spot the gap," Timmy shouted, taking hold of the handle above his door.

The space between the remaining Cadillacs was limited. Aim for the excavated spaces. The circled wagons were porous, so find the spot when the cars had left. There were two. One on the right, one on the left. The left was larger, but the right seemed to have no one nearby. Right it was.

Faster and faster in the quickening car, they were just thirty feet from the first Cadillac. A face turned. And another. The professionals switched their attention from the gang members, turning to face the car careering down the road. Alex felt the wheel twitch in his hands. He didn't trust it to react quick enough even if he wanted to turn. Hold the course. Drive straight into the space.

The first bullet chimed against the roof. Finn barked. Timmy shouted. Alex began to bellow, leaning down over the dash and tightening his grip. Another chime. The professionals were shooting at them. But the car was moving too fast.

They made the gap. A mirror cracked and smashed as it hit against a Cadillac. Adjusting the wheel, Alex straightened them out. The scrape of metal on metal meant the car was just about getting through. Pedal farther to the floor. Faster. The only way. The bellow continued, rising in volume.

Level with the professionals, Alex could see straight into their eyes. Not wearing sunglasses anymore. They were sweating. Worried. Not expecting this car. Trying to figure out whether it was even a target. One wasn't thinking, his gun raised. The muzzle flashed. More bullets chimed against the car. But all along the roof. Too fast to hit.

Passing, through the gap, Timmy waving, Finn barking: they were out the other side. Halfway down the Rockton street and heading for the horizon. The car picked up speed, more gunshots echoing around them. One caught the rear window, cracked the glass. Another followed it up, smashing its way through and burying deep in one of the heavy black bags.

A sitting duck heading in one direction. Alex turned left and then right, snaking the car. Harder to hit. Still a quarter of the road to go, still a distance before they could turn off the main street, the car was cornering sideways, the contents leaning one way and then the other. Almost there. Time to take back control. Time to slow down, make the turn.

A dirt bike broke out from an alley and into the road. A gang member, leaning forward over the handlebars had no chance. His friend, perched on the rear, firing backwards, never looked. The hood caught the front wheel, knocking the bike up into the air. It almost floated, caught like a plastic bag in a windy moment. No time to wait.

Alex hit the brakes. Behind them, the dirt bike fell back to earth. Joan was looking out through the smashed rear window.

"Are they okay? We hit them!"

"Drive! Drive!" shouted Timmy. "We'll mail them a check."

No need to say it twice. Alex wrenched the wheel to the right, easing off the gas. The car slowed but took the corner flat, feeling its way around the bend. Straightening the wheel, he saw that their route ahead was blocked. The road had one lane on either side, leading right out of town.

Away from the main street, the lots were bigger. On the edges, gardens stretched out in either direction. The porches of ranch houses with white crosses on the door. Like this all the way to the turnpike.

But the road was packed with people. Cadillacs on one side; torn out, stripped-down SUVs on the other. They circled around, skidding and shooting. There must have been three of the gang's cars and a single Cadillac, like lions trying to pull an elephant to the ground. The gang were quicker, the professionals better armored. Alex felt his own car twitch, switching into a higher gear.

"Timmy, give them some warning," he shouted to his friend.

Nodding, Timmy found one of the pistols. One of the larger ones, Alex noticed, which they'd not yet touched. If he'd been standing up, the kick would have knocked him right across the floor. But as he leaned out the window, watching down the barrel and holding tight to the roof of the car, Timmy prepared himself.

The crack of the gun filled up the car, the smell of cordite passing through and out the space where the rear window used to be. Again and again the gun fired. The road ahead shrank. Squinting to see, Alex saw faces dropping, hiding, and people hearing the gunshots from an unknown source. The Cadillac pulled to the side of the road; the gang's cars sat still in the middle.

They couldn't take a frontal collision. Alex had fitted the bull bars himself, and he knew the welding wasn't great. Hit hard square into the side of a car, even these lightened models, and they'd be in trouble. Three of them? They might as well get out and surrender now. Pulling to the right, heaving the wheel all the way, another route beckoned.

The suspension held firm as the car hit the curb. One clunking sound and then another, both sets of wheels passing over, and then a loud smash as the car hit a white picket fence.

Timmy jumped inside as the flying pieces almost caught him in the face. "Warn me when we're going off road next time, man."

They ploughed through the garden, the heavily-loaded car churning up chunks of the once well-manicured lawn. Righting the steering, Alex saw the gang members watching from the road, raising their weapons.

"Timmy!" he shouted. "We need a bit of cover."

His friend obliged. Whatever was left in the clip, he emptied it into the roadside. They were travelling too fast, no way of checking who was hit. But Alex saw every bald head duck down behind the cars. And then, like that, they were away.

The uneven yard was felt in the tires, then the suspension, working its way up to the seats, where everyone strained against their seatbelts. With a twist of the wrist, Alex turned them back toward the road, riding off the grass, over the curb, and onto the asphalt. The sign for the highway loomed large ahead. Now leaving Rockton.

"Exit, exit," shouted Joan, clinging to the dog. "It's up ahead. Get on there."

It was there; Alex could see it. That familiar green sign, leading them up and on to the highway. It must be deserted. Just like before. He could feel his heart skipping a beat. Once they were on the right road, it'd be easy to cruise straight through to Virginia. It wouldn't be easy at all, Alex knew. But he had to believe the lie. Even before they'd hit the road, he could see the problems which would slow them down at every turn.

Stopping for gas; stopping to administer medicine; stopping to sleep; stopping to eat; stopping to dodge around a turn-of-the-century Ford truck which had skidded across the road and taken up both lanes; stopping when it snowed or a storm hit; stopping to double back when a road was blocked; stopping anywhere that might possibly provide essential supplies, whether it was a gas station or a lumber yard; stopping to let the dog run free; stopping when Joan felt nauseous or when Timmy had to vomit; stopping when Alex's eyes were heavy and he couldn't drive another mile; stopping for every tiny reason. The road to Virginia was beset by a hundred hurdles, all adding hours and days to the drive.

With such a big car and all the extra gas, they could probably do it in a couple of days. If they were lucky. Alex allowed his imagination to run free and unfettered. Just driving with his mind on autopilot.

A flash of color in the mirror. Movement. Probably the gunfight back in town, Alex reasoned, watching the road ahead. The last thing they needed was to crash now or to hit a barrier. It caught his eye again. Quick. Flitting. Finally, he looked up. A gun muzzle flared, the bullet catching the brake light, sending chips of red plastic flying out behind the car.

A rider, chasing them down. Objects in the mirror are closer than they appear. So close, Alex could almost see him grin, late morning light catching off the skin of his head. As they approached the on-ramp to the freeway, short concrete walls lined the road. It would be like that all the way. Nowhere to dodge and weave. Sitting ducks. The sound of metal on metal. Timmy was loading another clip. Holding the barrel, he passed the gun backwards to Joan.

"Your turn, Joanie. Take 'em out."

Even in the rearview mirror, Alex could see her eyes widen. As she was about to open her mouth, about to lash her tongue in every which way, the snap of a shot and the fizz of another bullet overhead stopped her. Timmy motioned with the gun again, passing it across.

"Come on, just like we trained."

She accepted the gun in her hand, weighing it while Alex wrestled again with the wheel. The road into the turnpike was long and curved; he had to be careful not to push the car too hard, not to flip it on the side. But the bike didn't have this problem. The man was levelling his arm again, taking aim.

"Hold the dog," Joan ordered, turning in her seat.

Timmy grabbed hold of Finn's collar just as the dog felt a moment of freedom. He snapped his hands over the dog's ears. Watching in the mirror, Alex could see Joan turn in her seat, kneeling with an arm either side of the headrest. She held her arms out long, stretching, and looked down the barrel. She fired.

Missed. The bike trembled. The rider righted himself, taking aim again. His shot missed, taking a chunk out of the concrete barricade twenty feet ahead. The rubble crashed against the windscreen. They were travelling fast. Joan aimed again.

The backlash nearly knocked her into the driver's seat, the hot casing falling into Alex's lap. He didn't have time to watch the biker, trying to fish the metal from underneath his crotch. He threw it out the window, turning to see it go. The biker was still there, getting ready to fire again.

"Slow and steady, Joanie." Timmy shouted the instruction, trying to make himself heard over the gunshots and engine noises. "Take a breath."

The car had nearly reached the freeway. Nearly there. Once they were out of the bend, the biker would have even more space to chase them down. With all these bags and all these people, they were too heavy to outrun him. Joan took aim again, and Alex lifted off the gas just for a second.

Crack. The shot barked through the car. The dog whined. The casing flew. Joan shouted, her elbows in pain from the recoil. The biker, in the mirror, sat up. He slowed. He fell away, body falling off the saddle and onto the road. The car continued around the corner and soon he was out of sight. The road opened up. Only the freeway ahead. Timmy laughed and waved goodbye to Rockton through the smashed glass of the rear window. They were free.

CHAPTER 39

*N*ever slow down. Alex repeated the words to himself. Never slow down. An open road and a tank full of gas, the car hit a high gear and began to fly. Never an off-road vehicle, not built for the fight, it knew how to handle a flat stretch of asphalt and ate up the road ahead.

The rear window, smashed and left back in Rockton, whistled. The air swirled around in the car, their own private gale force winds. The dog bounced across Joan's lap as she passed the pistol back through to Timmy. Eyes on the road, hands on the wheel, Alex refused to turn. Focus. Drive. Get to Virginia.

"Slow down, man. Let's pull over and fix this," Timmy said, pointing to the whistling space at the rear of the car.

"We're not free yet," Alex shouted back. "We need to get further away."

The two others began to rumble back and forth, about conserving fuel and which turning to take. The right route to freedom, the right way to get out of here. But they didn't know everything. They were just along for the ride. Alex tuned them out, his attention glued to the road and the wheel.

Too many cars. Far more than there had been before. When they rode into Rockton, getting off the freeway by chance, they'd been on the bikes. Occasional vehicles had pulled up on the side of the road, some collided with the central barriers which separated the opposite sides. But they had been few and far between. Two every mile, maybe three. Alex remembered the cars, not the bodies inside.

But now, weaving between the stationary cars, he was counting. There'd been at least ten in the last half mile and there were more on the horizon. Had the world changed while they'd parked up in the small town for a few nights? How long had it been?

Maybe the entire world had tried to take to the road and had faltered. The road to Virginia was littered with failed attempts. The sick and the unsuccessful.

Alex didn't want to join them. Joan and Timmy argued while Finn had the pleasure of being able to fall into a deep sleep in the center seat. They squabbled over nothing much. Where to stop, where to eat, where to spend the night. Another world.

With the wheel between his hands, Alex didn't feel a part of the conversation. Since the car had burst through the gate at the church, he'd been in charge. Driving, directing, pushing harder and harder toward the farm, fixed in his mind. Now, winding between abandoned cars, he felt like Steve McQueen. Steve McQueen with a secret, striving to get home.

Signs for unfamiliar towns flew past every few minutes. Seneca. Clarion. Alex didn't know them. They were just distractions, keeping him from his destination. Temptations on the road to salvation. For the first time in days or weeks–hell, even in years–he felt good. In control. Master of his fate. Captain of his whole road.

With every mile that passed by under the tires, every half-read road sign that sat on the roadside, Alex felt his heart rate slow. For the last three hours, ever since he'd first heard the Cadillacs rolling into Rockton, every beat had been booming, trying to break out through his ribs. Finally, the rhythm started to slow. At the same time, the car slowed down.

As he eased off the gas pedal, the knots of cars and trucks and other vehicles became tighter. More frequent. Harder to dodge. At a slower speed, it was easier. The noise inside the car died down at the same time.

"Alex?" Joan placed a hand on his shoulder. "Is everything okay?"

The worst question. It ran laps around Alex's mind, turning into all sorts of shapes and transforming into all sorts of answers. Is everything okay? No. Nothing was okay. Not really. Not when looking at it from high up in the air, or even right up close. Plague. Chaos. People trying to kill them. No answers for anything. Nothing was okay. And these two people, arguing over the best campsites in Ohio, didn't know the half of it. He shook his head.

"Where do they get all these?" she said, stroking the dog's ears as it slept.

"Gang," Timmy announced, pumped full of self-assurance. "A cartel maybe. I've read about them. MS-13. Netas. They had a jail up here in Toledo, probably broke out and went on a rampage. We've been hearing about all these gangs roving the countryside. Maybe that wasn't just propaganda. But we got 'em though. Joanie with the crack shot. Dead eye."

He mimicked a pistol with his fingers, pointed it out the rear of the car, and fired. And again, making a gunshot sound by blowing air between his lips.

"It doesn't matter who they are. Sick, stupid gangsters with no regard for their lives don't matter." It was the first thing Alex had said in half an hour, and his mouth was dry. "It's the other ones. They're the danger."

"Weren't they just chasing down the criminals? I saw those men looting everything in town, and I assumed someone had sent the police. We don't have many gangs in Rockton."

"Who sent them? Who's left?" Alex asked her, turning in his seat. "I don't think there's anybody left to call the police. They didn't hesitate to shoot at me."

"So who are they?" Timmy chimed in. "Mercenaries? If the whole world's gone, then there's probably a killing to be made in real estate right now. Lot of property on the market, I bet. Might is right."

"No, I think Joan is right. I think they're government. American.

But I don't know who. That's the problem. Those gang idiots are just idiots, whatever. But the other guys? There's something deeper there."

The idea had been preying on his mind ever since one of their number had set up a small satellite dish in the middle of the street. They were prepared. They were well-equipped. There was something else happening here and it went deeper than just escaped prisoners stealing booze. Alex remembered the items he'd stuffed into his pocket earlier. He hadn't had time to check them.

"Here," he told the others, picking out the pieces. "I pulled this off one of the government guys back in town. Take a look."

To Timmy, he handed the earpiece and the device that was attached via a curled wire. To Joan, he handed a folded plastic wallet stuffed with papers. Turning his eyes back to the road, he noticed how much more he was having to avoid the other cars. This stretch of highway must have been the busiest in America. *Everyone wants to get to Cleveland*, he thought to himself. *But not us.*

Already, Timmy was turning the device over and over in his hands. It was a smooth plastic, totally black and about the size of a cigarette packet. But thinner. Much thinner. It had sat in the man's chest pocket and weighed nothing at all. Alex could see his friend fiddling with the switches and buttons, placing the earpiece to his head.

"There's something here," Timmy announced. "I can hear things. Let me try this."

Without warning, Timmy reached down to the car dash and began to press every button available. It was an old car, still fitted with a radio from back before the trade wars. Searching for a cord or an outlet, he found nothing. Taking the façade off the tuner, pulling out a wire and a knife from his pocket, he went to work. Focusing on the road, all Alex could see was a flurry of exposed wires and the sound of snipping. Then, through the dash, the sound of static.

"We're too far from the source, so it's choppy, but you can make out those words, right?"

Alex listened. His friend was right. Chopped up words and phrases, dribbling through between the white noise. Straining the ears, it was almost possible to hear certain fragments repeated again and again: Block. Back up. Help. Too much. Needed. Clear. I-80. Satellite. Sweep. Clear. Infected. Sick. Survivors. None.

Trying to assemble the scattered scraps into a cohesive whole felt like trying to complete a jigsaw puzzle with only a few of the pieces and no idea what the final image looked like. All jagged corners and edges which didn't fit together. But it was hypnotic, if only to hear the sound of a human voice over the radio once again.

Even if it sounded like another language, a communication from another world, it brought back memories of driving between cities. Arriving in a new state and fiddling with the dial, there'd be a country station or a rock station in an entirely new position. That old analog crawl through the noise. Only now, the voices on the other end didn't just have a different accent; they had a different purpose.

"I think some of that's Chinese," Timmy ventured. "It damn sure ain't English."

Enthralled by the voices, the sirens calling through the radio, no one had paid attention to Joan. Quietly, she'd sat with the papers, searching through the plastic wallet while the car picked its way between the deserted vehicles on the freeway. There were so many of them now. They must be approaching a turn off or a city. Joan spoke up, tearing Alex's attention away from the road.

"Er, guys," she ventured. "What's this?"

In the space between the two front seats, she held up a piece of plastic about half the size of a human thumb. Flicking a switch, a short metal protrusion emerged, gold plated for computer connectivity. A flash drive.

"I mean, I know what it is," she continued, "but why was it tucked in among all these papers?"

Alex had no answers. The device must have been tucked up inside the plastic wallet, hidden from view.

"What can you see? Is there anything written on it? Or on the papers?"

Timmy had been staring intently at the drive.

"I can see this little logo," he muttered, squinting, "painted in red. I think it's a biohazard sign."

"Exactly," Joan agreed. "But there's nothing else in these papers. They're all in some sort of code. I'd need to sit down and look at it properly."

In his seat, hands feeling the jittery steering wheel, Alex turned to take a look at the drive. There it was. The blood red logo. They were right. Biohazard. Recognizable all over the world. A triumph of branding. An advertiser's dream. They all knew exactly what it meant.

With his eyes fixed on the drive, his mind strayed into the far reaches of the world of possibilities, the urge to know exactly what was contained in the recovered documents. Billions of ones and zeroes that might hold the answer. An answer. Any answer. Any information which might make sense of this twisted world.

He guided the car along as the road became twisted and knotted, bend after bend slowing them down. There could be anything around the next blind corner, he thought. It could be an answer. It could be home. It could be the gang leader, Roque, with a knife and a gleam in his eye, moving straight for Alex.

As his foot rested firmly on the accelerator, taking the corners a little too quickly, Alex could feel his mind drifting. After all the insanity, it was nice to simply escape into his own thoughts.

To stop and consider everything. To not have to act on instinct. They had a dog now. Somehow, he still wasn't sick. There was still a long way to Virginia and plenty to talk about. He almost felt excited.

"Alex," Timmy shouted, interrupting the moment. "Watch out, man!"

Snapping back to the world, Alex saw the row of abandoned cars appear around a blind bend. He braked. The car teetered up on two wheels. It was too late.

CHAPTER 40

*T*he stiff strengthened steel of the bull bars crunched into the empty car. Alex felt the bit of the seatbelt chewing into his shoulder, squeezing the flesh tight. The sound of the engine cut out. It was quiet, for a second, and then the hurt started to catch.

All three people in the car took to rubbing their shoulders, cradling their chests. Joan's hands, Alex saw, were placed over her unborn child. She hadn't been wearing her seat belt. Timmy's hand thrust across her chest had kept her in place.

"Ah, man." Timmy clicked his tongue. "Click it or ticket."

Alex couldn't help himself: he started laughing. It wasn't funny. It didn't matter. So utterly absurd, so utterly dangerous, but he couldn't bring himself to stop. Soon, the others were joining in. The entire car began to rock, the laughter catching like a disease and infecting one another. Even Finn seemed happy, trying to lick the smile off Joan's face.

Wresting control back, Alex wiped a tear from the corner of his eye. In the moment, it occurred to him how little he laughed. The last time anything had swept him up like Timmy's joke, he must have been back in Virginia. Probably on Sammy's porch, possibly at the family dinner table. A different time. A different life. The memory was enough to jerk him back to the real world. It hurt.

Looking up over the dash, he tried to see what they'd hit. It was a car, turned sideways across the road. A beaten-up sedan, from the nineties or some time back. No one inside. Unlike every other vehicle they'd passed, it wasn't sitting right on the road. It had been turned at a right angle, forming a barrier. And it wasn't alone.

Looking up over the scratched sedan's roof, Alex could see other cars in the same crumpled condition. They'd been littered across the freeway, forming an obstacle course which would slow anyone down. The farther down the road he looked, the thicker the tangle of cars. About a quarter mile ahead, they were even stacked on top of one another.

Between the two sides of the freeway, the once-grassy space was now nothing but dirt. Dry dirt. On either side, the barriers which usually kept cars within the asphalt confines had been ripped up and laid across the road as obstacles. The tree line beyond was naked, almost encroaching on the road.

The key turned in the ignition, catching on the second attempt. Slipping the car into reverse, Alex began to back out of the wrecked sedan. The bull bars had done their job. Everything seemed to be working. Joan was scrabbling around on the floor of the car, hindered by her condition.

"Timmy," she asked, "can you help me? I dropped it when the car hit."

Turning in his seat, Timmy loosened his seatbelt. Before he could join the search, he tapped Alex on the shoulder.

"Man, look up. What's that?"

He motioned with his chin, and Alex followed his gaze. A hundred feet behind them, there were people in the road. They emerged from the tree line, walking toward the car. One of them raised a hand. A flash of light. A window in a nearby abandoned truck shattered.

"Crap. Crap, crap, crap. Get out of here, man."

Alex didn't need to be told twice. He was already trying to get the car away. But reversing meant getting closer to the attackers. The road ahead was just a maze of twisted metal. Picking a route through with the car might be possible but it would be slow and it would take time. Time they didn't have.

Another muzzle flash and another bullet whirring past. Time they didn't have. Eyes scanning the road, Alex spotted a space between the trees.

"Hold tight. Hold real tight."

The car reversed. In the back seat, Joan bent double, struggling to search around the floor of the car. The dog barked, catching sight of the men swarming toward them. Alex saw them too. The same outfits as the gang members back in Rockton. Bald skulls and white shirts, almost glowing in the sunset. They grew bigger and bigger as the car sped up.

The brakes screeched as Alex stopped. The gears clunked and groaned. The car began to crawl forward. Another gun shot, closer this time. On the roof of a distant truck, two men were setting up a large gun with a belt of bullets and two spindly legs. Objects in the mirror are closer than they appear. The mantra. He hit the gas, hard.

The smoke from the tires wrapped them in a cloud. The car lurched forward, heading for a space between two burned-out Hondas. It wasn't big enough. Alex smashed through anyway. When the front tires hit the grass, the whole car jumped, and again when the rear tires followed.

"I've nearly got it, nearly got it," Joan shouted from the floor.

The big gun was waking up. Checking his mirrors, Alex saw the first burst from the barrel, saw a chunk of turf explode to his right. They had to get to the trees. These were fall tress, shorn of their leaves.

Unwelcoming, gray and brown, they stretched away across the countryside. A wall of nature, hiding everything beyond. Get in there and they could hide. Or run. Or do something. Better than being sitting ducks, exposed in the road.

Riding over the rough ground was hard. Shaken like ragdolls, the passengers clung on tightly. All except Joan, still obsessed with snatching the drive up off the car floor. But it kept her flat, away from the shooting. They were fifty yards from the trees and the machine gun was warming up.

To the side, Alex could see the bullets eating up the ground. They chewed an arc from the road, following the car in a long loop, leaving only craters the size of buckets. Alex heaved the wheel to his left, lurching away from the swooping arc, and watched it follow. Away from the gap he was aiming for.

As the tracing curve almost caught up with the car, Alex flung the wheel back to the right, skipping ahead of the line and repositioning the car to sneak between the trees. A bullet caught on the bumper, sending shockwaves through the entire vehicle. But it worked. Ahead of the arc, just ten feet from the trees and travelling, they headed into the forest.

The attackers followed. There they were, riding in those same torn up SUVs. Jeeps which had been gutted and turned to dark intent. They had been pulling up along the freeway even as Alex had escaped and now chased him down into the depths of the forest.

"They're laughing, man," Timmy shouted. "Who the hell are these guys?"

He struggled to be heard over the sound of the car hurtling through the trees. They headed down a dirt path, barely flat and riddled with rocks and holes. Every time they hit a stone or a bump, Alex whispered a prayer for his welding. That suspension, he thought, was it tight enough? Every single turn of the wrench came back to him, each a possible fault that could ruin their chances of escape.

At the time, Alex had looked at the roll cage and the bull bars and every other change Timmy had made and wondered what the hell it was all for. He assumed that Timmy's mind was just chasing a pipe dream, lofty ambitions of creating the ultimate survival machine while struck down with sickness. They hadn't even managed to finish.

Right now, Alex could kiss his friend. He'd driven the car back before the changes. Like steering jello across an oily surface, barely fit to ferry kids back and forth to school. Now, everything was tighter, more controlled. Able to hold up to a thrashing. At least, as long as every weld held firm, as long as every nut and bolt stayed strong.

They headed down the hill. Not even a path, this must have been an old river bed. Nothing manmade could have been this uneven. This wasn't a world for vehicles. But the people chasing, they seemed to find it fun. Alex could see them, just like Timmy had said. Laughing, smiling. They had guns but they weren't firing. Enjoying the chase.

At least the path was straight. No steering, just keeping the car on an even keel. It wasn't easy. Every time they hit a bump, the wheel tried to whirl away, testing the wrists. Alex was fighting against the car, against gravity, against losing control. *Hold it together, hold it together*, he told himself.

"I've got it!"

Joan held up the flash drive, thrusting the prize up in the air, pushing her glasses back up on the bridge of her nose. Finn barked. Joan turned and saw the people giving chase.

"Who the hell are these idiots?" she yelled, trying to make herself heard over the clattering.

"Not people you want to meet," Timmy told her. "Just hold on."

The path had given way. Not even clear anymore, Alex saw plants and bushes and trees vanish under the bull bars and the hood. The car flattened everything in its path. To the sides, the thick trunks of the ancient trees blurred into a single brown smear. Hit one of those and they were dead. It was as simple as that.

Still, the ripped-up SUVs and the laughing faces chased them through the forest. This wasn't driving like Steve McQueen. This was being Steve McQueen. Alex tried to channel the old movies he'd seen, the way the characters effortlessly flicked the wheel this way and that, driving themselves out of danger.

There was a bend ahead. Alex steeled himself. Get a hold of the nerves. Time to shine. He tapped the brakes.

Nothing happened.

With the constant bouncing of the car, they were in the air. Too much momentum. He tried again. A little effect. They slowed slightly. Just enough to take the corner with any confidence.

A waiting game. Perfect timing required. Get this wrong and they would hurtle headfirst into the trees, ready to be picked off by whatever gang members were following behind. Careful. Careful. Alex tapped the brakes again, just the tiniest touch. And then, at the last possible second, he turned the wheel.

The car careened around the corner. The rear swung out but the front turned. The hood faced around the corner while the trunk struggled to catch up. They drifted sideways, the wooden wall rising up on their side. Hit the gas. Now.

Alex's foot stamped down. The wheels spun. Caught. The car pulled out of the drift, sending gravel and dirt flinging up behind them. Something for the chasers to deal with, swarming through a cloud of dust. The road straightened. And stopped.

CHAPTER 41

*T*he brakes shrieked. The car halted. The road had stopped and became a clearing, a river cut through the ground with huge boulders either side. Nowhere to go. Nowhere to run. Alex reversed, trying to find a new gap between the trees. Nothing. The only way out was back up the way they had just come.

From behind, the chasing pack stormed through the cloud of dust. The sound of laughter cut through the air. They didn't see the river. They didn't see the rocks. They didn't see the other car. Not until it was too late.

The first of the chasers hit Alex's car, catching it on a rear corner. Both vehicles were sent flying into the clearing. After that, three Jeeps rushed through the dust cloud and had nowhere to go. The first hit a rock, the second hit the first, and the third served to crush the first two up against the stone face.

The fourth and last car had tried to brake but caught against a loose rock, travelling too fast. It flipped, turning over in the air, and twirled in a loop across the clearing. It hit against Timmy's door, smashing the entire car into the tree line and trapping it.

Alex was the first to open his eyes. After the roars of the engines and the rush of the chase, the air was almost still. Almost, but not quite. Every particle creased up against the next, remembering the chaos and the fury of seconds ago. The world remembered the devastation and didn't let go.

Everything was sideways. The car had flipped, Alex realized. He looked to his right, downwards. Timmy was out cold. Behind, Joan was struggling, muttering to herself. The dog was gone. It wasn't quiet. A long, shimmering ring was occupying the ears. The only sound. It just felt quiet.

Unbuckling his belt, Alex opened his door and climbed out of the car. The clearing was about half the size of a football field. Long grass. River down one side, though with big rocks along the bank. Streaks of paint and white scrapes decorated each rock, an instant mural of the accident.

The other cars were in no better condition. People–gang members, Alex reminded himself–dangled out of crumpled cars and lay strewn across the ground. But they weren't all dead. Some were staggering to their feet. Some were even laughing.

Trying to straighten his mind, trying to keep the world stable, Alex ran back to the car. The others would have to wait. The best way to help them would be to keep them safe. That meant getting help out of the trunk.

Timmy had been right. Tying everything in place was important. As he reached in through the smashed rear window, Alex knew exactly where the guns were. As quickly as he could, he strapped a pistol to his hip and fetched the AR. A knife, too. Elsewhere, the laughter was getting louder once again.

Alex staggered back into the clearing, loading the rifle. The click as the magazine latched into place snapped him back to his senses, stopped the world spinning. A familiar noise, a central pillar around which to orientate himself.

"Hey, buddy," a voice called out, unseen. "What you doing with that? Can't you see you're in our world now?"

It was the same sickening singsong threat Saul had carried, the same terrifying timbre in the voice. But the speaker was invisible, the sound arriving from some unseen source.

The rifle whipped up to the shoulder and Alex looked down the barrel, scanning the trees. The crashed cars. There was nothing. Only those who were dead already and those who were trying to be alive. He watched a man stagger to his feet, coughing, spluttering, blood pouring down his face.

The bloodied man stood upright, his head swaying. Across his bare chest, the word Jesus was tattooed in cursive. Jesus opened his eyes and wiped away the blood. He ran straight at Alex, grimacing. Alex raised the rifle again.

"Stop," he shouted. "Stop right there!"

Running faster and faster, almost all the way across the clearing, Jesus ignored the instruction.

"Stop, now!"

Ignored again. Alex felt his finger on the trigger. Tilting his head, staring down the barrel of the gun, he saw the flecks of blood flying from the man's skin, the wide-eyed grin refusing to move. There was not an ounce of humor in the smile.

"Please, stop," Alex tried for the last time.

The thudding footsteps refused to halt. A breeze crept across the clearing. The grass swayed. Alex pulled the trigger, feeling the gun kick him hard in the shoulder. One round. It caught the man in the chest, right above the heart. Dead, instantly.

But the momentum kept him moving, falling forwards and backwards at the same time, landing right at Alex's feet. The alcohol could be smelled from five feet away, the real high proof stuff. Paint thinner, not the top shelf selection. Check the pulse. Nothing. But the man was not alone.

All around the clearing, men were beginning to crawl into sight. Looking along the barrel of the rifle, Alex could see them swaying, staggering, smiling, and cackling. Must be twelve of them, easy. Twelve bad men. *What happened to all the good people*, Alex wondered, *guess the good people don't have any reason to be out here. Except us.*

These men were hurt. Maybe their drugs were beginning to wear off. But they were moving, circling. Hard to track.

267

"I don't know who you are, but we just want to get out of here," Alex told the clearing.

No one said anything. Instead, they began to form into a wide circle, enfolding around his position as he stepped closer and closer to the center of the clearing.

The first thing to notice was that none of them were carrying guns. The second thing to notice was that none of them cared. They inched closer and closer, closing the circle.

Apart from one man. Up above, Alex noticed he had climbed up on to the top of one of the wrecked cars. Watching over the crowd, the dozen men and the man in the middle. Not like the others, this one was taller, rounder, heavier without being overweight.

A heavy bag of a man, built to take a punch. Bald, too, with black pants and a black jacket. Where the others wore only white shirts, he kept his covered. A single tattooed cross between his eyes was the only sign of marked skin. Alex had seen that same sign somewhere before, had seen the man himself back in Rockton.

While Alex watched the large man on top of the car, the first of the gang ran at him. He ran from the three, and Alex switched direction. A quick swivel, raising the rifle at the same time. No pause. Squeeze the trigger. Snap. The man fell flat. Eleven left.

Another ran, fell in the same way. Snap. The casing hit the floor before he did, lying nestled among the grass. Ten left. Nine left, as another ran right at Alex from the side, hoping to catch him off guard. The man caught a bullet in the forehead, the fine red mist spreading out from a shattered skull like sea spray.

Nine men left, lurching around Alex. Why weren't they afraid, that was all Alex could think. He had a gun. He had just gunned down four men. Their friends. But they were still shuffling in the same dazed way, still laughing and pushing one another like teenagers. Something was wrong here.

Was it the booze? If the gang had been drunk since the outbreak, their synapses were probably ruined. Rotted out. Meth or whatever else they were using to fend off the disease wouldn't help. Unable to transmit even the simplest thought. Fear. Fear was a disease all its own, able to infect individuals and crowds and bring them crashing to their knees. But these men knew nothing of it. They seemed immune. They'd embraced the disease. They'd embraced their own mortality. They laughed.

This time, two men ran together. Alex shot the first, but wasn't quick enough to hit the second. The man arrived on his side, swung a fist and caught Alex clean in the temple. He staggered back, only just holding on to the gun. A huge cheer erupted from the other men. This was sport, Alex realized. That's why they weren't afraid. They didn't think this was real.

The man who had hit Alex was jumping up and down on the spot, showboating, eliciting applause from the crowd. Then, he had his fists up, boxer style, and stepped in toward the duel. He was too close. No way to swing the rifle round, no way to keep a bead on him. Not while dodging punches at the same time.

Alex tried to keep the gun raised but he was only blocking. A blow to the shoulder, one to the ribs. The man was picking him apart. No space to find a shot. No room. Another crack to the ribs. *Don't shoot him*, he thought. *Try something else.*

Shaping up to shoot, Alex welcomed in the punch. Here's my face, he suggested, why not take a crack? The man obliged, swinging hard for the cheek. As the fist flew through the air, Alex stepped sideways and brought the rifle butt firmly up into the jaw. The man staggered, not expecting the counter. There was space. Alex shot him. Eight left.

This time, Alex didn't wait for them to move first. As soon as the bullet caught the dead man in the chest, the rifle was swinging around again. A person in the crosshairs. Close enough he barely had to aim. Pull the trigger, quick. Dead. Seven left. And another. Snap. Six left.

Altogether, they realized that the sport was ruined. This wasn't gladiatorial combat. Even in their drink-addled minds, the situation became clear. Alex had just wiped out half their number and they were next. They attacked at once.

The trigger squeezed twice. Both shots flew up into empty air. Alex felt a hand try to grab his shoulder from behind and he leapt forward, into the path of another. Ducking under one fist, he fired the rifle again. It caught someone in the shoulder, then a fist landed in the small of his back. They laughed, but not like before.

Alex kicked out, swinging a foot into a crowd of legs. As one fell, he smashed the rifle butt down on the stricken man's nose. He was out. Might as well be five, now. Kneeing the man in the jaw for good measure, he turned back to the crowd.

A punch knocked him backwards, a hand snatched the rifle away. Alex staggered and found himself pressed up against a rock. There were all five of them, arranged in a line. Breathing heavily. A drunken chase and a car crash, then watching their friends die in front of them. A difficult day for most people.

"Listen, I don't want to hurt anyone. I just want to get out. We want to get out. Please."

As Alex pleaded with the five encroaching men, one of them looked behind, turning his head up to the man who had been standing on top of one of the cars. No one there. He'd vanished. Between them, the gang members turned back to the one thing they knew for certain. This man had to be hurt.

The rock face pressed up against Alex's back. He was bleeding from his forehead; he could taste the trickle of blood which dribbled down into his mouth. The pain in his back was terrible, like the fist had reached through and smashed a kidney inside. The rifle was missing. There were five of them.

A man screamed. The others turned. A dog, biting down on his calf, tearing. Alex didn't look. No time. They were too close. Reaching to his hip, he pulled out the knife. Swung it at neck height. Caught one of them. Blood everywhere as the man sunk to his knees. The shower of blood sprinkled down on the rest of them. Alex danced forward. Four now.

No one knew where to look. Finn was sneaking between legs, sinking his teeth into anything that looked like enemy flesh. That meant the men had two enemies to watch. The knife was swirling, cutting down and diagonal. It caught against arms, against shoulders, against spines. Not quite enough to take people out of the fight but enough to make them take notice.

Finn dragged a man to the ground. Alex swung a foot, kicking him hard in the temple. Out cold. Three left, but they were scattered. One was now up against the rock where Alex had been trapped. Leave him there a moment. The other two were searching around, looking desperately. They wanted guidance. Their leader, that man from the top of the car, they couldn't see him. Not anymore.

Punching, Alex knocked the first to the ground, a blow to the neck and a jab to the chin. Lights out. The other ran, making straight for the trees. Let him go. Finn had the final gang member cornered up against the rock. Alex had a knife. Alex had questions.

"Who the hell are you people?" he snarled to the man, reaching down to drag Finn back.

Shivering, the man could barely speak. He wore the usual outfit. The black pants and the white vest, the same selection of prison tattoos, spread across the skin. A uniform.

"I-I-I-I... I just did what I was told. Roque told us to block the road."

"Who's Roque?"

Alex already knew the answer.

"I don't know, man," he whined, dragging out the syllables. "He just tell us what to do."

"And who tells Roque what to do?"

"How the hell should I know? We were just sitting around, and then, you know, I don't know man. You just do what people tell you, yeah?"

Lifting the knife, Alex wanted answers. He leaned into the cornered man, pressing the knife point up against his belly.

"Tell me what happened. Everything. Everything you know."

The man whimpered. Then his eyes widened, looking over Alex's shoulder.

"Roque, wait!" The desperation in his voice was clear. "I wasn't going to tell him noth-"

A shot rang out. Blood splattered against the rock. The man fell to the ground. None of them left, now. Apart from one. Alex turned around.

CHAPTER 42

The sun sat low, breaking a red haze across the tree-lined horizon. In the middle of the clearing, a man stood holding a woman, his arm wrapped around her shoulders and neck. Roque, Alex thought, that's what the man shouted. That's what Saul had said. The heavy man who'd been standing on the hood of a car. Now he had Joan by the throat, a flick knife pressing into her flesh.

Joan had dropped her glasses. The light caught the hint of a tear pooling in her eye. Finn growled, sitting on his haunches, ears pricked. Alex ran a firm hand along the dog's head, telling him to stay still. The animal obeyed; he knew the stakes. The stench of blood and fear hung in the air.

"Drop the knife," Roque shouted. "Throw it to the ground."

Alex obeyed. What option did he have? This wasn't just Joan being held prisoner. It was the child inside her. Whoever this man was, whoever had sent him, he ruled the moment.

"Let her go," was all Alex could muster. "Let her go and we'll leave peacefully."

Roque listened for a second, sniffed, and spat on the floor.

"No peace anymore. No time to leave. She stays with me."

There were a few essential truths: Roque, if that was his name, had

272

Joan. He had a knife. He had the height on Alex and he had the weight. He had a stance and an aura, no stranger to altercation. Alex, in every second, could feel the adrenaline thinning in his veins. He wasn't built for this.

For days and weeks now, he'd been endlessly propelled forward, crashing through the end of everything he knew with an interminable momentum. Only to find himself standing still, in a field, wishing he was anyone else. Just like being back in Virginia, he thought.

One of the crashed cars burned. The acrid smell of burning paint drifted across the clearing, stealing a ride on the breeze that blew between the trees. The grass swayed. A bird sang, alone. This was a single moment, an instant: everything in all recorded history had arrived to this one second. The pinprick pressing down under the weight of all the world.

The image of the empty warehouses. The sight of the lines at the ATM. The way the neon lights from Al's diner blinded pedestrians and kept them hungry. The panic in the President's voice as he lamented from aboard his private plane. The glacial eyes of the girl who'd caught them in the store. The sound of glass shattering as the stolen bikes rode off into the sunset. Joan stamping on his foot. Finn licking his face. Every memory whistled past the graveyard of Alex's mind, making itself felt.

There were decades where nothing happens and there were weeks where decades happen. The words floated up through the ether, arriving from some teenage sketchbook or motivational poster. Somewhere in the past. Back when everything was normal. When everything was boring. Alex had felt the decades of nothing, had seen them sidling by his whole life. A life lived in the last three weeks, all of it leading him here. The bird sang, still, alone.

"You're Roque?" Alex sent the question out into the world for lack of a better option.

"You may have heard that." Roque smiled. "But I couldn't comment."

"What do we do? Where do we go from here?"

"My friend, you really know nothing? There's nowhere to go from here. Nowhere to run. Nowhere to hide. We're all just waiting to die, in different ways."

Joan squirmed, struggled, pushed against her captor's arms. But Roque held firm. From ten feet away, Alex could see the man's arms were like girders: thick and inflexible. This was the closest he'd been to a gang member without having to fight for his life.

The man's upper lip quivered, Alex could see a dusting of white powder stuck to the skin. The eyes twitched. Roque smiled. There was no joy there.

This close, the tattoos looked different. Less religious. More intricate. Under his neck, Roque had painted a dragon, drawn in the Chinese style and wrapped twice around his throat. The monster's jaws opened wide just beneath the man's chin, about to swallow his head whole. Every time he spoke, the dragon's scales rippled.

"We're not going anywhere, you and me. Her," Roque nodded his head to Joan, "she might come for a ride. But we got nowhere to go. Nothing to see. We're at the end of the line for you."

"Just tell me why. Tell me who you are. Who were those people in Rockton?"

The big man laughed.

"Why would I tell you anything? You think this is a film? A story? Be quiet."

The end of the line. Roque's words. Alex agreed. This was it. This was life now. Not sneaking his cell phone under his office desk, waiting to stamp a signature on pieces of paper he'd never see again. Not retiring each day to an empty apartment and listening to the distant sounds of Detroit trying to stitch itself back together. Not lamenting every single piece of Chinese technology he'd ever bought and relying on it at the same time. Everything that mattered was in this clearing. They had to get to Virginia to make it all count.

The dog barked, Finn straining against his instruction. He'd picked up the paradigm pretty quickly, Alex thought. One moment he'd been locked in a room, topped up with enough food to get him so far, the next he was snapping at the tendons of gang members after a car chase along the freeway. Still just a puppy. A quick learner.

"Joan, listen to me. It's going to be fine. I'm going to get us out of this."

She tried to nod. The arm around her neck was too tight. Where was Timmy? Still out cold. With two of them, they could do something. Anything. People have plans. And people get punched in the face. A few weeks ago, a stray punch from a discontented vet in a disused warehouse was all Alex had to worry about. Freddy was probably dead now.

The pistol sat on his hip. But it was holstered. Not just a reach away, but held in place by a button. By the time he'd unclipped everything and trained the barrel on to Roque, the blade would be dripping wet. Even then, he'd have to make the shot without hitting Joan.

But what other option was there? Time had not just slowed down, it had almost stopped. There wasn't really a notion of time anymore. Before, Alex had arranged his life based on his work or other people's plans. There was none of that any more. The entire way he thought about the hours in a day had changed overnight. Changed for the better. Now, as he stood inside the atom of a moment and watched it turn from the inside out, time meant nothing. He had to act.

To get the gun from his hip, Alex needed time. Time to move, time to act. He needed Joan. He had to remind her of what to do, how to help. But first, he needed Roque's attention.

"Roque, you know, I think I met a friend of yours?"

"Oh yeah?" the man grumbled, uninterested. "What was his name?"

"See, that's the thing. There we were in the drug store. I'd met this swell girl there." Alex tried to speak confidently, nonchalantly, trying to press any button he could, trying to convey a message to Joan at the same time. "What she did to me that day, boy, I wish I could show you right now."

Roque wasn't watching. His eyes were trained on the cars, inspecting those which seemed most able to drive, still. Thinking about escape.

"Yeah. I wish she could show you herself. Anyway, I met a guy there. Saul."

The name caught Roque's attention. He tried to hide it. But it showed.

"I don't know no Saul," he muttered. Not looking at the cars anymore. Only looking at Alex.

"Met him in the drug store. He didn't like me. Reminded me of you. We had a fight. He's still down at the bottom of the basement steps. Wonder if the rats have got to him yet?"

"Why, you son of a b-"

The anger boiled up in Roque like the screech of a steam whistle. Joan stamped down on his foot. Alex's hand already had the holster unbuckled, brought the Glock up to eye level, looking down the barrel.

Roque shouted in agony. Turning back to Alex, he threw Joan to the ground, running forward with the knife. One shot. The trigger clicked. The hammer dropped. The firing pin hit into the primer. The powder caught. Everything inside burned. The pressure shot up. The bullet found itself riding the wave of an explosion, spinning and hurtling through the barrel, out of the muzzle, and slicing through the air.

It hit cloth, then flesh, then bone and buried itself in the chest of the charging man. Alex stood still, arm raised, gun smoking, and the breeze caught between the last remaining leaves of the fall tress. The grass rustled. The dog whimpered. Roque writhed around on the ground like a worm caught beneath a baking sun.

Alex ran to Joan first. She was bundled on the ground, her knees up as far as they could muster against her belly, her arms locked round in a protective loop. Finn sniffed at her hair and licked her ear.

"Joan? Joan? Are you okay, is everything fine?"

She looked up. A thin trickle of blood was drooling down her neck. The knife had caught her. Joan waved her hands, pointing to Roque.

"Don't worry about me, get him, stop him!"

The black clothes were stained with a deep brown blood. The color spread across Roque's chest as he tried to prop himself up from the clearing floor. Handfuls of dirt and nothing else. Alex stood over the man, holding the gun.

"Help me," Roque muttered, dying. "You got to help me."

"Tell me who you work for. Tell me who sent you. Tell me everything."

As Roque laughed, blood seeped up and between his teeth.

"No time. No time for that."

And he laughed again, each sound softer and softer until, at last, silence arrived back in the clearing. Not even the bird sang. The breeze didn't dare to blow. Just Alex and the world, quiet together.

CHAPTER 43

*A*lex Early felt the weight of the gun in his hand, felt the weight of the arm hanging in the air, and felt the weight of the heavy sky as day turned to night. He searched around the clearing, but no man moved to hurt him or his friends. Safe. Free.

As the last of the light left over the horizon, he left the body lying on the ground. Nothing more to be gained from asking questions to a dead man. The dead don't have a way with words, he thought, and now we've got more dead men than we know what to do with. Best to let them lie.

Holstering the handgun, he went to check with Joan. She was standing, picking with a finger at the fine line of blood scratched across her neck. A ring of crimson pearls. Nothing too deep. As he helped her steady, helped her breathe again, she left her arm hanging over his shoulders. Support.

With her, the dog seemed pleased. The tail swept from side to side, taking the hips with it. Finn with his fine nose could ignore the deluge of sweat and smoke and bodies that drowned out every sense. Alex had no such luck.

His heart slowing, his friend standing by herself, he began to notice the thick, dank fug which settled over the forest clearing. His stomach revolted, churning up a thin gruel which he coughed up onto the grass. All bile and adrenaline and memories. Not the start of a sickness, he hoped.

They found Timmy still unconscious in the car. Out cold, as diagnosed by the nurse, but more a result of the heady cocktail of medicines and viruses he'd endured over the past weeks. They dragged him into the fresh air, laid him comfortably down, and brought him back to the cruelty of the world.

"I had plenty of dreams," he admitted. "I can't believe I missed all the fun again."

There was nothing left to do but laugh. Pure hysteria, a breakdown in the thought process, the reveries of the world offering nothing else but the utmost absurdity. They told Timmy what had happened, covered every movement and action in the most minute of details and then understood where they were, once more.

Surrounded by the dead. The mysterious dead. Once Timmy could stand and walk, perhaps half an hour later, they began to search through the belongings of the gang members. They began with the cars, the stripped-out SUVs, the Jeeps which had chased them down and through the forest.

Guns and ammo, very little else. Some money, in various currencies, and plenty of questions. Anyone still breathing was knocked out with medicine and tied up together. They'd be untied when the time came.

Tucked inside the pockets of Roque, however, Alex found plenty to keep his mind racing. A government ID, not just a driver's license. A chipped strip of plastic which should grant him access to electronic doors and locks. Not that there were many of those around.

Whereas the other gang members had held small amounts of cash, Roque's pockets were packed with stacks of notes. Cold, hard currency. Not just dollars, but Yen and Renminbi, spread out across a palette of colors, fixed with the faces of other people's heroes. More than Alex could ever hope to spend.

But tucked away in the sole of his shoe, only found when Finn began to pick and chew at the dead man's foot, was a hidden device. A small black plastic drive. Flash memory, the very same as had been plucked from the pocket of the professional. Joan compared them: identical in every way.

It only meant more questions. Every find, every scrap of information, only put more space between them and the eventful truth. Each individual piece felt like the outline of a map, providing hints at the shoreline or the way the rivers ran without ever teaching them about the finer details, be it the tides, the winds, or the people who lived inside. Only raw information, devoid of context or explanation.

As the darkness fell down hard on the world, they decided to leave. The car, replete with the improvements Timmy had suggested, had survived. The roll cages and the bull bars had seen better days, but the wider shape of the vehicle and the machinery inside still worked perfectly. Once they flipped it over, set it on its wheels, they were good to go.

Driving up the hill was hard. The tires spun, the loose shingle of the surface often gave way. They'd fallen down the slope more than they'd driven down it before; the ascent was far more testing. Added to that, they had no idea what they would find at the other end of the path.

If the entire gang had given chase, they were now dead. There might be a crowd waiting beside the freeway. But the road was empty. Once at the top, Alex ran back down and freed the unconscious men. They'd wake up to a strange new world.

Back on the open road, the car ran perfectly. On the bikes, they'd stopped every night and made camp. On this night, they drove on and on. No time to stop. No quarter given to the hour. They needed distance between themselves and everything else. Distance can be the best medicine, for the soul and for the psyche.

Soon, however, Alex was alone. The others slept, their faces pressed up against the windows. Even the dog was curled and nestled into the side of a sleeping Joan. Hands on the wheel, eyes on the road, Alex would check on them occasionally. But they didn't move. Sleeping peaceful dreams. Sleeping, at least.

Alex felt his own eyes grow heavy. The constant drone of the rubber on the asphalt was hypnotic. The chips and damages in the tires gave the noise a pattern, a rhythm, which was repeated every second. It changed and evolved as the rubber was worn away. Eventually, with enough time, everything wears down to a single flat surface. For now, Alex enjoyed the noise. Quiet enough and calm.

The lights of the car picked through the dusk, lighting up the markings on the freeway. Soon, they'd switch to back roads, away from prying eyes. But, tonight, they just wanted to drive. Occasional cars perched on the side of the freeway, some stopping in the middle of a lane entirely.

Alex didn't look inside. He knew what was in there. The road was a census of people who had tried to do what had to be done, to head out away from the towns and cities and make it somewhere safer. The people in those abandoned cars had failed. For what it was worth, Alex realized, he was one of the lucky few. God only knew how many others there were wandering the country. But at least he was breathing.

In truth, he didn't need the lights. So full was the moon, hanging low, and so bright were the stars, without the electric lights to drown them out, that the night sky lit up the world ahead. In the distance, over the trees and the hills, the entire world stretched out. All under the same heavy sky.

It was the same world it had always been. The same combinations of minerals and chemical reactions, of different types of dirt being moved about by upstart slabs of oxygenated carbon. The same world now as it had been six months ago, six years ago, or the day Alex had been born. Maybe some of the stars had blinked out, switched off, or cooled down. But there were enough left that the effect stayed the same.

The same stars. Shining down on Detroit and Virginia both. They weren't even at the farm. What had been a simple journey in the minds of two men dreamt up in a desperate basement had become their one driving objective. Almost overnight, it had become the most important thing in the world. And they weren't even there yet.

That same Virginia under the same stars. Only time would tell whether it was a wise decision. Alex looked around the car, glancing at Joan, Timmy, and Finn. Not one of them knew what was waiting for them on the farm. They didn't know about Sammy, about Alex's parents, or about the ghosts he'd left behind in that house. It wasn't fair to inflict those ghosts upon them. Not yet. They'd find out eventually.

Alex looked down at his hands on the wheel. The same hands which had held a paintball gun and typed up meaningless documents in a bland and faceless office. The skin was rougher, dirtier now. The same hands but they'd changed. They wouldn't have been able to do the same things before that they could now. Even if they never made it to Virginia, Alex felt something kindling in his chest. Excitement. Hope. All it had taken was for the world to fall apart.

He looked around the car. Timmy was there. He'd changed, physically at least. A man who'd built his life on bluster and boasting, who'd been obsessed with the apocalypse and preparing for everything for as long as Alex had known him. Typical Timmy luck that he'd fall sick just as things got interesting. But he'd pulled through. He'd shown a kind of strength Alex never expected from him. They'd need that strength in the future, surely.

And then there was Joan. A mystery. A whole person he'd never expected to meet. Two people, really, he corrected himself. The mother and child, almost. The way she never talked about herself or her baby, Alex knew that kind of isolation all too well. A protective shell. A safe distance from other people. But she was warmer now. Friendlier. She was essential.

Even as his hands gripped the wheel, raising only to wipe the sleep from his eyes, Alex appreciated how little he'd thought about Virginia in the last few days. Even the ring lay untouched in his pocket. Back in Detroit, he'd grown used to tuning out, to filtering out the information he didn't want to hear. A comforting kind of numbness. It hadn't been necessary these last few days.

The devil was in the details. Details about the house they were driving toward and the people they'd find there. If there even was anyone waiting for them. At one time, Alex had been scared of his memories, scared of the emotions that could be dragged to the surface. Now he was curious. He'd taken on far worse, he now knew, and he'd survived.

The past and the future were colliding together, heading inexorably in the same direction, destined to crash. Inevitability had a reassurance all its own. Not just the people he'd left behind but the people he was taking with him. There were so many questions that were going to have to contend with so many memories.

How were they even going to look after a baby? No one had mentioned it to Joan but the problem was going to be very real, very soon. And the flash drives. And the documents. And all that money. And the gangs. And the government agents. And the virus. And the dead people. And the entire country, collapsing in on itself in an inescapable death spiral. They would need to contact the outside world, eventually, to find out what the hell had happened.

It was all too real, while at the same time seeming far too strange. Like living inside a book in the process of being written, the very idea of truth and reality turned infinitely over and over until nothing was the same and nothing was believable. But it was all too tangible. It was happening. This was all happening.

The night rumbled on and took the car with it, deeper into the unknown. Alex blinked his eyes as an abandoned truck appeared on the road ahead. As they passed, he could see inside. The dead were still sitting there, seatbelts working to hold them up straight. The virus had spread. The gray skin and bloody eyes were all too obvious. These dear and departed, they wouldn't be the last on the long road to Virginia.

A fire burned in the distance. A wrecked Chevy on the side of the road, no one at the wheel. Someone was setting fires. Someone was crashing cars. Someone, somewhere, knew something. The fire was drawing closer, the road heading in that same direction. The nearer it was, the fewer stars stood out in the sky.

But this was the only way forward, the only one they'd chosen. Driving toward the light, they could turn away later. Tired as hell and a slave to the wheel, Alex Early had no choice but to drive farther into the night. All he could do was drive.

A sign flew by. VRIGINIA, it called, along with a long list of states, 200 MILES. Gripping the wheel, gritting his teeth, Alex settled into his seat. No time to get comfortable. Plenty of road ahead. So near and yet so far, so much still to come.

THANK YOU FROM THE AUTHOR

Thanks so much for getting this far! I hope that means you enjoyed the book! I love talking to readers, so if you ever want to say hello, drop me a line at info@syndicatepress.pub.

It might take a while if I'm busy writing, but I'll get back to you as soon as I can!

Made in the USA
Middletown, DE
29 December 2018